CW01217273

Bloody Consequences

Bloody Consequences

Laura Hysell

The Isabella Howerton Series

Bloody Beginnings

Bloody Consequences

Dedication

To my family and friends for supporting me every step of the way

Acknowledgements

Dedicating time to write means there is less time for other things. Writing a book isn't just putting words to paper. That's just the beginning. There are a thousand tiny steps before a book is complete, and many people along the way that help.

First, my family has been my biggest help and biggest support. They have encouraged me every step of the way, even when I've gotten lost in "Twitter Land" or can't decide between two virtually identical covers. They keep me happy, and that's better than all the coffee and chocolate in the world!

I also have to thank my wonderful friends. These people understand my sarcasm, contain -or encourage- my coffee addiction, and are all completely different!

Last, but certainly not least, I have to say a special thanks to my BETA readers! Their input and observations were immensely helpful! I have some amazing BETA readers who sent me thoughtful and often comical commentary, which I thoroughly enjoyed. I love knowing my readers have connected to the story and the characters.

Thank you again!

"This above all: to thine own self be true." –William Shakespeare
HAMLET, (ACT I, SCENE III)

Chapter 1

We were sitting in Jed's living room, listening to my brother talk about the vampires. I had a thousand questions to ask, but Jed beat me to the vital ones. "Why were they still after you? They could have easily killed you, but they kept you alive and vampires keep coming after you and your sister. Why?" Jed asked.

Justin took in a deep breath and looked up, facing Jed. "They want my research. They want the project I've been working on," Justin replied, pausing. He glanced at me and pulled his hands out of mine, guilt etched on his face. "I've been working on making the vaccine airborne... and permanent."

The room went quiet and the only sound was the sudden intake of breaths. Then everyone was talking at once. Werewolves were standing up and yelling, pointing fingers at my brother. I stared at Justin, watching my brother take the wrath of a room full of werewolves. Justin looked down at his hands and hunched his shoulders, as though he was bracing himself for impact.

I looked over to Jed, waiting for him to get the werewolves under control. Jed was wearing his usual jeans and a flannel, looking relaxed despite the intense conversation. He sat back in his chair with his hands folded calmly in his lap, watching Justin with normal human eyes. Was he waiting for the werewolves to tear my brother apart? I moved closer to my brother and fingered the knife I kept on my side. I didn't want to battle werewolves, but I wasn't going to let them hurt my brother without a fight.

Mark had been sitting quietly beside me and I risked a glance at him. He was watching Jed intently, and his eyes had turned golden. Someone in the room growled, and I felt a cold chill run up my spine. I stood up and moved in front of my brother as my eyes roamed over the werewolves. Golden eyes greeted me from every face, but it was the face that was morphing into something inhuman that had me transfixed. Already, she was indistinguishable from the person I knew as fur quickly covered her body. She let out a piercing howl and I felt my heart speed up at the sound.

The other werewolves had quieted down and were watching Beth change. I was mesmerized, unable to tear my eyes away from her transformation. I had watched her change before, but through a video. This was different, and immensely terrifying. Loud cracking sounds accompanied her change as human limbs bent and twisted into wolf legs. Her face twisted and elongated into a muzzle, baring sharp teeth made for tearing. She howled again as her body completed the change from human to wolf, the sound echoing through the room.

Beth turned her large wolf's head toward me, her yellow eyes glowing like twin suns. No normal wolf could ever be confused for the giant creature she now was. She snarled, baring her teeth at me. I was afraid to move, using only my eyes to look around the room. Jed was still sitting quietly in his chair, but he was watching Beth. His face showed no emotion, and no hint at what he might be thinking. No one else in the room moved or spoke. The only sound in the room was the low growl emanating from Beth's wolf form. I wasn't sure what to do, or even if I could do anything.

Justin shifted behind me and I felt him clutch at the fabric of my jeans. He hadn't gotten over his fear of the werewolves, and this was only making things worse. I had spent more time around them than he had, and I wasn't sure if I was over my fear either. Beth growled again and moved deliberately toward me, her body hunched down as though stalking prey. No, I was definitely not over my fear. Despite the terror coursing down my spine, I felt a strange calmness come over me. I moved my hand slowly until it was resting against the hilt of my knife. I grasped the handle with sweaty palms and gradually pulled the knife free of its sheath.

Beth growled again and shifted her body, ready to spring. I wouldn't be able to move with Justin clinging to me, but I'd rather her get me than him. I bent my legs, ready to absorb the blow. There was no warning when Beth attacked. One moment she was hunched down, growling, and the next she was leaping into the air. I felt her front paws hit me in the chest, knocking the air out of me as I fell backward onto the couch. Bared teeth snapped at my face, but Beth couldn't reach me. Mark had his strong arms around her chest, holding her at bay.

Her wolf body was larger than any normal wolf, and far larger than Mark, but somehow he held her back. I gripped the rough knife hilt, and wondered if I could stab her with it. She was so close, and it would just take a single thrust. It would be like when I killed Patricia. I moved the knife in close to my body, ready to strike, when her weight suddenly lifted off me. I watched as Beth sailed through the air and crashed into one of the smaller couches, toppling it over. Mark was standing in front of me, breathing heavily. He looked me over briefly before turning his attention back to Beth, but I noticed his eyes lock onto the knife clasped in my hand.

I scrambled off the couch, pulling Justin with me. Most of the werewolves had scattered to the edges of the room, leaving only Mark between an angry wolf and me. Beth was back on all fours, looking angrier than ever as she snarled and snapped at Mark. I felt my skin prickle and I heard sick popping and breaking sounds from behind me. I now knew what that sound was; another werewolf was turning.

I grabbed Justin with my free hand and pulled him behind me toward the hallway. The only wolf I absolutely knew wouldn't hurt me was Mark, and he was still in human form. This room wasn't safe any longer. I reached the hallway and found myself stopped by Lucas. He stood poised like a bodyguard with his arms across his chest, blocking the way.

"Lucas, let them go," Jed called from somewhere behind me.

I breathed a sigh of relief as Lucas moved aside to let us pass. More snarling noises sounded from behind us, and we hurried faster, neither of us looking back. Justin stumbled behind me as I pulled him down the hall and into the closet. I pressed on the wall and waited impatiently for the security panel to pop up. As soon as the panel appeared, I punched in the code for Jed's security room and hurried Justin down the stairs in front of me while I closed the door behind us. We moved down the steps and I entered the code to get us into the monitoring room. Both security doors were thick steel, and I imagined they were werewolf proof as well. Of course, a werewolf in human form could easily follow us, but I was hoping Jed and Mark would prevent that from happening.

I sat down in one of the two chairs and tossed my knife onto the counter while I scanned the security cameras. I heard Justin sit down beside me, but my eyes were on the living room camera. It was hard to make out details on the small screen, but there were definitely two wolves in the room now. One of the wolves moved with lightning speed at Mark, who turned quickly to deflect the attack. The second, larger wolf took that opportunity to attack Mark from behind, launching onto his back. Mark dropped to the ground and rolled, shaking the wolf off him just before the first wolf sprung at him again.

They rolled to the ground again; Mark trapped underneath two snarling wolves. I watched nervously, my face pushed close to the monitor. Mark was still in human form when he came up from beneath the two wolves. He grabbed one wolf by the leg and hefted it into the air before hurling it across the room. He ignored the second wolf and raced after the first as it rolled to its feet. They moved out of the living room and I scoured the monitors until I found Mark and the wolf tangled on the dining room floor. The second wolf joined the fight, and the three of them tumbled across the floor toward the kitchen.

Mark managed to get to his feet and ran for the door, leading the two wolves outside. I swiveled in my chair until I was watching the monitors surrounding the house. Both wolves were stalking Mark, who still maintained his fully human form. One of the wolves leaped onto Mark's back, dropping him to his knees. The wolf latched onto his shoulder with strong jaws and even through the small monitor, I could see blood gush from Mark's shoulder.

Mark rolled and the second wolf joined the fray as they tumbled across the yard, fighting and tearing at one another. One of the wolves suddenly went sailing through the air to land on its back near the house. The wolf struggled and flopped on the ground, but failed to stand back up. With one wolf injured, Mark was able to turn his full attention onto the other, larger wolf. Mark wasted no time rolling across the ground to his feet. The wolf pounced, but Mark was able to grab it around the neck. He held the wolf off the ground with one hand before slamming the large wolf into the ground at his feet. Mark knelt over the wolf, his hand pushing the wolf's head down. The wolf thrashed its body around on the ground, struggling to stand. After a minute like that, the wolf finally lay quiet. Mark stayed still, holding the wolf down for several more minutes before he finally stood up and walked back toward the house.

The two wolves stayed where they were on the ground until Jed walked out and ushered them toward the barn. The remaining werewolves had all congregated outside to watch the fight, but they parted to let Mark back into the house. I was standing up before Mark had reached the back door. I grabbed my knife off the counter, sheathed it, and hurried toward the door.

"Izzy! What are you doing?" Justin asked as I grabbed the door handle.

"Mark's hurt. I'm going to check on him."

"Are you crazy? Did you just watch what happened? Did you see what Mark did?"

I stopped at the door and turned back to my brother. His blue eyes were wide with fear, and his sandy blond hair was a mess. "Mark won't hurt me. He just protected both of us. Please, just stay here. I'll be right back."

I left Justin with the monitors and quickly climbed the steps. I would have to deal with my brother later, but right now I needed to deal with the werewolves. This place was supposed to be safe for Justin, but it wasn't looking like that now. No matter what he had done, he was still my brother and I couldn't let a pack of werewolves tear him apart.

Mark was already in the small living room when I walked in. Blood dripped steadily down his arm and onto the floor. I looked him over briefly, taking note of the dark, bloody patches covering his clothes. He grinned weakly at me before limping toward the medical bed Hugo had been using earlier. I rushed over as he sat down and helped him pull off his blood-soaked shirt. The wound was worse than it had looked on the small video monitor. A large chunk of skin had been torn off, revealing white bone and raw flesh beneath. Numerous scratches and bites littered Mark's skin, but I noticed the smaller wounds seemed to be healing already.

"Where's Dr. Humphry?" I asked worriedly as I scrounged around underneath the hospital bed for bandages to staunch the bleeding.

"She's on her way," Mark muttered.

I found a box of bandages and pulled them out, wondering what to do next. The wound was far beyond my skills, but I could at least help with the bleeding. I swallowed down the bile that was rising in my throat and tried not to look too closely at the gaping wound. I opened one of the thickest gauze pads I could find and held it to the open wound. "Why didn't you turn into a wolf?" I asked as I watched the blood soak through the bandage at an alarming rate.

"It's complicated," Mark replied gruffly.

I waited for him to elaborate more as I swapped out bandages, but he just sat quietly. "I thought werewolves healed fast. This wound doesn't seem to be healing at all," I added as I put yet another bandage on.

"Some wounds heal slower than others, especially when made by another wolf. There's not much I can do without changing into wolf form," Mark added the last quietly.

I could feel myself growing light-headed and I looked away from the wound, concentrating on Mark's face instead. "Changing into a wolf would heal you?" I asked, and Mark nodded. "Well, go change then."

Mark sighed loudly and used his eyes only to look at me. "I'll change when my Alpha tells me I can."

"What? If you're hurt, can't you just go change whenever you need to? It doesn't make any sense to wait."

"It's wolf business, Izzy. You don't understand," he growled at me, his yellow eyes flashing.

"Well, why don't you explain it then?"

Mark turned his head fully toward me and gazed at me for a minute before answering. "I'm sort of on probation. For right now, I am not allowed to change into wolf form without the Alpha's permission."

"Do the others know that?"

"Yes," he replied shortly, turning his head away from me once more.

I could feel the blood soaking through the bandage again, and I quickly added another layer while trying not to look at it too closely. "Who was the second wolf?" I asked, wondering if the attack had been purposeful. Were the other werewolves mad at Mark for some reason? I felt like I was missing some crucial details.

Mark sighed loudly and muttered, "Logan."

"I thought you and Logan got along?" I was completely confused. Lucas seemed more the type to attack Mark than Logan. Logan had always seemed so cool and collected, and I knew he could control his wolf better than most. Why would Logan attack Mark?

"We do get along, but things are complicated right now," he said softly, pausing to take a deep breath. "I'm not feeling up to talking about it. Let's just say he's a little irritated with me right now. A lot of the wolves are."

"He took advantage," I stated.

"They're werewolves," Mirabelle said, startling me as she walked into the room with a medical bag in hand. I immediately moved aside to let the doctor examine Mark's injuries. The doctor was immaculately dressed as usual, in a button down blue blouse and black slacks. She rolled back her sleeves and slipped on gloves. She continued speaking as she pulled the bandage away. "Don't try to understand werewolf logic. You don't get the handbook unless you become one of them. Even being married to one, and being around them for years, I still don't understand it all."

I moved to the other side of Mark so I couldn't see the bite wound any more. My nausea was mostly under control, but that didn't mean I was comfortable seeing his bone exposed. The other side of Mark was littered with scratches and what looked like another smaller bite wound on his side. Blood was also seeping through the upper thigh of his jeans and I suspected there was a larger wound there as well.

Mirabelle sighed in frustration before yelling loudly, "Jed!" She turned toward me and shook her head. "Damn werewolves. I can't just patch him up like this. The smaller wounds aren't a concern, but this larger one is. He needs to change now, or there will be permanent damage. Jed!" she yelled once more.

I watched the doctor move around Mark to add a bandage to the wound on his side. She moved back to the larger wound once more, peeling back the bandages to peer at it again before adding another bandage and wrapping it tightly with gauze. “Any other major wounds?” she asked as she stepped back and peered at him, arms crossed under her breasts.

“Leg,” he murmured, even though Mirabelle’s eyes were already fixated on the bloody patch on his thigh.

“I need to check it,” she said shortly.

Mark nodded and slid off the bed, but had to clutch the bed rail to keep upright. I rushed over, putting an arm around his chest. He straightened up but I noticed sweat covered his skin and his face had a slight green cast to it. I waited until he seemed steady on his feet before moving in front of him and unbuttoning his jeans. His right pant leg was torn to bits and sticking to the wound beneath. I grasped the pants and slid them down his legs, gingerly pulling them away from his skin as I did so. Blood flowed freely down his leg from a large gash on his upper thigh. Mirabelle moved around me, efficiently wrapping his thigh in thick bandages and gauze once again without bothering to disinfect it.

I moved in close to Mark, holding him up with my body until the doctor had finished binding the leg wound. He leaned over me, resting on my slight frame more than I would have expected him to. Once done, we quickly helped maneuver him back onto the bed. I grabbed extra pillows, using them to prop him up so he could lie down on his side but still give the doctor easy access to his shoulder injury. I moved near to Mark’s side, watching him closely as he shut his eyes and laid his head down.

Mirabelle pulled a blanket out and I helped her cover Mark gently with it. She turned to me as she removed her gloves. “I need to find Jed,” she said softly, her eyes darting worriedly toward Mark. “I’ll be right back.”

I followed Mirabelle into the next room and pulled her to a stop. “What if Jed won’t let Mark change?” I whispered. “Won’t he still heal?”

Mirabelle looked at me and shook her head. "If he can't change I'll hook him up to IV's and hope he can heal fast enough in human form. Even if he changes, there's no guarantee he'll heal completely. For the most part, when they're in wolf form they can take more damage and heal at rapid speeds, but the transformation itself can be dangerous. You've seen it; the change can be violent and it's certainly not easy on the body, despite whatever magic is involved. It may be too late for him to change as it is."

I watched Mirabelle turn away and hurry toward the back door of the house before I walked back to Mark's side. "I'll be okay," Mark said faintly without opening his eyes.

"You don't look okay," I whispered back as I grasped his hand gently.

He smiled crookedly, but still didn't open his eyes. "I've had worse," he muttered softly.

"That doesn't make me feel any better."

Mark didn't say any more, and I wondered if he had fallen asleep. I stood by his side, watching the blood soak through his bandage as I waited impatiently for Mirabelle to return. After several minutes, the doctor finally returned with Jed following close beside her. Jed's flannel had splattered blood on it that hadn't been there before and mud caked to his cowboy boots. I looked from Jed to Mirabelle, trying to read the situation by their expressions.

Jed stalked toward me, and I had to fight the urge to run away. I held onto Mark's hand and squeezed gently, hoping he was awake but not daring to take my eyes off Jed. Jed didn't stop until he was toe to toe with me, and I was forced to lean backward in order to look up at his long, thin face. While Jed had always made me nervous before, he'd never caused the irrational fear that now gripped me and sent me into a cold sweat. He didn't say a word as he stared down at me with yellow wolf eyes. I lifted my chin and met Jed's stare bravely, or stupidly. I knew he could hear the pounding of my heartbeat and the quickening of my breath in fear, but I couldn't back down.

After what seemed an eternity, but was probably less than a minute, Jed backed up and walked casually around Mark's bed. I turned and followed Jed's progress worriedly with my eyes. Mark still hadn't stirred, which had me alarmed. I cast a worried glance at Mirabelle, but she was watching Jed as well. Faster than I could blink, Jed reached out and put his hands on Mark's torso. He growled low in his chest and I felt the hairs on my arm stand up.

Mirabelle suddenly grabbed my arm and pulled me back. I released Mark's hand and stumbled backward, my eyes glued on the two men. Jed growled again and Mark's eyes shot open, glowing a brilliant green color I had never seen before. He thrashed on the hospital bed, held down only by Jed's hands on his chest. Jed growled again, and this time Mark responded with a growl of his own as fur began to coalesce across his body. Mark's face elongated and his limbs bent and snapped. Each dramatic change was punctuated by a piercing howl from Mark's mouth that sent chills down my spine.

Mark howled one last time before he settled onto the bed, breathing hard. He was no longer human, but he wasn't a wolf either. Mark had mentioned the wolf hybrid form, but I had never seen it before. He mostly looked as he normally did, just covered in fur and much larger. His feet were a strange mix between human and wolf, and his hands were longer with sharp claws on the ends. His mouth was a strange mix of human and wolf, with a shorter muzzle and long teeth that jutted over his lips.

Jed stepped back from Mark, panting as though he had just run a marathon. He stumbled toward one of the chairs and sat down heavily. Mark was still lying on the bed, breathing hard but not moving other than that. Mirabelle hurried toward Mark, pulling back the bandages on his shoulder to inspect the wound. I followed her cautiously while still watching Jed from the corner of my eyes.

"He seems to be healing much faster," Mirabelle said softly as she turned toward me. She quickly replaced the bandage, and I felt a swelling of relief when blood didn't gush from his wound as it had before. "We'll still have to keep an eye on him though."

I stopped beside Mirabelle and looked down at Mark in his strange hybrid wolf form. This form must have been what inspired all the werewolf horror stories, despite how rare it was. Perhaps it was also the cause of the Bigfoot stories. I touched Mark's head, feeling the soft fur run through my fingers. "Why isn't he awake?"

"I had to force the change on him, and it can be draining," Jed responded.

I turned toward Jed, who still sat in a chair breathing heavily. "You forced him to change?" I asked, not understanding. "Is that why he's not a full wolf?"

"He's not a full wolf because I didn't choose for him to change into one. I am the Alpha, and as such I can force my wolves to change as I see fit," Jed said bluntly.

"Or not allow them to change at all," I retorted.

Jed looked up at me and his eyes were once again normal human brown, but that didn't make him any less scary. I bit my tongue, knowing I had probably gone too far with that remark. "You are not Pack, so you do not understand," he said roughly as he stood up and walked toward me. "Mark has proven himself within the pack. He has reclaimed a place, albeit a lower one than he was used to before. Be careful you do not ruin things for him further."

I heard the threat in his words, whether I understood it fully or not. "Is Mark allowed to change now?" I asked in what I hoped was a polite tone.

"Yes, he is allowed to change as needed from now on," Jed replied as he moved around me to stand beside Mirabelle. "Keep me apprised on his condition. If need be I'll change him into full wolf form later."

Jed started to walk out of the room, but stopped when he reached the hallway. "Isabella, make sure you keep your brother in the security room for now. I have ordered my pack not to harm him, but there's no sense testing anyone's limits right now. Oh, and don't get any ideas about leaving," Jed added, his silent threat hanging in the air.

Chapter 2

By dawn the next day, I was tired and cranky. I had gotten my brother set up in the bunker with food, clothing, bedding and a small television while I spent most of the night on a couch in the small living room monitoring Mark's condition. Hugo was still recovering, so Dr. Humphry spent the night with her husband in one of the spare rooms down the hall. I hadn't had the chance to check on Jared yet, and worry gnawed at me, but Jed had ordered me not to enter the barn under any circumstances. Considering what had happened with the wolves, I was more than happy to oblige. The last thing I needed was a confrontation with an unfriendly werewolf, especially while Mark was still recovering. On top of that, Jed scared me and I really didn't want to cross him.

Mark still hadn't woken up, and Jed had come back around midnight to force Mark to change into his full wolf form. He said it would speed the healing process faster and I just had to trust his judgment on the matter. I watched Mark all night, afraid to fall asleep for multiple reasons. First, I was worried about Mark since he still hadn't woken up, despite the fact that his wounds were healing rapidly. The second reason I didn't sleep was because I was worried about someone sneaking past me and going after my brother, despite

Jed's orders. In all honesty, the main reason I was afraid to sleep was more due to the fact that there was a great wolf a mere three feet away from me. In my heart, I knew Mark would never hurt me, but that didn't change the fact that he currently appeared to be a very large, very scary, injured wolf. Injured animals could be far more dangerous, and certainly more unpredictable, than uninjured ones. I wasn't sure if this held true with werewolves, but I figured better safe than sorry. Therefore, I spent most of the night in a worried state of unrest.

I did eventually doze, but not for more than fifteen minutes at a time. By five in the morning, I had decided sleep wasn't going to happen and I started a pot of coffee in the hope that the caffeine would keep me functioning for a few hours more. I was mixing my coffee with creamer when strong arms suddenly enveloped me from behind. I squeaked and almost dropped my coffee before I realized the muscular and hairy arms belonged to Mark. Thankfully, they were simple human hairy, and not werewolf hairy.

I turned in his arms, holding the coffee carefully out to the side while I hugged him with my free arm. I buried my face against his bare chest, listening to the steady beating of his heart and trying to contain the tears that were welling in my eyes. "You're awake," I said softly, "and human."

Mark chuckled softly and kissed me on top of my head before pulling back. "I'm good as new," he said.

I stepped back and sipped my coffee as Mark moved around the kitchen preparing his own coffee. His stomach growled loudly and he turned to the refrigerator, pulling out an assortment of foods. I stood back and watched, my eyes roaming over Mark's 6-foot plus body. He wore only a pair of boxers and moved easily as though he'd never been injured. Mirabelle had removed the bandages after he had taken wolf form, but he had been too furry to examine the wounds closely. I discreetly looked for his injuries, particularly the shoulder wound, but there was no visible trace.

I set down my coffee and began making pancakes while Mark

cooked the bacon and eggs. Mark didn't speak as he maneuvered around the kitchen, grabbing utensils out. He opened the egg carton and cracked egg after egg into a large glass. I watched him out of the corner of my eye as he cracked over a dozen eggs into a glass before tipping the glass up to his mouth and drinking them down. I shuddered and quickly turned back to the pancakes I was cooking.

Mark set his glass in the sink and moved back to the stove. Once more, I heard the unmistakable sound of cracking eggs, and I shuddered before I heard the sizzle as they hit the hot frying pan. "I don't normally eat raw eggs," Mark commented into the silence.

I flipped the cooked pancakes onto a plate and poured more batter onto the griddle before responding. "Is it because you changed into a wolf?" I asked, keeping my eyes on the pancakes.

"It's more that I was injured, my Alpha forced a change on me, and then I didn't hunt to replenish my strength. The change healed me, but it also weakened me temporarily. Luckily, it's nothing a little food can't fix."

We cooked enough food to feed a small army, but no one joined us as we sat down at the small kitchen bar to eat. We didn't speak as we ate and drank our coffee. Despite the caffeine and food, I was feeling more tired than before. As soon as we finished eating, Mark excused himself to shower and get dressed. I made up a plate of food and took it down to my brother, along with a thermos full of coffee.

Justin was already awake and sitting in the monitor room, watching the barn intently. I moved up beside him and set the plate of food down in front of him. The barn held several cages for wolves to change in during the full moon if they didn't have full control. The full moon was past, but there were three full cages. John sat outside the farthest cage, watching the wolf inside intently. The wolf was making circles around the cage, randomly jumping toward John as though to attack him. The wolves in the other two cages both appeared to be sleeping.

Justin dug into his food eagerly, while still keeping his eyes on the monitor. I sat down beside him and watched the monitor as well, until Justin had finished scarfing down his food. He turned to me as soon as he cleaned the last food off his plate. "Thanks, Izzy. I was starving."

"Did you sleep at all?" I asked, observing the dark circles underneath Justin's eyes and his tousled hair.

He shook his head. "Not really," he replied, his eyes moving back to the monitor. "I kept worrying one of the wolves would come for me."

"Good thing wolves can't turn doorknobs," I retorted.

Justin turned toward me and rolled his eyes, a small smile playing at his lips. "Oh, very funny. Don't tell me you weren't worried too. I could see you on the monitor. I think you got less sleep than I did."

"Hard to sleep in the same room as an injured wolf," I replied, and instantly regretted it. Justin's face fell and he quickly turned back toward the monitor, worry etched on his face. Justin was scared enough of the wolves without me adding to his fears. "Mark would never hurt me though," I added hastily.

"Doesn't mean you let your guard down," Justin countered, and I had to agree. Of course, I wasn't about to say that aloud.

"Is that Jared?" I asked as I pointed at the wolf John was watching.

"I think so. These are the two wolves Jed brought to the barn yesterday," Justin said, indicating the two sleeping wolves. "Jed was in the barn with them for quite a while. It wasn't pretty."

"What do you mean?" I asked, remembering the blood I had seen on Jed's shirt the previous day. "What did Jed do to them?"

Justin glanced back at me and I noticed how bloodshot his blue eyes were. "You know how Mark turned into that weird wolf-man hybrid?" he asked, and I nodded. "Well, that's sort of what Jed did. It was like he was still human, but with these weird wolf elements. Then he used his teeth and claws to…" he stopped, clearing his throat.

"He punished them."

Justin nodded, "I suppose that's what you'd call it. Looked more like torture to me. And the wolves didn't even fight back!"

We were quiet for a while; both of us lost in our own thoughts. I watched the monitors with him for a short time. I didn't see Jed, but Mirabelle and Hugo eventually went to the kitchen and helped themselves to breakfast. Mark came downstairs, dressed in jeans and a t-shirt, and joined them. I watched them for a few minutes before my eyes automatically went back to the barn. I was worried about Jared still, wondering when he'd come back to human form. He was alive at least, but until I spoke to him and saw him in person, I'd worry.

"Are you mad at me?" Justin asked softly, startling me out of my internal worries.

I took a deep breath before turning toward him, collecting my thoughts. "I love you, Justin. I can't say I understand though, and I get the feeling there's a lot more to your story."

He nodded and looked directly at me. "There is a lot more, but I don't know how much I should divulge. If my research was destroyed in the fire, then that's good… and bad."

"Justin, if you can trust anyone, it's me."

"It's not that I don't trust you, Izzy, because I do. There are just a lot more groups involved than I was ever aware of. It changes things." He stopped and sat back in his chair, tapping his fingers on the chair arms nervously. "Can we trust these werewolves?"

"Well, they hate vampires, so that's a big bonus in my book," I replied with a smile. I knew he wanted more than that, but I didn't know the werewolves much better than he did. Mark was the only one I really knew, and up until recently, I hadn't thought he was anything other than human. Of course, I had never had reason before to think werewolves and vampires were real.

"The wolves may hate the vampires, but they're almost as

brutal," Justin muttered in response.

"You think they're brutal?"

Justin shrugged his shoulders, but his fingers continued tapping nervously on the armrests. "I think the only difference is they seem to have a set of rules, whereas the vampires don't."

"I don't know enough about them either. I do know Mark though, and I trust him. And he trusts Jed. Besides, who else is there?" I added, realizing I was trying to convince myself just as much as I was trying to convince Justin. How much did I really know about the wolves, or Mark for that matter?

He stared at me for a minute before sighing loudly. "I guess I don't have much choice. Sarah will force me to continue my research if she finds me."

I flinched at Sarah's name and leaned back in my chair, staring at my broken fingernails. "As if this vaccine isn't bad enough already," I muttered.

"I get the impression not all the vampires are on board with this vaccine being dispersed," Justin began, shaking his head. "Unfortunately, the vamp in charge is apparently very old and very powerful. He used his own blood for the vaccines, so he gains power for each human linked to him. From what I was hearing, he's already too powerful for any of the other vampires to disobey him."

"Who is this big vampire?"

"The owner of Petri Co. His name is Petrivian; the man who we met in the mountains."

"Are you sure it's just *his* blood in the vaccines?"

Justin nodded. "Yes, according to what I overheard with Sarah, it's a death sentence for any of the other vamps to use their blood. Wait, why do you ask?"

"What does he look like?"

Justin frowned at me, obviously curious as to my line of questioning. "He has dark hair and big eyebrows," Justin shrugged. "He looked like a nice, regular guy. Not too tall, not too short. Sarah thought he was good looking, but I thought he looked sort of average. I never would have looked twice at the guy, and he certainly didn't look like an ancient vampire."

I thought about that. I had wondered if Henri Donovan was actually Petrivian, but it didn't sound like it now. Although I had only met him in dreams, I got the impression his dream-self was his true form. This man sounded like the complete opposite of Henri. Henri was tall, muscular, blond, and gorgeous. He certainly wasn't average. "You said yourself that there were more groups involved than you realized. You weren't just talking about werewolves, were you?"

"Sarah kept talking about other vampires disobeying orders, like that Patricia vampire. The ones who disobeyed were punished or hunted. Of course, Patricia is dead now. Although, I did get the impression that Patricia had a boss. Maybe there are other vampires fighting against Petrivian," Justin shrugged. "That doesn't mean they'll help us. Maybe they'll kill each other off though, if we're lucky."

"Let's hope there are other vampires out there making things difficult for this Petrivian guy," I replied softly, my thoughts turning from Patricia to Henri Donovan again. Was Henri working against Petrivian? To what end? How had I wound up with his blood in my system and not Petrivian anyway? Or did I have Petrivian's blood in me already, and I just wasn't aware of it? I shuddered at the thought.

"I need to get my lab up and running again," Justin said suddenly, catching me off-guard and pulling me quickly out of my thoughts.

"What?"

Justin opened his mouth, then closed it again as though re-thinking what he was going to say. He was quiet for a minute, but I stared him down, arms crossed, until he finally sighed in defeat. "I wasn't just working on making the vaccine airborne. That's what the vampires had me working on, but I was doing my own research on the side; research which is now burnt to a cinder."

"What research, Justin?"

"To save her," he replied, more to himself than me. He was quiet for several minutes before he looked up at me, his blue eyes swimming with unshed tears. "I was working on reversing vampirism, or at the very least trying to reverse the effects of the vaccine."

"Why didn't you say so earlier?" I exclaimed, jumping to my feet. "If the werewolves knew this earlier, they probably wouldn't have been trying to tear you limb from limb! Damn it, Justin!"

Justin stood and grabbed my arm, shaking his head. "I didn't know if I could trust them, and after seeing what they did to each other...."

"So you'd rather keep this information to yourself! What good would that do, Justin? At this point in time, I don't think there's much choice in *who* you can trust. Any human who has had the vaccine is a potential threat, including me! Werewolves are immune to vampire blood! They're pretty much the only ones we can trust won't be influenced by vampires."

"They're immune?" Justin asked wide-eyed. "This could change everything." Justin grabbed a notepad sitting on the counter and began hurriedly scribbling in it.

"What are you doing?" I asked exasperatedly.

"Making a list of everything I need to get my lab going again. Do any werewolves have strong science backgrounds? Are there any scientists, researchers, or doctors? I could use some help. This could change things, Izzy."

I stared at him, but he continued to jot down his list. "So, I take it you're going to trust the werewolves now."

He stopped briefly to glance up at me and nod his head. "Like you said, it's not like I have much choice. Plus, if werewolves are immune, I may be able to synthesize an antidote with their blood. Damn, I wish I could find Ron. He'd be a big help."

"Ronald Dawson?" I asked, frowning. "From your company?"

Justin nodded without looking up from his note pad. "Yeah,

he didn't go on the expedition. He came down with pneumonia and had to stay behind. Last time I saw him he was in a hospital in New York."

"When you called me all those months ago I got a strange phone call just after I hung up with you. It was Agent... something. I don't remember his name, but he was asking about your team, including Ron, George, Jin and Sarah. At the time, I thought they were all dead," I added slowly.

"Most of the team is dead," Justin said softly as he stopped writing to look at me. "George is either dead or a vampire. I haven't seen him, so my guess is he's dead. I don't know why anyone else would be looking for Ron. He wasn't on the expedition, so he doesn't know anything about vampires or vaccines. He was a very good researcher though; probably the best."

"I can ask John to look for him, if you think he can help you."

"Assuming he hasn't gotten the vaccine himself," Justin muttered in reply. "For all I know, he could be working for Petri Company. Hopefully, he just retired like he kept threatening to."

"I'll go talk to Jed and John," I said as Justin put his list in my hand. "Stay here until I've smoothed things over. I imagine the wolves will be more agreeable if they think you're on their side and not working *with* the vampires." I stopped at the door, one question still on my mind. "Justin, why were you working on making the vaccine airborne and permanent? Did you realize what you were doing? Were the vampires forcing you? Please, help me understand, so I can explain it to the werewolves."

Justin stilled before he looked up at me, guilt etched on his face. "I made a mistake, Izzy. I trusted Sarah, despite what she had become. I never got the vaccine. I never drank vampire blood. I was fully aware of what I was doing, but by the time I realized my mistake, it was too late. Remember, Sarah and Jin were both researchers as well. They're not the same though. It's as though they remember their lives as humans, but they're disconnected. They needed me to do their research, but they knew enough to understand what I was working on."

"Do they know you were working on a cure?"

"No, I don't think so. I hid it when I could, and I wrote all my notes in code. They started watching me more when I hadn't made any progress on making the vaccine airborne. I stalled and destroyed research when I could, and I think that's when Sarah realized I had stopped helping her. She tortured Jared and Kirk, turned Jin into a vampire, and I still wouldn't help her."

"So she came after me," I stated.

"I think so," Justin replied, nodding his head. "I think something else was going on with Sarah though. We started moving around a lot more, not staying in one place for more than a few weeks. New vampires showed up that didn't take orders from Sarah and seemed to have their own agendas. Things were quickly growing chaotic. Sarah grew more aggressive, too," he added, looking away from me remorsefully.

I stared at my brother, thinking about the things he was saying and the things I was sure he was omitting. Our mother had died in a car accident when I was eight, leaving me as the only female in the household. Dad did his best, but ultimately he died of a broken heart. The doctors said it was heart disease due to years of drinking, smoking, and just plain unhealthy habits. I had been 17, and Justin at 20 stepped in to take care of me. The reality of it was that I had been taking care of Justin since our mom had died. For years, it had just been the two of us, and I could read him like a book. Now, I wasn't so sure. He had learned to lie while he'd been with Sarah. I knew he loved her, but even when she'd been human they hadn't had a healthy relationship. How much had he helped her willingly, thinking she was still the same person?

"Is there anything else I need to know?" I pushed softly.

"No, not right now," Justin replied quietly as he turned away and sat back down to watch the video monitors.

I stared at his back for several moments, gathering my thoughts. Poor Justin, I thought. He put his trust in the woman he loved, and she turned into a creature of evil. Not his fault, but he was bearing the guilt nonetheless. He had followed Sarah blindly one too many times, and this time he paid the ultimate cost. Sarah was gone as far as I was concerned. Maybe she wasn't technically dead, but a vampire was close enough.

I turned and left the room, closing the door behind me. Justin was living in his own fantasy world, and he was definitely keeping secrets. I'd let him keep those secrets for now, and hope they didn't come back to bite us later. I had enough secrets of my own that I wasn't sharing, so I just had to trust him. One thing I knew for sure though, Justin would work on a cure. He'd want Sarah back. I didn't know if he could cure vampirism, but if he could at least counter the vaccine, it was a step in the right direction. What else could we do?

Chapter 3

I meandered back through the house to the kitchen, where Jed, Mark, and Hugo were chatting as they cleaned up the breakfast dishes. I stood in the doorway awkwardly, not wanting to interrupt them. They acted very human, as though they hadn't all heard me walk into the room. They probably smelled me as well, which reminded me I still needed to take a shower. Mirabelle walked in the back door, carrying empty plates in her hands. She smiled at me and handed the dishes off to her husband before walking over to me.

"My work is officially done here," the doctor said grinning widely, and showing off perfect white teeth. She casually tossed her dark tresses over her shoulder as she glanced back into the kitchen. "I've given everyone a clean bill of health, and now I have to go treat my human patients."

"Everyone?" I asked.

"Well, Jared seems to be healed, but he's still in wolf form. That's Jed's territory," she added with a look toward the Alpha.

Jed stood at the sink with his hands in soapy water, washing dishes. He was dressed in his usual flannel attire, and I briefly wondered if he owned any other clothes. He didn't turn around as he spoke. "Only time will tell," he said simply. I didn't know what that meant, but decided to let it go for now.

"Thank you for all your help, Mirabelle," I said, taking the doctor's hands.

Mirabelle smiled again and nodded her head. She gave Hugo a quick kiss before excusing herself to go to her clinic. Jed moved away from the sink, drying his hands on a towel as he walked toward me. Mark moved to take his spot automatically, but I kept my eyes glued on the Alpha.

"Did you need something?" Jed asked as he stood before me. He was too close, invading my space as he looked down at me.

I nodded, my mouth suddenly going dry. Even at his most casual washing dishes, he was still intimidating. "I spoke to my brother again, about the vaccine." Jed blinked, but didn't say a word. I licked my lips and blurted the words out. "He was working on a cure."

"A cure?" he asked incredulously, his eyebrows shooting up.

I nodded, not entirely trusting my voice. I held out the list of supplies my brother had given me, hoping to keep things simple. "If he can get some supplies, he thinks he can continue his research. Not the research to make the vaccine airborne though," I added quickly. "He might be able to stop the vaccine's effects, particularly if the Pack is willing to help out. He also mentioned another researcher who could help him, if John can track him down. And if any of the Pack has a good science background that you think might help, he could use assistance."

Jed's eyebrows rose further at that last remark and he suddenly seemed to relax as he stepped back a step, finally moving out of my personal bubble. "He would willingly take assistance from a werewolf?"

I nodded, "Yes. I think he's still a little nervous, but he'll come around." Of course, I was still nervous around the werewolves. Any sane human would be.

"Do you trust him?"

"He's my brother!"

"That's not what I asked," Jed replied sharply. "I need to know if he can be trusted."

I sighed and glanced at Mark still washing dishes. "He wants Sarah back. I think he'll do whatever it takes to save her. He blames himself for her becoming a vampire, so, yes, I think in this he can be trusted. He claims he never got the vaccine or drank vampire blood, so he's not being influenced by vamps."

"That's assuming he's telling the truth. He could have been given vampire blood and have no recollection of it, or have been ordered to lie about it. For now, I'll trust your judgment on this. I hope it's not misplaced," he added, pointing a finger in my direction. Jed looked down at the list, perusing it briefly. A small smile played at his lips as he got to the end of the list. "I have a place that should work for Justin to conduct his research. It's not far from here, and there's a house he can stay in as well. I'll send some people to get it set up, and acquire these supplies."

"Thank you," I replied.

"Who is this person he wants John to search for?"

"His name is Ronald Dawson. He and Justin worked together at NuvaDrug. He was supposed to be on the expedition as well, but he got sick and stayed behind in New York. I think someone else was looking for him too."

"Someone else?"

I shrugged. "When Justin's expedition first went missing, I was contacted by someone I thought was a government agent. I'm not sure whom he was working for, but he was asking a lot of questions about Justin's team, including Ron. He seemed to know quite a bit as well."

Without another word, Jed nodded and stuffed the paper into his pocket before turning on his heel and exiting through the back door. I watched him walk toward the barn through the window and had to resist the urge to follow him. I wanted to know what he was thinking. More than that, I wanted to check on Jared. I pursed my lips as I stared at the distant barn.

"Jared will be fine," Hugo said in his deep, rumbling voice as he moved up beside me to peer out the window. "The first change can be difficult, but most of us were injured when we were changed. The survival rate is pretty high by day two."

"Some don't survive?" I asked softly, a lump forming in my throat.

"Each day he's alive his odds improve. He handled the change well. Now we just wait for him to return to human form," Hugo finished, patting me on the back awkwardly. Mark moved up next to Hugo, drying his hands on a towel. Hugo glanced at Mark, then back at me. "I'll leave you two to talk."

Hugo walked out the back door and headed toward the barn. I turned away from the window and walked through the dining room. I could sense Mark following right behind me. I moved through the rooms and into the hallway, where I stopped, debating which way I wanted to go. My eyes were heavy with exhaustion, and I wanted nothing more than to sleep, but I had heard the emphasis Hugo had put on his last words. Mark wanted to talk to me, but I wasn't eager to talk to him.

"I'm exhausted, Mark," I said as I put my foot on the first stair. Maybe if I avoided him long enough, he'd leave me alone.

Mark sighed loudly behind me and put his hand on my arm. "Izzy," he began, but I stopped him.

"Please, can we talk later? I didn't get any sleep last night and it's catching up to me. I'll just take a short nap. Can you keep an eye on Justin for me?" I added, hoping I would appeal to Mark's protective nature.

Mark stared at me, and I watched his eyes soften bit by bit until he finally nodded. "Of course I will," he replied. "I wanted to have a chat with Justin anyway. We'll talk later."

Mark waited until I had made it to the top of the stairs before he turned and walked away. I swallowed the lump that seemed stuck in my throat and opened my bedroom door. The bed was made and the curtains had been thrown open, letting in the early morning sunshine. I closed the door and pulled the blinds before settling onto the clean bed. The room wasn't as dark as I'd like it, but I doubted it would matter. I could feel sleep pulling at me the moment I closed my eyes.

Sleep did come quickly, but it was not restful. The dream pulled at me as soon as I drifted off. All around me was darkness, and cold. I hunched down, shivering around my naked and dirty body. I reached a hand out to feel the bars of the cage. I knew this cage, but it was much smaller than I had remembered it, and seemed to shrink with each passing second until cold metal pressed painfully against my flesh.

I hunched down further, as small as I could go, and the cage shrank with me. There was nothing but the cage and the darkness. I tried to scream, but I had no voice. My hands clawed at the cage, but there was no room to move. A small light appeared in the distance, but it didn't illuminate anything. I needed to get to that light, I knew. The light was the way out. The light was my salvation.

I pushed against the cage again and tried to reach through the bars. That's when I really looked at myself. I had thought I was covered in dirt or mud, but when I looked closer I realized it was blood. The blood was too bright! I shouldn't be able to see the blood in the darkness, but it was all I could see. Suddenly there was blood everywhere, coating the cage as well as my body. Then I was falling. The floor disappeared beneath me and I felt myself sinking down into an endless pool of blood. The cage was gone and I was able to stand, but the blood was rising quickly. The blood was up to my knees in seconds, and ascending to cover my thighs.

I looked up toward the distant light, trying in vain to reach out toward it as I sank deeper into the pool of blood. The blood was like quicksand, pulling me down faster the more I struggled. With each beat of my heart, the blood rose, surrounding me. Then the thought came to me, as though someone had spoken, even though I heard no voice. I needed to drink the blood. If I drank it all into me, I would be free. The light twinkled again, urging me to go to it. The blood had reached my chin, shining brilliantly in the darkness. I held my hand out toward the light as the blood rose higher, but I still couldn't reach it. The light was too far away and too difficult to reach. I tried to swim in the blood, but it thickened around me, making each movement that much harder. The blood churned around me like the waves in an ocean, covering my lips. I finally opened my mouth, letting the salty blood swirl in, before I drank it down.

I shot up in bed, drenched in sweat. My heart was pounding so loudly I could hear it echoing in my ears. The sheets had tangled around my arms and legs, and I struggled to yank them off. I finally succeeded in removing the blankets and climbed out of bed. The bedside clock indicated I'd only slept for a little over an hour, but I knew I wouldn't be able to go back to sleep despite how tired I still felt.

I grabbed clothes out of the dresser and headed to the bathroom to finally shower. The steaming hot shower helped refresh me and I felt more awake afterwards. I took my time getting ready, fixing my hair and putting makeup on before going downstairs. Vanessa had supplied me with clothes and makeup, which I put to good use. I wore tight jeans that conformed to my body tucked into knee-high brown boots and a long cream-colored shirt that just covered my hips. The shirt had a scoop neck that showed a fair amount of cleavage. I wasn't very busty, but I was able to use the push-up bra to full advantage.

I reached the bottom of the stairs and didn't immediately see anyone, so I decided to check on my brother. John was with Justin in the control room when I arrived. John had his laptop out on the counter, typing as Justin spoke. I entered the room quietly and perused the monitors while they spoke. The camera for the barn showed only one wolf, Jared, in a cage. The remaining cages were now empty.

"Hey, Izzy," Justin said and I shifted my attention to him. "John's going to work on finding Ron for me."

"That's great, Justin," I replied.

"Mark wants to talk to you," he said as he shifted uncomfortably in his chair.

I stared at my brother thoughtfully, taking in the clean clothes and freshly shaven skin. He looked better already, with a hopeful light on his face. My eyes darted toward John, dressed in his usual black attire. He appeared immersed in his computer, but I had the feeling he was latching on to every word said. "Did he say what he wanted to talk to me about?" I asked nervously, darting a look back at my brother.

He shook his head, "No, but he seemed worried." Justin stared at me with blue eyes that were so similar to my own. "Are you okay?"

I smiled and nodded my head. "Of course I am. I just wanted to check on you first and make sure everything was alright."

"Everything's fine," he replied. "I'm going to stay down here for now, until Jed can get my lab set up. I guess he has a place in mind that I can use, and there are a couple werewolves already willing to help."

"That's great. I guess I'll go find Mark now," I said, even though it was the last thing I wanted to do.

"He's playing pool with Beth," John said. He looked up at me finally and I found myself involuntarily backing up at the intensity of his gaze. John had a way of finding things out, and the look he gave me said he knew every deep secret I had.

I shot my brother another quick smile before hurrying out of the room and up the stairs, away from John as quickly as possible. John would be watching me on the monitor, so I turned toward the bar room. The door to the room was open, and I could hear the familiar sound of pool cue striking ball from the hallway.

I walked into the room slowly, my eyes adjusting to the dim lighting. Mark and Beth were at the far end of the room with Logan and Lucas, playing a game of pool. It was an odd group to be playing pool, I thought, but they all seemed at ease. Mark looked up at me and grinned widely. I found myself grinning automatically in return as I walked toward them. Mark was dressed in jeans and a Captain America t-shirt that fit snugly, accentuating his physique. He still had the sexy goatee around his mouth that somehow made him look even more attractive than his usual clean-shaven look.

Logan and Lucas were standing together at the opposite side of the pool table, and I found myself having a difficult time telling them apart. Both men had day old facial hair and were dressed similarly in casual jeans and shirts. I eyed them, looking for the smallest detail to set the twins apart. One of the twins laughed at something the other said, and I immediately knew the laughing twin was Lucas. Lucas had a carefree vibe about him. His hair was also slightly shaggier and more tousled.

Beth was setting up a shot as I walked up, her eyes focused down the length of the pool cue. She wore a blue skirt that swished when she walked and a cream blouse that was simple but matched perfectly. I walked up next to Mark and watched as Beth sunk a solid ball. She moved around the pool table, her eyes flickering up to me briefly. She settled on another ball and shot, just missing her mark. She walked over to stand on the other side of Mark while Logan moved up to the table to make his shot.

Logan sank his last remaining pool balls in a matter of moments, and lined himself up for the eight ball shot. I watched the game, but my eyes kept flickering to Beth on the other side of Mark. She had inched herself closer to Mark until her arm was touching his. I turned my attention back to Logan as he called out his shot. He sighted down the pool cue and took his shot in one smooth move, sinking the eight ball exactly as planned. He stood up and turned a wicked grin on Mark.

"Well, brother, it looks like we win," Logan said softly. "Drink up you two!"

Mark chuckled and shook his head before walking over to the bar, with Beth following closely at his side. I followed behind them while keeping my distance from Logan and Lucas. Lucas jumped behind the bar, laughing as he pulled out two beer mugs. Mark and Beth sat down at the bar while Lucas pulled out four bottles of alcohol all with high proofs, including Absinthe. He grinned maliciously and pulled out a mason jar of clear liquid, setting it beside the others.

"Alright, who's going first?" Lucas asked.

"I will," Beth said.

Logan dropped a die on the counter and pushed it toward Beth. "Let's consider these one through five," he said, pointing at the bottles in a row. "If you roll a six, you get to pick your poison."

I sat down on the other side of Mark, and Logan followed me, sitting down on my other side. "Loser does werewolf shots," Logan whispered and I turned to look at him. He was sitting close beside me and had a small grin on his face.

"Werewolf shots?" I asked.

"Fast metabolism means we have to consume large quantities very quickly. So, werewolf shots are in beer mugs. Then you spin in a circle for one minute to hopefully speed things along. Not sure if that actually does anything or not, but it sure is fun to watch."

"Ah," I responded, looking back at the beer mugs in front of Beth and Mark. I didn't ask why they were playing their game, but figured it was some sort of werewolf bonding.

Beth cupped the die in her hand and shook, before tossing the die onto the counter. We all watched it bounce and roll until it settled on four. Lucas counted off the bottles dramatically and picked up the fourth bottle. "Ooh, tequila. Excellent choice!" He laughed as he poured half the bottle out into the beer mug.

"We'll drink together," Mark said as he rolled the die. The die bounced and came to a stop on two, the bottle of Absinthe.

Mark groaned loudly as Lucas poured the Absinthe into the mug. "No diluting this down for you," Lucas said. "We all agreed on pure shots. No sissy human stuff."

Mark nodded, picked up his mug and turned toward Beth. Beth smiled at Mark and leaned toward him, placing a kiss on his lips. "For luck," she said as she grabbed her mug and pressed it to her mouth.

"On three," Lucas said. "Three!"

Logan snorted beside me, but my focus was on Mark and Beth. They both quickly drank down their respective drinks, gulping loudly. Mark slammed his empty mug down first, followed quickly by Beth. Mark let out a breath and pounded his hand on the counter several times before standing up. Beth kept her mouth closed, but tears swam in her eyes. She took a deep breath through her nose before standing up as well.

Beth stumbled and grasped onto Mark. His arms immediately wrapped around her as he pulled her to her feet. I swiveled around in my seat as I watched Mark and Beth spin in a circle while Lucas timed them for one minute. At the end of one minute, Mark and Beth stumbled back to their seats at the bar.

"So, are you two ready to play again?" Lucas asked as he played with the bottle of Absinthe, spinning it across the counter. "Maybe Izzy wants to play."

"No way," I replied immediately. I had never been much for drinking games or pool, and this seemed like the worst of both.

"What, are you chicken?" Lucas taunted as he made clucking noises. When I didn't immediately respond, he began flapping his arms in addition to the clucking.

I rolled my eyes at him and grinned in spite of myself. "I know the basics of pool, but I've only played a few times. I don't think it would be a fair game."

"I would never take advantage of you, my sweet," Lucas said sincerely as he placed a hand on his heart. He grinned and added, "Okay, I would definitely take advantage, but not of a pool game. We can make this fair. We'll give you an extra shot when you miss."

"I don't know. I'm not sure I can handle werewolf shots," I added. I eyed the bottles on the counter, wondering if I still had enough vampire blood in my system to handle the alcohol. Nothing would save me from the awful taste though.

"With all that vampire blood you drank, I'm sure you can take a little alcohol," Beth said suddenly. "You can be on the twin's team, but you don't get extra perks because you're a novice. I'll give you one extra shot, that's it." She stared at me pointedly, then stood up and walked over to the pool table as though everything had been decided.

I didn't like the extra pity shot Beth was giving me, but I was going to take it anyway. I stood and followed her to the pool table, where she had begun setting up the game. When had I agreed to this idiotic game? Mark moved up behind me and placed his mouth next to my ear. I could smell the alcohol on his breath as he whispered to me. "You don't have to do this."

"Yes, I do," I replied as I turned to face Mark. I stood on my tiptoes and snaked an arm around his neck as I pulled my body close to his. He lowered his face to mine and I kissed him thoroughly, tasting the burning Absinthe that still lingered on his tongue.

I released Mark and immediately turned and walked around the pool table to Logan and Lucas. Lucas was grinning widely as he held a pool cue out to me. I grabbed the cue and turned back toward the table. Beth stared at me, her expression icy.

"So, same stakes as before?" Logan asked into the uncomfortable silence.

"Absolutely," Beth replied immediately. "Izzy can break."

Mark opened his mouth to argue, but I quickly moved into position to break. Lucas moved beside me and snaked an arm around me. "Let me help you, sweetheart," he said softly as he put a hand over mine.

I shook him off and stood up. "I've got it," I replied tartly.

He held up his hands in surrender and grinned. I turned back toward the pool table, but Beth moving up beside Mark drew my attention. She stood in front of him and leaned back until she was casually resting up against him. I took a deep breath and focused on the pool table. Beth was trying to get under my skin, and it was definitely working. Well, two could play this game.

I focused back on the game in front of me as I carefully took aim. I took a deep breath in and held it. Using all my strength to break up the balls, I took my shot. The cue ball jumped into the air, bounced off the table and rolled across the floor. The rest of the balls scattered across the pool table. Lucas laughed as he retrieved the ball off the floor.

"Well, Izzy gets one freebie! I guess this'll be it," Logan said as he patted me on the back.

"Not with this ball," Lucas said as he walked over with the cue ball in hand and held it out for me to see. In the place I had struck the ball, there was a crack originating from the impact point. "Looks like you still have some vamp blood in you after all. I guess you got super strength and super healing!"

My face burned with a combination of embarrassment and fear. Why couldn't I just be normal? I waited while Lucas grabbed another ball and handed it to me. Outwardly, I tried to appear calm, but my heart was racing and I knew the werewolves could all hear it. I took the new cue ball and placed it back onto the table. I hadn't sunk any balls, so I lined up the easiest shot I could see.

I tried to gauge my strength better as I tapped in an easy shot. The ball sunk, and I moved around the table to line up another shot. My second shot missed and I moved away from the table so Beth could take a turn. Beth walked around the table, wobbling slightly as she moved. The alcohol was obviously taking effect, and I only hoped it hindered her pool game. She sunk four balls easily before her fifth shot went wide and Lucas moved in for his turn.

"This is where the game ends, folks," Lucas said arrogantly as he lined up for his first shot. He sunk the first ball and moved around for his next shot.

Lucas sunk ball after ball in quick succession, until all that was left was the eight ball for the win. The shot was trickier, requiring him to lean awkwardly across the table as he called up his shot. He took a deep breath and let it out slowly as the rest of us moved in closer to watch. Beth moved in front of Lucas so she was right in his line of sight. Just as Lucas pulled back to shoot, Beth lifted her shirt up, exposing her ample breasts. Lucas sliced across the edge of the cue ball. The ball tapped the edge of the eight ball, sending it spinning the wrong way across the table.

Mark laughed loudly and knocked Lucas off the table. "Looks like it's my turn," he said. Mark moved around the table, lined up his shot, and sunk the first ball. He aimed his second shot and missed completely.

I blinked, wondering how he had missed such an easy shot. "Damn," Mark muttered as he stumbled backward. I looked up at him, taking in the glassy eyes. Apparently, the alcohol had taken hold on him as well.

I looked over at Logan, but he shook his head. "Your turn, Izzy. I'm not playing this round."

Great, the game was riding on me. I moved around the table, wondering how I could possibly make such a difficult shot. Lucas shadowed me, whispering tips in my ear. I took the shot he indicated as the easiest, lined up, but in my fear I didn't give it enough power and the cue ball barely tapped the eight ball. I sighed in frustration and moved out of the way so Beth could shoot.

She wobbled slightly, but seemed in better shape than Mark as she aimed and took her first shot. She easily sunk the ball and lined up for her last ball, sinking it just as quickly. All that remained was the eight ball, and Beth had a direct shot. She grinned in triumph as she effortlessly sunk the eight ball, winning the game.

Chapter 4

The last thing I wanted to do was get drunk with the werewolves who had attacked me, my brother, and Mark, but I didn't have much choice. It was either play along, or run for the hills. I followed the others back toward the bar, where Logan played bartender this time. If the vampire blood was still prevalent in my system, I wouldn't actually get drunk, but I would still feel the burn going down. I tried to take comfort in that small fact. How had I gotten myself into this situation?

I reached the counter and sat down between Lucas and Mark. Logan set a mug down in front of me and handed me the die. I didn't waste any time shaking it and tossing it onto the counter. I rolled a five, and Logan slid the mason jar across the counter to me. Lucas chuckled beside me as I unscrewed the lid and took a whiff of the potent alcohol.

"What is this? Turpentine?" I asked, scrunching up my nose.

Lucas snorted in laughter and patted me on the back. "That, my dear, is the homemade stuff. Drink down the whole jar!"

"The whole jar?" I asked, sizing up the jar with my beer mug and thinking I had definitely rolled wrong.

"That's the rule," Mark muttered beside me. "Sorry, we should have told you. You can roll again."

"No, it's fine," I replied, even though it was definitely not fine. The drink smelled worse than rubbing alcohol. I could sense Beth on the other side of Mark, waiting for me to give up. Jealousy was a powerful motivator. I took a deep breath, trying to push down the emotion. Mark wasn't mine to claim, so I couldn't really be jealous, could I?

Lucas picked up the die beside me and rolled it across the counter, where it stopped on five as well. "Damn," Lucas muttered, as Logan pulled another jar out from under the counter. He unscrewed the lid and turned to me with a small smile on his lips. "Well, let's do this thing. On three?"

I nodded and swiveled toward Lucas, holding the jar aloft. Lucas smiled suddenly and leaned forward to plant a kiss on my lips. He lingered there, trying to tease my lips open with his tongue. I leaned backward, trying to put distance between us as I clamped my mouth shut. I felt Mark's arms reach around me and push Lucas backward. Lucas laughed as he fell back, sloshing some of the alcohol over his hand as he did so.

"Hey, Mark and Beth kissed for luck before their drink. Shouldn't we do the same?" Lucas asked me, his eyes twinkling with laughter.

I gazed at Lucas, wondering at his game. He was staring at me pointedly, as though trying to communicate with me silently. Mark growled behind me and I risked a glance over my shoulder at him. He still looked a little tipsy, with his glassy eyes focused angrily on Lucas. Beth sat close beside Mark, her hand resting casually on his thigh as she gazed at him in obvious adoration.

I felt a strong jealous wave come over me at the sight of her hand on Mark's thigh. I set my mason jar down, stood up, and grabbed Lucas with both hands. My lips made contact with his and he responded immediately, exploring my mouth with his tongue. His hands trailed around my body until I felt one hand grab my butt and squeeze. That was the last straw for me. I pulled away from him and sat back down as though nothing had happened.

"Let's drink," I said, reaching for my jar and holding it to my lips.

I glanced at Lucas, waiting for him to pick up his jar as well. He held the jar to his lips and I took my first sip of the burning liquid. I tried not to breathe as I drank the alcohol down as fast as I could. About halfway through the jar, I had to stop and take a breath; this was a mistake. My throat immediately burned as though fire had coated it and I struggled to breathe clean air into my lungs. I coughed and sputtered while someone pounded on my back, as though that would help.

I held up my hand to stop the person pounding on my back, as I regained control of my breathing. My vision blurred with tears, but I could just make out my drink. I picked it up, ignoring Mark as he implored me to stop, and put the drink to my lips again. I took a deep breath and drained the remaining liquid. When the last drop was gone, I slammed the jar onto the counter and stood up, carefully keeping my mouth closed this time as I breathed through my nose.

The room spun around me, and I grinned suddenly at the feeling. I actually felt drunk already! Maybe I didn't have as much vampire blood left in me as I had feared. Could I be free soon? Lucas moved up beside me and we spun in circles as Logan counted down the time. At the end of one minute, I stopped spinning and walked unsteadily back to the bar. Mark steered me onto the bar stool, but I found it difficult to stay in one place as the stool swiveled back and forth beneath me.

"Well that was a rush," Lucas muttered as he took his place beside me.

I nodded and found myself giggling. I turned toward Mark and grinned widely. "I think the alcohol test worked," I said slowly as I concentrated on my words.

Mark nodded and smiled, but the smile didn't reach his eyes.

"We'll see. It is promising though."

"Shall we rack up another game?" Lucas asked.

"No more," Mark replied as he stood up and pulled me to my feet.

"No hard feelings?" Logan asked as he walked around the bar to stand before Mark.

Mark shook his head and clasped hands with Logan. "All is well, brother," Mark replied before he turned back to me. "Izzy, care to join me for a walk?"

"Sure," I replied, nodding my head and immediately regretting it as the room spun around me. I grasped onto Mark's arm to steady myself, feeling him flex his muscles beneath my hand.

"Who wants to play another game?" Lucas asked loudly and I watched him stumble toward the pool table.

Logan shook his head and smiled at his brother. "I'd best keep an eye on him. He can do a lot of damage in the short amount of time that alcohol will be in his system."

I watched Logan walk over to his brother, who was attempting to rack up the pool table for another game. My eyes roamed toward Beth, still sitting at the bar. She turned her pixie-like face toward mine, a scowl marring her delicate features. I smiled at her and her scowl deepened briefly before she turned away from us.

Mark pulled gently on my arm, and I let him lead me toward the back door. A cold gust of air met us as soon as Mark opened the door, and I shivered as goose bumps covered my skin. Mark stopped and snagged a denim jacket out from behind the bar. He pulled the jacket around my shoulders, and I shoved my arms through the sleeves as we walked outside.

I stumbled on the uneven ground as I tried to keep pace with Mark's long strides. We wound our way past the lines of laundry and toward a large copse of trees. Frost lingered on the ground in the shadows of the large fir trees, where the sun had yet to reach. I followed Mark deeper into the trees, where the absence of a biting breeze made it warmer despite the lack of sunshine. We continued for several minutes until Mark finally stopped in a small glade.

The ground was immaculately cultivated, with bright green grass cut short. Wooden benches lined the edge of the glade. Amidst the beautifully manicured lawn, rows of headstones were set into the earth. The closest headstones were newer, with bright flowers adorning them. Mark walked purposely to the most recent grave and knelt down, pressing his knuckles to the headstone. I stood back and read the headstone. It was simple, with just a name and dates stating 'Peter Sanderson 1975-2005'.

Mark knelt there for several minutes, and I stepped back to give him some space. He finally stood and took my hand, leading me to the closest bench. "Has the alcohol worn off yet?" he asked.

It hadn't been more than thirty minutes, but already I could feel the alcoholic buzz diminishing. I sighed and nodded my head. "Mostly," I muttered as I wiped the dew off the bench before sitting down.

"I had a feeling," Mark responded quietly as he sat down beside me. "Especially after you took out that cue ball."

I looked at Mark, who stared out across the graveyard, his face serious. He didn't look at me as he spoke. "This is where we bury our own, especially when the circumstances around the death are peculiar. Peter was the last member of our pack to die. He was Beth's brother, and my best friend," he said the last slowly.

Mark took a deep breath in and ran his fingers through his thick brown hair as he gathered his thoughts. He finally sighed and turned toward me, his eyes roving across my face as though trying to read something there. "I was the one who had turned him initially. It was my decision, my choice, to make him a werewolf."

Mark stopped talking, his eyes distant with memory. When he finally spoke again, his voice was thick with emotion. "It was just a stupid accident. Beth and I were... we were dating at the time. There aren't many female wolves, so most of us date humans, which is what

Beth was at the time. Neither of them knew what I was.

"The three of us were driving over the pass to go skiing up at Hoodoo. We had been joking around when we hit a patch of ice and our car went tumbling over a cliff. Beth was in the back seat with me, and I managed to protect her with my body. Peter was driving though, and he wasn't so lucky.

"By the time the car finally stopped rolling; Peter was on the brink of death. I made the decision right then and there to bite him, hoping to save his life by giving him the healing benefits of a werewolf. He wasn't conscious and it was a long journey back to Jed's house. Needless to say, by the time we made it there, the bite had taken hold and Peter turned into a werewolf." Mark paused, looking at me pointedly.

"The bite killed him?" I asked carefully.

Mark shook his head. "No, he spent four amazing months as a werewolf. He was great at it! He learned quickly, and by the fifth full moon, he was ready to be out of the cage and roaming free. Jed was against it, but I insisted he would be fine. We changed as a group here on Jed's property, but Peter took off away from the rest of the pack. Several of us followed him, trying to get him to come back to the hunting grounds, but he was so fast. He had picked up a scent, and he was following it.

"The scent led us to Beth. I don't think Peter knew what he was doing. I think his wolf wanted to make his sister part of the pack. She had been walking her dog like she did every evening. Peter as a werewolf was ruthless. He killed her dog and attacked her. When I arrived, he was tearing at her throat and she was on the brink of death. He didn't know that he was killing her. His wolf had completely taken over." Mark grew still as he remembered the events. When he spoke again, it was in a hushed voice. "I had no choice. I attacked Peter."

Mark stopped, tears glistening in his eyes. I held my breath, waiting for him to continue, but knowing where this story would end.

My eyes flickered toward the headstone marking Peter's grave. I reached out and grabbed Mark's hand, trying to comfort him. He didn't acknowledge my hand as he took a deep breath and stared out across the graveyard again.

"Peter was wounded pretty badly, but we figured he'd heal from it. We brought him and Beth back here and locked them up. Women don't survive the change often, but she did. Peter eventually turned back into his human form, but his wounds were too much. Injuries from other wolves don't heal as fast, and he didn't have the strength or ability to change back into wolf form again and speed the process. Jed tried to force his wolf, but it was just too much for his body. He died that night," Mark finished.

My heart ached for him and his obvious sadness and guilt. "Is that why you left the pack?"

"I had killed my best friend, my Pack member, my brother. It was too much," he muttered, finally turning toward me. His eyes glistened with unshed tears. "The bond in a pack is strong. If you have control, you can feel other members of your pack. You can sense their feelings, their thoughts, and their injuries. I felt him die."

I leaned into Mark, resting my head on his shoulder. I was glad he was finally letting me in. It was difficult being in a house full of werewolves and feeling like the odd man out, not understanding the strange dynamics at play. Why was he telling me about this now? Was it because of Beth, because of Jed or was he opening up to me now because he wanted me to open up to him? It would be something he would do.

"Jared is back in human form," Mark said suddenly, and I sat up in surprise.

"Is he okay? Wait, can you tell because you're back in the pack?"

Mark nodded and smiled crookedly at me. "Yes, we're both in the pack now. He's fine. I felt him change while we were playing pool. He seems to be himself," Mark added with a laugh.

"Why didn't you say something sooner?" I asked as I stood up, ready to go see Jared. No matter what Mark said, I needed to see him for myself.

Mark pulled gently on my hand, urging me to sit back down. "He's not going anywhere, Iz. Please, we need to talk first."

I didn't like the look he gave me, as though he could read me like a book. I hesitated, but finally sat back down. My arms crossed over my chest and I leaned away from him. "What do you want to talk about?" I asked testily.

Mark grimaced, and I regretted snapping at him. I unfolded my arms and tried to look less defensive, even though that's exactly how I felt. He sighed and ran a hand through his hair nervously. "Jared's thoughts are loud and clear right now. It's part of the change. When we invite a member into the pack, we usually get a rush of emotions and thoughts. New wolves don't have control over these thoughts, so we get overloaded. Those of us who have been around a while can tune others out, and control our own thoughts, but it can be difficult."

"Why are you telling me this?"

"When we found you in Washington, Jared told us a little about what had happened, but he held back a lot. All those thoughts are now rushing to the surface. His emotions are heightened, and it can make him dangerous."

"So you want me to stay away," I stated, and was surprised when Mark shook his head.

"No, I think he needs you, Izzy. And, I think you probably need him," he added slowly. He stopped talking and looked down at his hands, gathering his thoughts. My heart sped up as anxiety gripped me. "I know what Sarah did to you," he said softly, his eyes glancing up at me with concern.

I swallowed hard at his words and felt tears building inside me. No, I wouldn't cry anymore! Flashbacks of Sarah's wickedly smiling face haunted me. Once again, I felt the sting of her whip on my skin as the scent of lavender filled my nose. "She tortured us," I said finally, blurting out the words. "If I hadn't been so full of vampire blood, I'd be dead right now. She flung me around like a rag doll, put me in a cage, whipped me, had sex with my ex in front of me, and she would have done it all again the next day!"

Mark reached toward me, gathering me into his arms. I resisted, pushing against him until he let me go. I saw the hurt and confusion in his eyes, but I couldn't be comforted by him right now. All the anger I had been keeping in bubbled to the surface. "Mark, don't!" I screeched at him.

"Izzy, a lot has happened to you. Don't push me away. Talk to me," Mark pleaded softly.

"Why? You apparently know it all now anyway," I retorted angrily.

He shook his head. "No, Izzy, I don't. I know this is hard, but please, you need to talk to someone. If you can't talk to me..." he stopped talking and looked down at his hands again. He took a couple deep breaths before continuing. "Talk to someone, Izzy. I don't know if Jared is the right person to talk to or not, because of what he went through, but you need someone. I want to be that someone for you, but I can't if you keep pushing me away."

"I don't need or want to talk to anyone about anything. Got it?"

"Iz, if you keep this bottled up, bad things can happen."

"Bad things already did happen, Mark, and I handled it! Don't push me!"

Mark looked up at that, anger etched plainly on his face. He schooled his face quickly, and plastered a blank look on his face. "How did that vampire, Patricia, die?" he asked suddenly.

I reeled, not expecting that question. My hand instinctively went to the knife I kept on my side. "What?" I asked, my words failing me.

"Justin told me you stabbed her," Mark said deliberately, his eyes darting toward my thigh, where I was caressing the knife hilt. I stopped touching the blade at his look, and crossed my arms as he continued. "A normal blade wouldn't destroy a vampire like that, even if you got her in the heart. We bless all our ammo to give it a bigger kick in case we run into vamps, but we didn't have any blessed knives with us. Where'd you get the knife?"

"Patricia gave it to me," I muttered.

Mark barked a laugh and shook his head. "Ironic, that you used it to kill her."

I smiled in response, but there was no humor in it. "I suppose so," I replied, shivering as a gust of wind cut through the trees.

"Do you have the knife on you now?" he asked.

I frowned, wondering why he was asking such a stupid question. Clearly I had it on me. My shirt wasn't long enough to cover the knife sitting down, and he'd seen me touching it. "Obviously, Mark," I retorted, shaking my head.

"Show me."

I sighed and pulled the knife from its sheath, holding the blade up for Mark to see. He held out his hand and I handed the blade to him, hilt first. He examined it, turning it over in his hand. "There's some silver in it," he muttered, running his hand lightly over the blade.

"Patricia said it was blessed," I said as he held the knife up, examining it from every angle.

"It looks old," Mark said softly, his eyes looking at me over the knife. "I don't think you should be carrying this around until we figure out what it is."

"Excuse me?"

Mark lowered the knife and stared at me. "I don't think this knife is blessed, Izzy."

"What are you talking about? Wouldn't it have to be blessed to have killed Patricia?"

"I'm not sure. I could be completely wrong. Maybe the knife is fine. Maybe it's the sheath. Can I see it?"

I swallowed, wondering why he was acting so strange over a knife. I untied the bindings on the sheath and handed it to Mark to examine. "It's just an ordinary leather sheath, Mark. What's the big deal?"

"I can't see it," he replied, his eyes still focused on the sheath. He put the knife back in the sheath and examined it as a whole. I waited impatiently while he looked it over, tapping my nails against the back of the bench. He finally set the knife down in his lap and looked back at me. "When you're wearing the knife, I can't see it."

I stared at him blankly while the words sunk in. He picked up the sheath and strapped it around his arm, and I gasped when the knife and sheath both disappeared. He pulled the knife out, showing it to me. When he did, the knife and sheath both reappeared. He replaced the knife, and it disappeared once more.

I held my hand out to him. "Let me see," I demanded.

Mark hesitated, running a hand through his hair. I kept my hand held out toward him, willing him to hand the knife back to me. He finally sighed and unstrapped the knife, revealing it once more. "I don't like you carrying this around, Izzy. Can you promise me you won't wear it until I've had someone look at it? Please," he pleaded.

"That knife saved my life, Mark."

"Please, Izzy, just humor me. Keep it, just don't wear it," he added as he set the knife back in my outstretched hand.

"On one condition," I said as I gripped the knife and pulled it from Mark's grasp. He looked at me curiously, and I smiled. "Teach me to shoot."

Mark grinned and nodded his head. "I don't like you needing to defend yourself, but I get it. A gun is the great equalizer."

"Especially where vampires and werewolves are concerned," I replied as I clutched the knife. I wouldn't wear the knife, but I also wasn't letting it out of my sight for a minute. Especially now that I knew it would disappear when worn.

"You don't need to defend yourself against werewolves," Mark stated. "I'll protect you."

I rolled my eyes at the statement. Sure, I knew Mark would protect me. That was definitely his style. I thought about how Beth had attacked Justin and me. Mark had stopped her, even in human form, but I had been ready to use the knife on her. "What would this knife do to a werewolf?" I asked softly, not sure if I should ask him or not, but needing to know.

"There's enough silver in it that I can sense it just touching it, so it would definitely hurt a werewolf. A vital wound would probably kill." He stated. I had my eyes on the knife, turning it over in my hands as Mark spoke. "I saw the knife in your hand when Beth attacked. Were you going to use it on her?"

I looked up at Mark, trying to read his face. He looked worried, with frown lines between his eyes. I trusted Mark, maybe more than I trusted anyone, but I wasn't sure if I could tell him the truth. "It was just a safety measure," I said, settling on the safest version to tell him. "I'm just human, remember. What else could I do with a giant werewolf on top of me?"

"You're right," Mark agreed, relaxing back in his seat. Just like that, the tension eased from Mark. "Don't worry; no one will try something like that again. Jed dealt with them, and I'll always be here to protect you."

There he was, protecting me again. I bit my lip to keep from saying what I really thought. He had relaxed and wasn't grilling me on Sarah, so I needed to keep conversation away from any sensitive subjects. I grinned and sat back casually. "So, what was the deal with the pool game?"

"Mending fences," he replied with a smile. "What was the deal with you kissing Lucas?"

I laughed and scooted closer to Mark. "Jealous?" I whispered in his ear.

"No."

"Well, he really was an amazing kisser," I said dreamily as I tried to keep the smile off my face. "After his first kiss, I knew I needed to try again. I'm not sure I've ever had such a wonderful kiss before."

Mark growled low in his chest, and I looked up at his face worriedly. He may have been growling, but there was a small smile playing at the corner of his lips. He knew the game. Mark leaned over me, blocking my escape with his arms. I felt my heart speed up at his nearness and I licked my lips in anticipation. He moved his body closer, and I instinctually angled backward until I was sitting awkwardly on the bench with my back pressed against the arm railing. Mark moved with me, closing the distance between our bodies. I shut my eyes as he leaned his face toward me and placed a chaste kiss across my lips.

I opened my eyes when no more kisses came, to see Mark staring at me from mere inches away. I waited, my heart pounding in my chest. He moved in closer again, rubbing the roughness of his beard across my neck. His lips found my earlobe, and he nibbled it gently before laying a stream of kisses across my cheek. Finally, his lips found mine once more. He urged my mouth open with his tongue as his soft lips melded with mine.

I moved my hand up to his chest, but he growled and pushed my hand back down. He held his body above mine, his powerful legs pinning me to the bench. He didn't touch me with his hands, except to push my own wandering hands back down. My hands ached to touch him, to feel his strong arms, to touch his muscular chest, but he wouldn't let me. Instead, he put all his passion into this one amazing kiss, until I was panting with desire and gasping for breath. He placed one last kiss on my lips, and quickly moved away until no part of his body was touching mine.

I almost fell off the bench when he moved, catching myself at the last second awkwardly and struggling to sit upright. I glared at Mark, daring him to comment, but he didn't seem to notice. He was breathing heavily and I could see a fine sheen of sweat across his brow, despite the cold breeze whistling through the trees. I pursed my swollen lips, feeling the echo of his kisses still on my skin as I struggled to get my heartbeat under control.

Mark stood up and held a hand out to me. I gripped my knife in my left hand, and reached my right out to his. He pulled me up in a quick movement, jerking me toward him. "So, what was that you were saying about the best kiss you've ever had?"

I laughed and pulled myself against Mark's body as I circled my arms around his waist. He draped an arm around my shoulder and I noticed how comfortably I seemed to fit there. "Well, it's a close one, but I guess yours might have been better." Mark growled, and I laughed and punched him playfully in the side. "Just kidding! Yours was the best!"

I looked up at Mark's face, noticing the smug smile fixed there. He looked down at me and kissed me on the top of my head. "Shall we head back?" he asked.

I shook my head, not liking the prospect of spending all my time with a bunch of werewolves. I knew I'd have to get used to it, since Mark and I were still wanted by the authorities, but I needed a break. "I don't want to go back just yet," I said before my thoughts turned back to Jared suddenly. I tried to push the worry for Jared aside, but couldn't help thinking about him and my brother. Jared was a werewolf now, and could hold his own, I hoped. My brother, on the other hand, was a human.

Mark must have read the worry that crossed my face, because he pressed another kiss to my head and said, "Everyone is safe, Izzy."

"I know, but..." I trailed off and pressed my face against his chest. How did I stop the worry? I felt safe in Mark's arms, but worry began gnawing at me once more as I remembered the pain inflicted on me by Sarah. Every time I closed my eyes, I saw flashes of her pink trench coat and felt the sting of her whip.

"I have an idea," Mark said suddenly and I looked up at him.

"Jed has a place that's maybe a ten minute walk from here. It's where he's planning to get Justin set up for his research. There's a house attached to a shop. The house isn't as big as Jed's is, but it would probably be good for us to get some distance from the rest of the pack. Plus, you could keep an eye on your brother from there. We could move your stuff in there. Want to take a look?"

I nodded and Mark took me by the hand, leading me through the graveyard. I glanced at the names and dates on the tombstones as we passed. There were several graves together with the same date of death, in 1934. The further back in the graveyard, the older the dates were. I also noticed that most of the birth dates indicated the person buried there had lived much longer than any human I had heard of. The longest indicated the person had been over 300 years old at the time of death. I kept my thoughts to myself as I followed Mark down a winding path behind the graveyard. We walked through forest for most of the way, following a path that looked unused and overgrown with brush. We emerged from the forest and I spotted a small cottage in the distance. The house was beige with a dark green trim, and seemed to blend into the landscape. Next to the cottage, a large metal building stood that dwarfed the house in size. Overgrown fields surrounded the tiny home. A light snow began to fall, and we hurried to seek warmth inside the small house.

Chapter 5

The inside of the cottage wasn't much warmer than the outside. The front door opened into a modest living room that was clean and furnished with two small cream couches, a dark mahogany coffee table and a wood fireplace in the corner. The walls were pale birch paneling, but there was no artwork or decoration to speak of. I shivered and closed the door behind us as Mark moved immediately to the fireplace. I wandered around the tidy house, taking in how clean and immaculate it was despite the fact it had obviously been vacant for some time. Cream carpet stretched from the living room and down the single hallway. The house had a large kitchen, which doubled as a dining room, complete with a mahogany table that would seat six comfortably and matched the coffee table in the living room.

Down the single hallway, I found one bathroom and three furnished, but plain, bedrooms. Each bedroom had a queen size bed, dresser and nightstand. The back room was slightly larger, with a large glass door leading onto a small back porch. The only colors throughout the house were cream, white, black and dark brown, giving the house a very Spartan feel to it. I meandered back to the front of the house, where Mark had a small fire started. I followed him outside and helped him bring armloads of firewood in from the wood shed beside the house. Snow fell quickly, changing the scene outside to reflect the changing season. Before I had seen an abandoned field, and now I saw fresh beauty as the pristine snow covered the dead ground.

I set down my bundle of firewood and stood before the small fire, warming my hands. Mark added another log to the fire, and disappeared down the hallway toward the bedrooms. I pulled my borrowed jacket tighter around me as I stared into the flames, waiting for the fire to heat up. Mark walked back in with a thick, black blanket in his hands. He moved up behind me, slipping the damp jacket off my shoulders before settling the blanket around me. I ran my hands along the soft blanket as I pulled it tighter, shivering. Mark wore no jacket, but it didn't seem to bother him as he stood staring into the fire with his hands casually in his pockets.

"Well," he said, finally breaking the silence. "What do you think?"

"It's cozy," I replied as I pulled the blanket tighter and sat down on the thick carpet. I pulled my boots off and set them off to the side to dry, carefully placing my knife inside one. The fire crackled loudly and I smiled at the bright flames. "I think this will work. It's not like I can go back home, or rent an apartment, since I'm still a wanted criminal."

"When you're ready, we'll go back to the main house, get a truck, and bring our stuff back here," Mark replied as he sat down on the floor behind me.

"*Our* stuff?" I asked, looking at him quizzically over my shoulder.

Mark sighed loudly and ran a hand through his hair. "You're not staying here without werewolf protection, Izzy. The main house is too far. Besides, there are three bedrooms. I'll take the third."

I wasn't entirely sure I liked the idea of cohabitating with Mark. I found myself breathing faster at the prospect as anxiety gripped me. How awkward would it be sitting on a couch between my brother and Mark? Could I handle sleeping down the hall from him, with no other werewolves in hearing range? I wasn't sure I'd be able to keep my hands to myself. I blushed at the thought and turned my face quickly toward the fire.

"What are you thinking?" he asked softly as he brushed a hand across my back. I shivered at the sensation and blushed even brighter. Good thing I wasn't facing him.

Mark moved his body closer behind me until I could feel him pressed against my back. Out of the corner of my eyes, I watched him. He lay down on his side, with one hand propping him up. I turned my head slightly towards him as he ran a hand through my dyed chocolate hair, the color still catching me off guard. My heart sped up at his touch, and I knew he must have heard it because his mouth quirked into a smile. His brown eyes met mine and he wrapped his arms around me, gently tugging me down until I was lying awkwardly on top of him. He grinned just before he flipped me over, settling me carefully onto the floor.

I stared up at Mark, feeling his heart pounding as he pressed his body against mine. He leaned forward and kissed me softly, tenderly. After a minute, he pulled back, looking at me as though asking for permission. Normally, this would be my cue to pull away. We weren't in a relationship. We hadn't expressed our feelings. The last man I'd been with had been Kirk, and I hadn't given myself to him until we'd been dating for almost six months.

Mark started to lean away from me at my hesitation, but I pulled him back. Life was too short to wait. I touched Mark's face and smiled before tugging him toward me. He kissed me with renewed passion, while his free hand ran the length of my body as far as he could reach before coming back up. He stopped at my stomach, pushing my shirt up so his hand was caressing the bare flesh of my stomach. His hand moved up further, toying with the edge of my bra before coming back down.

He broke off from the kiss and sat back to pull his shirt off in one quick movement. I stared at him in awe, marveling at the perfect lines of his body. I splayed my hands across his stomach, feeling every muscle inch by inch. Mark let me explore briefly, before he reached forward and tugged at my shirt, sliding it over my head. I lay back as he ran his hands around my bra, playing with the edges before reaching behind me to unhook the clasps in one deft move.

Mark tossed my bra behind him and stared at me, his eyes soaking in every inch of my body before he moved his hands over me. I closed my eyes as he leaned across me and began kissing me vigorously. His lips moved from my mouth and down my chin, hungrily seeking out new areas to explore. One hand moved to my jeans and stopped there, as though he was silently asking for entry.

I felt a moment of panic, as memories of my torture at the hands of Sarah suddenly came back to me with force. I felt the sting of the whip where Mark's hands lingered on my skin. Mark stilled, somehow sensing my anxiety as he pulled back to look at me curiously. I grabbed his face and pulled his lips back to mine, determined to keep my mind occupied. I kissed him fiercely, feeling the rush of desire quickly return.

Mark responded just as eagerly, his hands once again roaming down the soft skin of my stomach to stop at the top of my jeans. I felt brazen as I moved my hands to my jeans and quickly unbuttoned them. Mark took the cue, pulling my remaining clothes off in quick succession until I lay naked on the blanket before the fire. Mark stood and stared down at me, before pulling off his clothes and lying carefully on top of me.

Heat rushed down my body at the sight of him unclothed and more than ready to go. I stared down the length of our bodies, where he held himself above me, waiting. I looked up into Mark's eyes, and read the desire there. He leaned forward and kissed me again, gently pressing his body against me. "Condom!" I croaked out suddenly. "I'm not on birth control."

"Crap," Mark muttered as he rolled off me and scurried

through the house.

I heard a flurry of banging doors as Mark searched at top werewolf speed through the house. He returned within seconds with a full box of condoms in hand and a grin on his face. He tore the box open, but carefully opened the first condom and put it on. He crouched on all fours over me and began kissing me with renewed intensity.

My body responded immediately, and I arched toward him, allowing him access. It had been too long since Kirk, and I felt nervous and excited at the same time. Mark pressed himself against me, slowly filling me inch by inch until he had sheathed himself fully inside me. He stared down at me, his eyes speaking volumes. He moved slowly at first, taking his time as though he were afraid to hurt me. I closed my eyes and let the pleasure consume me. My body moved in time to his, and he began to quicken his pace until all other thoughts left my mind. I put the torture and death behind me as I concentrated on the pure ecstasy.

Several hours and multiple condoms later, I lay exhausted before the dying fire. We had spent most of the day alone together exploring each other's bodies, and it was finally time to go back to reality. Mark pulled on his jeans and searched the room for our clothes. He tossed my underwear to me playfully and I slowly pulled it on, my body sore and tired. I crawled to the couch and snagged my bra, while Mark continued his scavenger hunt for our clothes. I spotted my pants and socks underneath the couch, and pulled those on as well.

Mark finally returned with our shirts, and I pulled my cream blouse on and grabbed my boots. I carefully pulled the knife out of my boot, and set it on the ground while I pulled the boots on. While Mark straightened the living room, I scurried into the bathroom to freshen up. I examined myself in the mirror, wondering how I could possibly fix my hair. A quick search of the bathroom revealed a hairbrush, which I hurriedly ran through my hair.

As soon as I was presentable, I walked back to the living room. Since I had agreed not to wear the knife, I had to find something to do with it. I had tried tucking it into the pocket of my jeans, but the jeans were too tight. I didn't want to carry it everywhere, so I tucked it into my boot. Since I hadn't actually strapped it to me, I figured this would have to do as a suitable compromise until I could put it somewhere safe. Mark had cleaned up the living room, and it looked as it had when we had arrived, but it felt different to me. I smiled as I trailed a hand across the back of the couch and walked to the front door. Mark held the borrowed jacket out to me, and I slipped it on before we left the cottage.

It had continued to snow while we'd been in the small house, and now several inches of soft fluff covered the ground. I followed Mark through the snow, hoping my boots were waterproof enough to keep my feet dry on the long trek back to the main house. We walked silently until we reached the forest edge, where there was only a slight covering of snow on the ground.

Mark stopped under the sheltering branches of a large fir and grasped my free hand. "What's going on in the pretty head of yours?" he asked as he pulled me close.

I laughed softly and looked up at him. Small worry lines marred his face, and I realized I'd been silent too long. "Not a whole lot. I think I'm too exhausted to think."

"Want me to carry you?"

"Aren't you tired at all? My legs are shaking so bad I can hardly walk!"

Mark chuckled and scooped me up in his arms, cradling me close to his chest. "I could run a marathon," he replied with a kiss.

"Werewolves," I muttered. He laughed loudly at that before quickly moving through the forest.

After a minute, I relaxed into Mark's strong arms and let him carry me down the forest path. He didn't seem tired at all, and had more than proven his stamina. I stared at his face, examining the strong jaw and the small laugh lines around his eyes. Mark's eyes darted to mine and he smiled. "What?" he asked as he ducked beneath a low branch.

"How old are you?" I asked, still examining his face. He looked like he was in his thirties, but I couldn't be sure. After seeing the graves, I had begun wondering how long werewolves lived.

Mark frowned slightly and looked away from me, his eyes focused on the path ahead. He took a large breath in and darted a look at me. I could feel his heart beating faster, and I grew worried he wasn't going to answer me at all. He stopped suddenly, and I looked around. We were at the edge of the small cemetery. Mark paused for only a moment, before hurrying through the falling snow to the other side of the graveyard and stopping.

He was silent for a minute, staring off into the distance. He finally turned toward me, his chocolate eyes imploring. "Does it matter?" he asked.

"Please, Mark, just tell me."

He sighed loudly and closed his eyes, his head bowed. "I was born in 1923, and changed into a werewolf in 1949. Age is... irrelevant. We're not immortal like vampires. Werewolves do age, just slower," he replied without looking at me. "Much slower."

I reached out a hand and caressed his face until he opened his eyes and looked at me. "It's okay, Mark. So, how old do werewolves live to be?" I asked curiously. I was desperately trying not to think about the impact of what he'd just told me. He was old enough to be my grandfather!

He shrugged and started walking once more. "I can't recall a werewolf who died of natural causes. Jed is a couple hundred years old. He's the oldest I know personally," he added.

"How old is the oldest you've heard of?" I asked, knowing Mark would avoid actually answering the question if he could. He was good at evasion, but not outright lying.

Mark walked for several more minutes before he finally

stopped and set me down on my feet, sighing loudly in defeat. He leaned back against one of the large fir trees and placed his hands in his pockets. "Vanessa has a relative that's close to 500 years old. From what she's said, he looks like he's maybe fifty and he's still as spry as the newer wolves. As I said, we do age. It's just a much slower process."

I tried to keep my face blank as I soaked in this information. Mark would outlive me by several lifetimes. Maybe I shouldn't have pushed him for an answer. I could have been blissfully unaware. No, I couldn't have been. This new world was too strange for me not to ask questions. I hugged Mark, putting my arms around his waist and my head on his chest so I could listen to his pounding heartbeat.

Mark stood still for a moment, before I felt his body relax. He pulled his arms around me, holding me tightly to him. We stood like that for several minutes, before I finally pulled away and looked up at his face. "You still owe me a date," I said, abruptly changing topics.

He grinned back at me and scratched at his beard. "That wasn't a date?" he laughed.

I punched him playfully and turned down the path. "No, that wasn't a date," I retorted with a backward glance.

Mark followed behind me as we cleared the forest and slogged through the knee-high snow to the house. The house was blissfully warm and the sounds of talking and laughter could be heard coming from the kitchen. Mark and I shared a look before following the voices. John, Vanessa, Jed and Jared were in the kitchen, preparing dinner. My stomach rumbled, and I realized Mark and I had missed lunch.

Jared looked up at me, a huge smile plastered on his face. I rushed to him and threw my arms around his neck. He wrapped his arms around my waist and nuzzled his face in the crook of my neck, holding me tight. I felt tears well in my eyes, but I didn't stifle these tears. These were tears of joy.

"You okay?" I asked softly as I pulled back to see Jared's face.

He was clean-shaven and had cut his hair short, making him look almost respectable, if you didn't notice the mischievous twinkle in his eye.

Jared smiled crookedly and pulled me tight to him again. "I am now," he whispered in my ear.

We stood there clutching each other for several minutes, until someone cleared their throat dramatically. I smiled and pulled back, but Jared clung to me still, with his arms wrapped around my waist. I let him keep his grip on me as I turned toward the rest of the room. John was standing nearby, his eyes focused carefully on Jared. Vanessa and Jed were across the room, seemingly engrossed in the process of making dinner. My eyes moved to Mark worriedly, where he leaned against the doorframe with his arms folded across his chest.

Mark smiled at me reassuringly. "Izzy, you and Jared should go talk."

I nodded and pulled Jared's hands off my waist, taking him by the hand as I led him out of the kitchen. I stopped beside Mark and rested a hand on his arm. "Thank you," I murmured. He smiled down at me and nodded his head.

I led Jared through the house and into the smaller living room, which no longer looked like a hospital room. We sat down on the couch, and I looked up to see that John had followed us. He moved to the corner of the room and leaned against a wall, his eyes targeted on Jared and his hand resting on the gun on his side.

I opened my mouth to speak, but John had obviously read the confusion on my face and answered my unasked question. "He's a new wolf, Izzy. I'm just keeping an eye on him. If he gets too emotional, it could trigger the change. You don't want to be close if that happens."

I didn't like the idea of John listening in on our entire conversation, but I figured it was for the best. If any of the wolves wanted to hear our talk, it would be easy for them to eavesdrop anyway. Then there was the whole werewolf mind reading thing. I wasn't too sure about that. I turned to Jared, attempting to pretend John wasn't just a few feet away. Jared had a quirky smile on his face, but his sweaty hands clutched mine desperately, relaying his anxiety.

I squeezed his hands reassuringly and attempted to casually lean back into the couch cushions. "So, how are you really?" I asked, my eyes scrutinizing him carefully. He was dressed in a plain black t-shirt and black sweats, no shoes. The look didn't suit Jared, but I figured they were probably borrowed clothes anyway.

Jared kept one hand clutching mine, while he moved his other hand to lift up his shirt. His skin had completely healed; all signs of his torture gone from his body. "Go ahead," Jared began with a smile, "I know you want to touch me."

I laughed, but reached out to run a hand across his chest. He was still muscular, but thin due to his captivity. I ran my hand over the areas of his stomach where he had been burned, thankful that all injuries appeared to be healed. Tears began to well up in my eyes as I thought of how close Jared had been to death. Then, inevitably, I thought of Kirk and his broken body.

Jared pulled me into his arms, reading me like a book. "I'm alive, Izzy, and Kirk's in a better place," he muttered into my ear.

"I wish I could have saved him too," I whispered back.

"You did, Izzy. In the end, he was himself again. What better way to die, than fighting to defend someone you love?"

I shook my head. "Kirk never really loved me, but he was himself in the end. He fought hard."

"He did fight hard," Jared agreed.

"We should do something for him. A funeral, I guess," I added, shrugging. "Did they... did the wolves get his... body?"

Jared nodded. "They did. We can talk with Jed about a funeral, or something."

"Let's do that," I replied, attempting a weak smile. "You know, I did love him too, despite everything that happened between us."

"There are all kinds of love, Izzy."

I smiled wider at Jared, feeling my heart swell at the sight of him, whole and healthy. "Yes, I know."

"I don't know how I can ever repay you for saving me, Izzy. Jed explained that it had been your decision to turn me into a werewolf. I want you to know that you made the right decision. It's what I would have asked for, if I could have."

I sat back and grinned at Jared, managing to contain any threatening tears. His words lifted a small weight that had been on my chest. I still felt the burden of Kirk's death, but I was thankful I didn't have Jared's added to it.

"Do you like being a werewolf?" I asked softly.

Jared leaned back, his face serious for a change. "It's... odd," he shrugged. "I can't really describe it. I vaguely remember being a wolf, but it's like trying to remember a dream. I can catch glimpses, but can't grasp it completely. The heightened senses though, are going to be a big plus. I like the feeling, but it's taking a bit of getting used to. It's hard to tune out everything. I'm overwhelmed with smells and sounds mostly, but I can't decipher everything. Honestly, I have a bit of a headache from it all."

"A headache is not a good sign," John said from the corner of the room. "You need to tune down your senses. Don't let yourself be overwhelmed."

Jared nodded and held his breath, his eyes closed in concentration. After a minute, he let out a big breath and looked at John. "It's not working," he said. "In fact, I think the headache is getting worse."

John pushed off the wall and walked toward us, his feet not making a sound. "Concentrate on one thing. Focus and shut out everything else," John said as he stopped before the couch. "Pick one scent, and focus on that. Tune out the rest of the world."

Jared grasped my hand harder and shot me a worried look. His eyes had taken on a golden ring around the edge of brown, indicating his wolf was surfacing. "Jared, it's alright. Look at me," I said in a slow, soothing voice, as though I was speaking to a frightened animal. Perhaps I was. "You're safe here. Listen to my voice only. I'm here for you."

Jared's eyes focused on mine, bringing back memories of our shared torture. He locked eyes with me and took in a deep breath before slowly letting it out. Again, he took in a slow breath, and released it just as slowly. I could feel John hovering beside us, but I kept my focus on Jared. I watched in fascination as Jared's eyes turned back to their usual light brown. He smiled suddenly and looked to John.

"Headache seems to be subsiding," Jared said to John. "No need to shoot me."

I shot a look at John, who had pulled a gun out. After a closer look, I realized it wasn't a normal gun, but a tranquilizer gun. Still, I felt better when John put the gun up and moved silently back to the corner of the room.

"Well, that was exciting," Jared stated with a chuckle. I rolled my eyes, but couldn't help but smile. Seeing Jared with his humor intact made me immensely happy. "I think you're my good luck charm."

"I think maybe you're mine as well," I replied, smiling.

"Well, I'm glad we got this mushy crap out of the way. Obviously, you hold an undying love for me. Please, please, contain yourself," Jared added, placing a hand over my lips before I could reply. "I'll just go let Mark down easy for you. Oh, Mark!"

Jared turned toward the hallway and feigned surprise at seeing Mark standing in the doorway. Mark was frowning at Jared, trying to read the situation. I laughed and stood up, but Jared grabbed me and pulled me down onto his lap. He wrapped his arms around me and rubbed his face across my neck, sniffing loudly.

"Jared!" I laughed as he tickled me when I tried to pull away.

"What?" Jared asked, his voice straining to stay serious as he tickled me again.

"Am I interrupting?" Mark asked as he pushed his way onto the couch beside Jared.

"You could help," Jared stated as he tickled my ribs, causing me to wiggle in his lap.

Mark grabbed my legs, pulling me onto my back across Jared's lap. I thought he was going to pull me away from Jared, but he surprised me by tickling the back of my knees. I wiggled and laughed, struggling to free myself from the two werewolves. They tickled me relentlessly, until I finally fell to the floor and rolled away from them. The two men laughed, nudging each other as they stood simultaneously and held hands out to help me up. I ignored both of their hands and stood on my own before stomping out of the room. I stopped at the hallway and shot a look over my shoulder at Mark and Jared chatting and joking. I glanced at John, who smiled and nodded, before I left the room.

I followed my nose back to the kitchen, knowing the men would soon follow behind. Today was a good day. I smiled, allowing myself to feel happiness no matter how brief. Sarah was probably trying to track Justin down, but at least for now he was safe. Kirk was dead, but Jared was alive. I wasn't sure if him being a werewolf was good or bad yet, but at least he had a chance now. As for Mark, I felt my heart pound faster at the thought of him. I was seeing him in a new light, and I had to admit that I liked what I saw. It was too soon to use the L word, but there was definitely the possibility.

Possibilities. Yes, there were still possibilities. I nodded to myself, as though I could convince myself with force of will alone. Today, right now, life was good. I relished in the moment, knowing deep in my heart that it wouldn't last.

Early the next morning, Jared, Justin, Mark, Jed and I made our way to the werewolf graveyard. Jared and I had spoken briefly with Jed about arranging a funeral for Kirk, but Jed surprised us by having the details already arranged. Hugo had buried Kirk's body, and was waiting for us at the graveyard when we arrived.

We lined up near the fresh mound of dirt, dressed for the occasion. There was no priest officiating over his burial, just a simple affair of friends. Several werewolves had complained openly about burying a human in their graveyard, but Jed had overruled them with a simple admonishment. Kirk had given his life fighting vampires, and he deserved respect. I hadn't heard a single word of complaint after that simple statement.

Hugo cleared his throat loudly and brushed the dirt and mud from his hands. "Kirk Daughtry was a brave man, who died at the hands of some spineless, blood-sucking vampires. I didn't know him, but I know it takes a special kind of person to willingly stand up and fight monsters. Kirk, I hope you find peace!" Hugo bellowed as he grabbed a handful of dirt and poured it across the ground marking Kirk's grave.

"Well said," Jed commented softly. Jed's attire was a slight change from his usual, with him wearing a black button-down shirt in place of his standard flannel. His jeans and boots were the same though. He looked at our small group and said, "Would anyone like to share some words about Kirk?"

Justin squeezed my hand before taking a small step forward and clearing his throat. "Kirk was one of my best friends. He was always jumping from job to job, and seemed to have the worst luck, but he did it all with a smile. I'm going to miss you, buddy," Justin choked out.

I stepped up beside my brother and hugged him from the side. He sobbed quietly, clutching me with one arm as he bowed his head. Justin had never been much for funerals. "Kirk and I were engaged once," I began softly, "but I don't think I ever really knew him. We were young and thought we were in love. I'll never forget him..." I trailed off, unable to continue. What could I say? I'd broken his heart, and he'd broken mine. "He died well..." I stopped again. He died well? Who dies well? You either live or you die, and he died. Before his death, he'd been driven insane. Sure, in his last moments he had fought hard, but he was still dead. "He was... he tried to be..."

"Kirk was a crazy-ass, story-telling bastard," Jared cut in. "You couldn't believe half the stories he'd tell you. He was always on the lookout for a new quick fix, whether it was with money or girls, but never drugs. And it always, and I do mean always, turned out badly. Particularly with the ladies," Jared added, winking at me. "But Kirk would just shake it off and move on. Even when things were going horribly wrong in his life, he would be there in a second if you needed him. He was there when we needed him, in the end. That's what I'm going to hold on to and remember."

"Rest in peace, Kirk," I whispered, and everyone else followed suit.

"Rest in peace."

* * *

In the rush of events and my captivity, I had completely forgotten about everything mundane. November had flown by, and the werewolf house was celebrating Thanksgiving. Most of the wolves spent Thanksgiving with their families, but a few came to Jed's house. My last Thanksgiving had been spent at a homeless shelter, serving meals. Justin and Sarah had gone to her parent's house, and there was no one else for me. Now, despite the odd circumstances, it seemed I had more people than I'd ever had before.

Everyone in the house was up early on Thanksgiving morning, helping prepare in one way or another. Justin left his room to help Jared and John organize the house to accommodate extra guests. The large dining room table wouldn't be enough for everyone, so the closer living room was rearranged with another large table and chairs. Beth and Jed ran the kitchen, assigning tasks with ease. I sat on the back porch with a giant bag of potatoes, quietly pealing, while werewolves bustled around me. With the oven on all day, it was hot in the house, so the cold outside was refreshing.

"You're awfully quiet," Vanessa whispered as she plopped down beside me on the wooden bench.

I glanced up at her to flash a quick smile before returning my attention back to the potatoes. "I was just thinking about last Thanksgiving."

"Oh, what'd you do last year?"

"Izzy served meals at a homeless shelter," Mark chimed in as he passed into the house with a large crate in his hands.

I shot him a glance, frowning. "How did you know that?" Mark shrugged and continued inside, letting the screen door slam gently behind him. I rolled my eyes and turned back to my potato peeling.

"What about your family?" Vanessa urged.

"Justin was with his girlfriend, Sarah, and we don't have any other family," I replied.

"Sarah? As in the psycho vampire?"

"That's the one," I replied.

"Well, family is what you make it."

I looked up at her and smiled, but my eyes caught her newest hairstyle. Her hair was striped black and white, and made me immediately think of a skunk. It also brushed past her shoulders, and seemed considerably longer than the last time I'd seen it. "Did you get hair extensions?"

Vanessa grinned and shook her head, running a hand through the lengths. "Nope, just let it grow."

"Your hair must grow fast," I commented.

"You know how werewolves heal fast?" she asked, and I nodded. "Well, some of us grow hair really fast when we change shapes. Also, the hair dye goes away."

"So you get a new hairstyle every month."

She laughed and ran a hand through her hair. "Precisely! If I don't cut it between shifts, I could probably get my hair to my butt in a couple months. Faster, if I change shape a lot."

"That's handy," I responded ruefully. "So, not everyone gets this side effect?"

"Everyone does to an extent. Beth's hair grows maybe an inch, but John's grows a good foot! You should see it right after a change," she giggled and stood up, brushing her hands off. "Beth will start yelling if I don't go help her, so I'd better run."

I resumed my potato peeling after Vanessa left, until I had peeled the entire bag. Beth took the potatoes from me without a word and shooed me back out of the kitchen. She wasn't my favorite person, so I didn't waste any time leaving her to the kitchen. No one else needed my help, so I wandered into the living room and turned on the television.

The usual Thanksgiving parade was on, along with various holiday movies and the football pregame coverage. I flipped through channels idly, stopping on a news announcement about Petri Company. The announcement had me hooked. The founder and CEO of Petri Company, Mr. Petrivian himself, was visiting with the President in the capitol. The report didn't show Petrivian, but stated that his private jet had flown to the White House and he was currently dining with the President and his family for Thanksgiving.

"Dining *with* them, or *on* them?" Jared asked wryly as he joined me in the living room.

I shushed Jared as I resumed watching the news broadcast. There wasn't much more to it, other than statements about how close Mr. Petrivian had become to the President. From the sounds of it, they were the best of friends. The last statement before going to a commercial was that Petrivian would be the guest of honor at a New Year's Eve banquet in New York City. The guest list would include many foreign dignitaries who hadn't yet had the privilege of meeting the esteemed Petrivian.

I clicked the television back to the football pregame show and sat down in one of the wooden dining chairs. "None of that sounds good," I commented softly.

"The blood-sucker is certainly getting around," Jared responded. "I wonder how fast they're distributing that vaccine."

"He doesn't need the whole world under his control," I began softly, shaking my head as the scope of things came into focus. "He just needs the world leaders."

"Your brother needs to get working on a way to counter that vaccine."

"How long will that take? And, assuming he can make something, how do we distribute it to people like the President, who are surrounded by security?"

"By making the counter-vaccine airborne," Justin said as he walked into the room.

"Do you think you can do that? Can you even make something to counter the vaccine? That's a lot of variables, Justin."

"If my research hadn't been burnt to a crisp, it would go faster. As it is, I'll have to work from what I remember," he added, crossing his arms defensively. "I wasn't exactly putting all my effort into making it airborne, you know. I don't want the vampires to rule the world, or whatever the hell it is Petrivian is up to."

I nodded and tried to put a smile on my lips to soften the sting. "I know, Justin, it's just that there's a lot riding on you making a cure. Things are escalating quickly, it would seem."

"Don't worry about things you don't understand. I have a plan in mind to expedite my research," Justin responded curtly before storming out of the room.

I sat back, stung by his words and tone. My trust in Justin was the only thing keeping the werewolves at bay, but it was a tentative thing. He was right that I didn't understand anything about his research, but that didn't cease my worry. We had a lot riding on Justin's skill, and he had only been a junior researcher. Petrivian, by now, probably had hundreds of scientists working on his goals. Could we move fast enough to stop him?

Jared interrupted my thoughts by gently patting me on the arm. "More werewolves just arrived," he said just before I heard the front door open. I schooled my face into what I hoped was a pleasant look, and went with Jared to meet the other werewolves.

Thanksgiving progressed quickly, and thoughts of vampires were pushed to the back of my mind. Most of the werewolves joining us, I already knew, but there were a few new editions. Those who wanted to watch the football game ate dinner in the living room, while the rest ate in the dining area. I ate in the living room, even though I didn't care much about the game. In all honesty, it was to stay away from Beth, but she ended up following us into the living room as soon as Mark indicated that's where he was eating. Leaving the living room then would seem petty, so I sat, picked a team to root for, and tried to enjoy myself. After all, it was Thanksgiving and we were supposed to be thankful for the things we had.

Jed led a round of thankfulness, making each person state something they were thankful for. Most comments were about family and friends. I sat silently, listening to the statements from the dining room, before Jed moved into the living room and asked the rest of us to state what we were thankful for.

"I'm thankful for my new Pack family and fast healing. Without it, I'd be dead right now. I'm also eternally thankful for Isabella," Jared stated as soon as it was his turn. He grinned widely and looked at me. "Because of you, I have this Pack. Because of you, I am alive. I owe everything to you."

I swallowed back tears as every werewolf in the room looked at me. Mark patted my leg under the table and quickly spoke up, taking the attention off me. "I'm thankful to be back in the Pack. At first, I was hesitant, but it feels good to be home again."

A loud round of hurrah's and cheering echoed Mark's words. I smiled and squeezed his arm gently. When the noise finally died down, eyes turned toward me again. What could I possibly be thankful for? Sure, I was alive, but that was because of the vampire blood. Could I be thankful for vampire blood? That probably wasn't a good thing to say to a room full of werewolves, and it wasn't precisely true. I was thankful my brother was alive, and Jared, but at what cost?

Kirk was still dead.

I closed my eyes, unsure what to say. The smell of lavender wafted to me, and I felt transported back to Sarah's torture room. Even now, I could feel the sting of her whip, and hear her Southern accent as she taunted me. Everyone was waiting for me to respond, and I sat there like a fool. I opened my eyes and ran my hands through my hair, looking around the room for some sort of inspiration.

Mark stared at me worriedly, a frown marring his brow. Jared had his head down, but I could see enough of his face to see the sad, forlorn look there. I looked up at Jed, who was waiting patiently for me to speak. He nodded encouragingly, and I attempted a weak smile back at him.

"I'm thankful for... werewolves," I blurted. Mark barked a laugh beside me, and several others chuckled. Jed stared at me, and I felt as though he could see right through me. He nodded once and turned to Justin, who sat quietly on the other side of me.

"I'm just thankful to be alive," Justin murmured.

"I'm thankful for Mark," Beth stated as soon as Jed turned toward her. Jed scowled down at her, and she quickly hurried on. "Thankful that he's back in the Pack, where he belongs, I mean. It wasn't the same without you."

"Thanks," Mark muttered.

I rolled my eyes and pretended to listen as the rest of the werewolves said what they were thankful for. When everyone had taken a turn, Jed cleared his throat loudly. Silence descended on the room as everyone listened to their Alpha.

"I am thankful for my Pack. You are my family and my friends, and I couldn't ask for anything more. We are complete once more, with the return of our brother, Mark. Not only have we grown in number this year, but we haven't lost any members of our Pack since the death of Peter. This, unfortunately, may change with the recent developments among the vampires. I hope not, but we all need to be prepared. Today is a day of celebration and reflection though.

Today is not the day to worry over things we cannot change, but to be thankful for the people in our lives."

The room was silent for several minutes before food was passed around, and merriment returned. I reflected on Jed's words, and tried to keep my thoughts on the people in my life. I had my brother beside me. Jared was alive and well. Then there was Mark. I glanced up at his handsome face beside me and smiled.

Chapter 6

The weeks that followed were busy helping Justin move into the cottage and adjoining lab. The snow had continued steadily, making travel between the two houses more difficult. Jed had several vehicles, and left a Jeep at the cottage for our use, since we frequently traveled between the two houses getting things organized. There wasn't a direct road between the houses, so we made our own through the deepening snow.

Jed had a few werewolves helping Justin set up the large metal building beside the cottage as a research laboratory. Justin spent most of his time in his new lab, tucked away with a wolf named Marshall, who had a PhD in three different subjects. I didn't ask how old Marshall was, but I figured he was one of the older wolves in Jed's pack. He was certainly the only wolf with grey hair, even if it was only at his temples.

As soon as Justin had settled in at the cottage, I began the process of moving to the cottage with him. I had been putting it off, wondering how it would work with Mark and Justin in the same house. Mark seemed to be waiting for me. The only belongings I had were the clothes, makeup and toiletries Vanessa had given me. I felt bad depending on other people, but I had no access to my bank accounts. According to John, all of my assets had been frozen, along with Mark and Justin's as well. Even if I could access my accounts, going to the store wasn't a risk I was willing to make as a wanted criminal. Was it too late to move to a tropical island and start all over?

John had taken a crew to check out my apartment in the hope he could retrieve some belongings for me. He was due to return any day. I wasn't optimistic after his run to Justin's place had yielded less than satisfactory results. Justin's house had been burned beyond recognition, destroying all of our family mementos. Clothes and things could be replaced, but our childhood pictures couldn't. I tried not to dwell on that as I packed my clothes into the jeep.

Mark walked up behind me, placing a hand at the small of my back as I shoved a box into the jeep. We hadn't been alone together since that day in the cottage. Every time we had a few moments together, it seemed as though someone sought us out. I turned toward Mark, and he moved his body close to mine, trapping me between him and the jeep. I smiled up at him and ran my fingers across his chest. The front door of the house slammed, and we both jumped apart as Beth sauntered toward us with a box in her hands.

"You forgot this," she said, thrusting the box toward me as she pushed her way between Mark and me.

I took the box, which contained my bathroom belongings. A box of tampons I was sure I had packed in the bottom of the box, was now sitting predominately at the top of the box. I blushed and hurried to put the box into the jeep, my eyes darting to Mark. I slammed the door of the jeep and turned around to glare at Beth, who had moved so close to Mark her arm was brushing against his. "I didn't forget it," I said testily. "I just hadn't grabbed it yet."

"Well, I didn't want you to forget it. It's obviously that time of the month, so you'll need those tampons. Are you sure you don't need the super large ones?" Beth asked with a smile plastered on her pixie face.

I imagined smacking the sickly sweet smile off Beth's face,

but it would probably be a bad idea to get into a fight with a werewolf. I took a deep breath in as I tried to calm down, knowing my face was probably bright red. I darted a glance at Mark, daring him to say anything. He stood resolutely looking at his shoes with his hands behind his back.

I faced Beth and returned her smile with one of my own. "Did I leave the box of condoms upstairs too?"

Beth's smile disappeared and she glared openly at me. "I'm sure you have boxes all over the house," she retorted. "You probably buy them by the dozen."

"What do you mean by that?" I blurted, my anger bubbling up and ruining any intelligent response I could have had.

"Do I need to spell it out for you?" she sneered, taking a step toward me.

"If you have something to say, maybe you should just come out and say it," I responded, taking a step toward her. My hand moved unconsciously to my thigh, but I wasn't wearing my knife. It was in my box of belongings in the jeep behind me.

Beth moved closer, until we were toe to toe. She was taller than me by a few inches, and used that extra height to glare down at me. She spoke in a harsh whisper, emphasizing each word. "You. Are. A. Whore."

Werewolf or not, I wasn't going to let anyone speak to me like that. I pulled my arm back, ready to punch Beth in the face, but Mark was suddenly between us. He had a hand on my arm, keeping me from punching Beth. He gently lowered my arm and pushed me back into the jeep. His other hand was on Beth's chest, holding her at bay as she glared at me with yellowing eyes.

"Izzy," Mark said softly, shaking his head at me.

"Are you kidding me?" I responded angrily, pushing his hand away before he had a chance to say any more. I stormed away from Mark and back to the house without a backward glance.

Jared stood in the doorway, waiting for me. His golden eyes

were transfixed on Beth, and he gripped the doorframe with enough force to splinter the wood. I tapped Jared on the arm and pushed him into the house without a backward glance at Mark and Beth. Jared stared at me, breathing hard as he tried to contain his wolf. With John gone, Hugo and Mark were in charge of keeping Jared's wolf under control. I had no idea where Hugo was, so I took it upon myself to calm Jared down.

I pulled him into the small living room and settled him onto the couch beside me. He growled a deep rumble that shook the couch. "Jared, it's alright. Look at me," I said softly.

Jared leaned in toward me and sniffed my hair. I froze, trying to keep my heart rate under control. Jared sniffed again loudly, breathing in my scent. I sat still as he scooted closer to me on the couch and wrapped his arms around me. We sat like that for several minutes, and I felt my tension slowly ebb away. I wasn't afraid of Jared, no matter how much the others warned me about new werewolves. We anchored each other back in the real world.

Finally, Jared sat back and looked at me, his eyes once again his normal light brown. He smiled and took my hands in his own. "I wanted to rip that bitch's throat out," he said calmly, with a smile on his face.

I laughed and nodded my head. "Me too," I replied.

Mark walked into the living room, and I glared up at him angrily. Jared shifted and turned toward Mark, his hand tightening on my own. "Jared, can I have a minute with Izzy?" Mark asked.

Jared squeezed my hand and looked back at me, his demeanor indicating loud and clear he wouldn't leave unless I asked him to. I nodded my head and Jared stood up, but he didn't leave immediately. He stared at Mark and crossed his arms over his chest. "Where's the bitch?" he asked bluntly.

I snickered, but immediately plastered a blank look on my face when Mark's eyes darted to me. Mark looked back at Jared and sighed loudly. "Beth is with Jed in the barn," he responded carefully.

Jared nodded and started walking out of the room. "Jared, stay in the house."

Jared stopped at the doorway and turned back around. "I wouldn't think of leaving Izzy here unprotected," Jared retorted. "I'll be in the kitchen."

Mark waited until Jared had left the room before moving to the couch and sitting down beside me. "I'm sorry about Beth," he said immediately, taking my hand in his.

I pulled my hand away and crossed my arms under my breasts, pulling the fabric down in the process. I was wearing a low cut white shirt and a push-up bra, revealing ample cleavage already. Mark's eyes flickered to my breasts, as I had intended. I tried not to smile at his reaction, remembering why I was irritated with him.

"You're sorry about *Beth*?" I asked, frowning at him. "What exactly does that mean, Mark?"

"I, uh, it means I'm sorry," he mumbled carefully.

"Don't be sorry for Beth. She's her own person, and you have no control over her. What you do have control over is yourself."

Mark frowned, drawing his brows together. "What did I do?"

I sighed in exasperation. "She called me a whore and you didn't say a damn thing," I began, my voice raising as I spoke. "Then you held me back, like I was the one attacking her! She's a werewolf!"

"Exactly, Izzy, she's a werewolf. What were you planning to do? Punch her?"

"That's exactly what I was going to do!" I screamed back, jumping to my feet. "I certainly wasn't going to stand there and let her insult me! She's been a bitch to me since the moment we met, and it's only gotten worse!"

"I already had a chat with Beth. She's sorry about what she said. For now, I think you need to calm down," Mark said slowly as he stood up. "If it's that time of the month..."

"Are you kidding me?" I shouted, cutting him off. "Did you really just go there?"

Mark stared at me like a deer caught in the headlights. "Werewolf, Izzy," Mark said, as though that explained it. I stared at him blankly, hands on hips, waiting for an explanation. "I can smell blood on you."

"It's not that time though, Mark," I replied, feeling a trickle of confusion, followed quickly by fear. My period had ended four days ago. I took a deep breath and turned down the hallway toward the bathroom, shutting the door on Mark before he tried to follow me.

I stripped, examining myself in the mirror for any wounds or anything indicating I was bleeding. There was nothing there. Not a mark or scratch. There was no blood anywhere. "Mark," I called softly through the door.

"I'm here, Izzy," he replied.

I opened the door and peeked out at him. "I think your werewolf sniffer is broken. Are you sure you smell blood on me?" I asked.

He sniffed the air and nodded. "Yes," he replied carefully. "I thought you were on your... um... thing... last week, but the smell of blood is stronger now."

"I *was* on it last week," I replied, debating what to do. I blushed even as I moved behind the door and ushered him into the bathroom.

Mark walked into the bathroom and I immediately closed the door behind him. Mark stared at me, a smile slowly forming on his face as he stared at my naked body. He immediately moved toward me, his arms encircling my waist. I pushed him away and crossed my arms beneath my breasts.

"You're still mad at me?" he asked.

"Yes, I'm still mad, but I'm more concerned than anything. Do I still smell like blood?" I asked, fear causing my heart to beat faster.

Mark's face turned serious as he leaned close to me, sniffing his way across my body. He paused at my neck, sniffing loudly before moving down to my stomach, where he paused again. He stayed there, running a hand across the soft flesh of my stomach as he sniffed my skin. After a minute, he moved on, sniffing his way down the length of my body. He gripped my thigh, pressing his face close to my skin. He growled suddenly and I backed away into the door.

"What?" I asked as Mark stood up.

"It's as though you're covered in blood, but there's not a mark on you. I can smell it, but you're not injured."

I grabbed my clothes and quickly pulled them on while Mark stood back, staring at me. "I don't understand," I replied as I pulled my shirt on. "I haven't been injured. Am I bleeding internally? Is something wrong with me?" I asked as fear suddenly gripped me.

Mark pulled me into his arms, holding me close. "No, Izzy, you're not injured," he replied matter-of-factly.

"Are you sure? If it's internal..." I trailed off. How would I even get internal injuries?

Mark muttered into my ear, "I'm sure it's not internal."

"Then what is it? Is it from when Sarah had me? Is it something to do with the vampire blood? Do you have any ideas?"

Mark breathed in deeply and held me tight to him. I could hear his heart beating fast in his chest. He knew something, but he wasn't telling me. After several minutes, he pulled away and opened the bathroom door. I followed him into the living room, still waiting for an answer. He continued through the house, and I had to run to keep up with his long strides.

"Mark, wait," I said as I rammed my knee into the edge of a couch, wincing at the pain that shot up my leg.

Mark stopped in the hallway and glanced back at me. "I need to talk with Jed," he said simply. "Why don't you go to the cottage and get your stuff organized. I'll meet you there later."

Mark walked away before I had a chance to respond. I stood there rubbing my knee, when Jared walked back into the room. "I'll go with you," Jared said, moving toward me.

"Do I smell like blood, Jared?" I asked softly.

Jared sauntered toward me, stopping when he was inches from me. He sniffed the air above me and sneezed. He backed up and covered his nose, his eyes quickly changing from brown to gold. "What is that?" he asked softly, narrowing his eyes. He moved back toward me, wrinkling his nose as he sniffed the air around me.

"Jared?"

"You did smell like blood earlier, but now..." he trailed off as he walked around me, sniffing loudly. "The smell of blood is fainter, but now there's something else. I'm not sure what it is, but I don't like it."

I swallowed hard, fear and anger speeding up my breathing. Mark knew what it was, I was sure of it. What could be so bad that he wouldn't tell me? This had to be because of the vampires. I knew not all of the vampire blood had left my system, but I hadn't had any vampire dreams since Patricia had died. Maybe that wasn't true. I thought of the dream where I was drowning in a pool of blood. I hadn't told anyone of the dream, but it had recurred nightly. Each night I tried to reach the light, and each night I failed. The dream only ended when I drank the blood. I had thought it was a regular dream, or nightmare, brought on by the trauma I had experienced. What if it wasn't? Perhaps there was more to it.

Jared was watching me curiously, so I shrugged and walked past him, attempting to shake off the bile that had risen in my throat. There was no sense panicking yet. I walked with an air of calm out the front door with Jared on my heels. I wasn't sure if it was a good idea for him to leave the house without another werewolf, but I didn't think Jared would hurt me. Mark's story about Beth's brother came to mind, but I shook it off. Probably, I should feel more anxiety where Jared was concerned, but I just couldn't muster up the appropriate fear.

I climbed into the jeep with Jared in the passenger seat. No other werewolves jumped out to stop Jared from coming with me, so I backed the jeep out and drove along the path we had made to the cottage without a backward glance. This year Oregon was experiencing one of the worst snowstorms in a century, and it was only early December. It wasn't currently snowing, so the drive was fairly quick through the packed route we had made. I parked the jeep in front of the cottage and grabbed as many of my things as I could carry. Jared grabbed what I couldn't manage, and trailed me into the house.

The house was cold and empty when we entered, and I figured Justin was once again in his laboratory. I walked directly to the back of the house, dumped my belongings on the bed, and claimed the large bedroom for my own. The bedrooms were all identical, but this one had a sliding glass door leading onto the back porch and was slightly larger. I imagined it would be lovely in the summertime, but this time of year the porch was slick with ice and snow.

"So," Jared began as he set the boxes he carried onto my bed, "which room is mine?"

I had been staring out the glass door, and turned to look at Jared curiously. "What?" I asked, wondering if he was joking.

Jared quirked a smile and bounced down on my bed. "We could share a room," he smirked, rubbing his hand across the lavender bedspread. "I wouldn't mind."

"Jared," I said in exasperation.

He laughed and sat up. "I suppose I could take the other bedroom," he said solemnly.

"This house only has three bedrooms, Jared."

"Exactly," he responded. "You, Justin and me. It's perfect."

"We have Mark to think about."

"He's not really my type," Jared responded, straight-faced.

"Jared," I laughed, shaking my head. "You know I'm talking about Mark and me."

Jared grinned and wiggled his eyebrows. "Well, I've never really given thought to that. It's not that I'm opposed to threesomes, but I'd prefer two girls and one guy, or better yet, three girls."

"Jared!" I shouted, smacking him playfully on the arm.

"What?"

I laughed and shook my head as my fears and worries seemed to diminish. Jared had that effect on me. I walked away still laughing and Jared followed behind me into the living room. Justin had moved in a few days prior, but the place still seemed empty. I shivered, thinking it was almost as cold in the house as it was outside. The fireplace was empty, but I hurriedly grabbed paper and kindling and started a fire. As soon as a small fire was going, I retreated back to my bedroom to throw on a sweatshirt.

Jared was feeding the fire as I walked back in, pulling a thick black sweatshirt over my head. I sat down on the couch closest to the fire, watching the flames grow as he added pieces of fir. He shut the glass door, but I could still hear the gentle crackling as wood caught fire. I stared at the flames, enjoying the peace a simple fire brought me.

Jared stared into the fire and didn't turn around as he spoke. "Is Mark moving in here too?"

"I don't know," I replied honestly, sighing. "He wants to, but I'm not sure if it's because he wants to be with me, or he wants to keep me safe. I'm not even sure what I want."

"All joking aside, I do want to move in here," Jared said, surprising me. The fire was blazing, but Jared kept his focus on it as though it would go out at any minute. I studied his profile in the firelight. He'd been keeping his hair military-style short, but his facial hair seemed to be a constant fixture no matter how much he shaved. I wasn't sure if that was a werewolf side effect, or just a Jared thing.

I waited for him to elaborate, but he didn't say any more. I finally asked, "Why?"

Jared was silent for a few minutes, seeming far away. He finally sat down on the floor, with his arms across his knees, and looked up at me. The expression on his face caught me off guard. Jared was seldom serious, but the look on his face was grave. "I think I need to stay close to you," he said softly, quirking a small smile at the corner of his lips that didn't seem to touch his eyes. "I owe you my life."

"Jared, you don't owe me anything," I said earnestly.

"Yes, I do, Izzy," he sighed loudly, all trace of a smile vanishing from his face.

I leaned forward, touching Jared's shoulder gently. "We saved each other."

"Do you have nightmares?" he asked softly, but not waiting for an answer. "When it was just Kirk and me, we would sleep in turns. Then Kirk stopped being Kirk, and I was on my own. The nightmares got worse then. After you came along, it was different. The nightmares have slowly quieted down."

I swallowed hard and pursed my lips. What could I say to him? Nightmares still plagued me every night, and they definitely weren't quieting down. In fact, I worried they were getting worse. "They say that time heals all wounds. That's all it is. I don't think I did anything. Like I said, we saved each other," I muttered.

Jared laughed humorlessly and shook his head, his eyes focusing on me finally. "It's not just for saving my life, but for saving me from myself. You kept me sane while Sarah tortured us. I was disappearing, Iz. If you hadn't shown up when you did, I don't think I would have been *me* any longer. I was just one torture away from where Kirk was."

His words broke my heart, and I had to stifle the tears that were filling my eyes. I kept forgetting how much Jared had endured, and how strong he truly was to have survived it with his sanity intact. How long had Sarah tortured him? What else had she done that I knew nothing about? If he needed me, how could I possibly deny him? Not that I wanted to. He kept me grounded, and he made me laugh. I kept eye contact with him as I nodded my head. "Of course you can stay here, Jared. We'll figure this out. Don't worry."

He smiled in return, and this time it reached his eyes. The sadness on his face slipped away as he nodded his head. I sat down beside him on the floor, watching the fire and getting warm. He leaned his body against mine, and we sat in companionable silence. Jared made me feel safe and whole, and I supposed I did the same for him. I relied on him more than I wanted to admit to anyone, including myself. Fear had become my close companion these days, and I worried that it would seize control completely.

Chapter 7

I hadn't seen my brother in some time, so Jared and I decided to walk down the short pathway to the shop he was using as a lab. The building was a large, rectangular metal structure with no windows and only two doors. It was separated from the house by about ten feet, and the doors were both facing away from the cottage. I turned the doorknob on the small door, but it was locked shut. I shivered and kicked the snow off my boots while Jared knocked on the door. We waited under the small overhang as snow lightly fell to the ground around us. The other door was a large rollup door on the side of the building, but we'd have to wade through deep snow to get to it. The door locked from the inside anyway, so there was no point trying it. No one answered, and Jared and I exchanged looks. He hammered on the door again, leaving a small dent in the metal with his fist.

"Maybe he's not in there," I surmised, even though I could see the glow of lights from under the door.

"He's in there. I can hear someone talking," Jared said as he put his ear to the door. "There are a couple people in there, I think. It's probably Justin and Marshall."

Jared pounded his fist against the door repeatedly, until finally we heard someone turn the lock on the door. Jared put his hand down and I stepped toward the door when it opened slightly. Justin peered out at me, his eyes bloodshot and his blond hair disheveled. He sighed loudly when he saw me, irritation clear on his face. What looked like blood stained the collar of his white lab coat.

"Hey, Justin," I began with a smile on my face. "Can we come in? It's cold out here."

"Now's not a good time," Justin said bluntly. He didn't say any more as he began to push the door closed.

Jared moved in front of me and shoved his foot into the gap, holding the door open ajar. "Who's in there?" Jared asked as he put his hand on the door and began slowly inching it open.

Justin struggled against Jared, unsuccessfully trying to keep the door closed. Jared's werewolf strength won out quickly, and Justin jerked back as the door swung open. The door was only open for a few seconds before it slammed closed in our faces. I stepped back, my heart pounding in my chest as I tried to wrap my mind around what I had seen of the lab in those few moments before the door had shut.

The laboratory had several long tables, containing the usual things you would expect to see in a science lab. Those things weren't what had me staring blankly at the closed door before me. The walls were all pristine white, with the exception of the far wall, which was more red than white now. Bright red blood gleamed over the darker, drying red. On the floor were strange piles of black, like ash. Against the wall stood a man, chained by thick, black manacles to the wall. I didn't know the man, who was slumped naked in his chains and covered in blood.

I stumbled away from the lab as bile rose in my throat. I felt Jared's arms around me, leading me back toward the house. I swallowed hard, choking down the urge to vomit. Darkness began to descend, and I realized I was going to pass out soon. I stopped walking and sunk to my knees in the thick snow. The cold helped refresh me, and I sat there breathing slowly until I regained my composure.

Jared hovered behind me until I stood up. My jeans were soaked through at the knees, but I ignored it and continued into the house. I hadn't thrown up or passed out, so I took that as a win. As soon as we were in the house, I moved to the fireplace. Jared put a new log on the fire while I shivered in my wet jeans and tried to make sense of what was happening in my brother's lab.

"That was a vampire," Jared stated as he stood up from the fireplace, dusting wood splinters from his hands.

I jerked my eyes toward Jared, seeing the surety in his eyes. The thought had crossed my mind as well. The man hadn't moved, looking almost dead. His skin was pale, and seemed to glow eerily under the harsh fluorescent lighting. Then there was the ash. It was those piles of black and gray that stood out in my mind the most, almost as much as the blood did. "How many piles of ash did you see?" I asked Jared, hoping his werewolf eyes had noticed more than my human ones in the few moments we had seen of the room.

"Three," he stated matter-of-factly.

I nodded and shivered again. Jared walked down the hallway and came back a minute later with a new pair of jeans for me. I held them in my hands, but didn't put them on. All I wanted right now was a thick pair of sweats, which I didn't currently own. I sighed and moved closer to the fire, kicking my boots off in the process.

"Did you know about this?" I asked as I stood and pulled my wet jeans off.

"No, of course not," Jared replied.

I nodded, not looking at him, as I pulled on the dry jeans and sat down on the couch nearest the fire. Jared took the wet jeans from my hands and disappeared down the hallway. I felt unhinged. Part of me wanted to yank my brother out of that lab and tie him up so he'd be safe. The other part of me wanted to go back into that lab and kill the vampire myself. I shivered at the thought.

I heard Jared in the kitchen, and used the opportunity to go back to my bedroom. I rifled through the box that contained my clothes, haphazardly tossing them into the dresser. At the bottom of the box were my shoes. I reached into the pair of knee-high black boots and pulled out my dagger. I had let John examine it and run some tests, but he hadn't said anything about the results to me yet. John had additional people lined up to examine the knife. I didn't know their qualifications, and didn't care at this point. Knowing vampires were in the next building changed things in my mind. I strapped the dagger to my side, feeling slightly comforted by its presence.

I scooped the rest of the clothes and shoes out of the box and stared at the last two items remaining. Mark and John had been teaching me the basics of firearms, but things had been too busy for me to get any real target practice in. The first gun was Mark's choice, a 40 caliber Glock that I could hardly hold because the grip was too big for my hand. The second was a 9mm Browning. I loved the way the Browning fit in my hand, but it didn't have the power of the Glock. Stopping power and speed were necessary when dealing with vampires. In addition, the Glock held more bullets than the Browning did. Both guns were equipped with John's special blessed ammo. The ammo could kill the newer vamps easily, burning them from the inside out, but they had both told me to empty a clip into a vamp just in case. Some vamps could withstand more than others, and it was always better to err on the side of caution.

I grabbed the Glock and strapped the holster on so the gun fit at my hip, just above the knife. Feeling paranoid, I grabbed the Browning and put it in the shoulder holster so it rested rather uncomfortably under my arm, then I put my jacket back over it. I moved to the mirror hanging on the back of my door and looked at my reflection. The jacket was loose enough that it helped cover the guns up, but I still felt ridiculous. How was I going to sleep tonight, knowing there was a vampire next door? I'd be too paranoid to sleep with a gun under my pillow.

I grabbed the knee-high boots and pulled them on before

heading back to the living room. Jared sniffed the air when I walked in and looked toward me curiously, his eyes surveying me. He didn't say anything as he carried a mug toward me. I smiled at the delicious aroma of hot chocolate and took the mug. He had even put whipped cream on top.

I followed him back to the couch and sat down beside him, licking the whipped cream off the top. "Better?" Jared asked, smiling.

I grinned back at him and nodded. "Yes, the hot chocolate helps."

"Do the guns help too?"

"Yes," I replied simply.

Jared chuckled and pulled up his shirt, showing me the gun at the small of his back. "They help me too. Guns have a calming effect on me."

"I'm surprised they let you have a gun," I muttered.

"I'm surprised they let *you* have one," Jared responded quickly. "You can't hit the broad side of a barn! I'm a trained professional. If I lose control of my wolf, I'm not going to be pulling a gun out."

I conceded his point and shrugged as I took another sip of hot chocolate. I did feel calmer, but I think it was more because of the knife than the guns. I resisted the urge to pat the knife with my hand and concentrated on my hot chocolate as my thoughts turned. What was my brother doing in his lab?

"That scent I smelled on you before; I think I know what it is," Jared said, startling me out of my thoughts. I looked at him sharply, narrowing my eyes as he continued. "I smelled it in that lab, too. It was vampire."

I took a deep breath in and let it out slowly as what he said clicked into place. "That explains why Mark reacted the way he did. He knew exactly what it was."

"What I don't get is why? Why did you smell like blood and vampire? I don't smell it on you anymore," he added.

I wasn't sure either. Although we had suspected I might still be linked to Henri, none of us had spoken of it. Henri hadn't invaded my thoughts or dreams since I'd killed Patricia. I hadn't actively sought him out either, thinking that perhaps my connection to him was fading. I certainly didn't heal as fast as I used to.

The front door opened and Mark trudged in, kicking snow off his boots. He pulled his jacket off, which was coated with a light dusting of snow, and hung it on a peg by the door. He didn't make eye contact with me as he walked across the living room and slumped down on the opposite couch. I watched him quietly, but my anger began bubbling the moment he walked into the room. Did he know about my brother's experiments? Did he know why I smelled like vampire and blood? Was he going to tell me, or keep it secret? I couldn't even drum up anger over the Beth incident anymore. It was minor in comparison.

I tapped my fingers anxiously on my mug, waiting for him to speak. "Did you know there's a vampire in my brother's lab?" I blurted out angrily, unable to keep my mouth closed any longer.

Mark's head jerked up and his eyes darted automatically toward the lab, as though he could see through walls. He started to stand up, looked back at me and shook his head. "There is?" he asked, and I felt a slight tension in me ease. He didn't know about it, that much was obvious. He was still halfway standing up. "Are you sure?"

I nodded, but Jared was the one to respond. "We went to check on Justin. He wouldn't let us in, but we saw a vamp chained up on the wall. I think there have been a few vamps, if the blood and ash are any indicator," he added.

Mark swallowed visibly and darted a look back toward the lab. "The lab has been off limits to everyone except Jed, Malcolm, John and your brother for the last week. I guess Jed didn't want a panic on his hands. It makes sense, I suppose, for Justin's experiments. He's asked for vials of werewolf blood as well." Mark sat back down, but he didn't look completely relaxed. "I haven't smelled vampires around, so I'm guessing they collected them elsewhere and brought them directly to the lab."

"So, you're okay with all this?" I asked angrily.

"Jed is Alpha," he replied with a shrug, as though that explained it all. Jared shifted uncomfortably next to me. He had been learning about the werewolf hierarchy, and hadn't seemed happy about it.

"Okay," I said, even though it wasn't okay. They wouldn't explain much in the way of werewolf rules, so I was better off just dropping the subject. Besides, I had another worry on my mind. "What was the deal earlier with me smelling like blood?"

Mark ran a hand through his hair and leaned back on the couch, stretching his legs out in front of him. He looked up at me, flicked his eyes toward Jared, and back to me again. Several minutes passed in silence, while I waited rather impatiently for him to say something. I sipped down the last of my hot chocolate and set it on the small table. Mark finally stood up and scooted in next to me on the couch, his leg pressed tight against mine. He leaned in and sniffed the air around me noisily, moving his face in close to my body. I stayed as I was, waiting.

"The smell is gone," Mark whispered softly in my ear. He turned his body sideways on the couch so he was facing me. He seemed relaxed outwardly, but I suspected he was acting that way for my benefit. "You smelled of blood strongly, but then I smelled something else on you. It smelled like a vampire."

"Why didn't you tell me earlier?"

He shrugged and glanced away, looking uncomfortable. "Jed wanted to be informed immediately if something like this happened."

"So instead of telling *me* first what's going on with *me*, you ran off to tell your Alpha?" I responded irritably. I didn't even try to keep the anger out of my voice.

"He's my Alpha."

I nodded and smiled ruefully. That seemed to be his answer for many of my questions these days. "You and Jed suspected this would happen. My connection to the vampires isn't gone."

Mark shook his head and sighed. "Your connection with one vampire in particular isn't gone," he said softly. "Vampires are like people in the sense that each one smells differently. They still smell like disgusting vampires, but each scent is unique. The scent I smelled on you is the same scent I've smelled on you several times before."

"I haven't had any contact with him," I replied immediately, knowing exactly to whom Mark was referring.

"Any dreams?" he asked, and I could see the pain it caused him to ask that in a tightening around the eyes.

I blushed and turned my head away, thinking back on the dreams of Henri. He was usually in some state of undress or completely naked. "No, he hasn't come to me in any dreams."

He nodded and sat back, bouncing his leg anxiously, his demeanor changing. He was far from calm, and doing a poor job of hiding it. "Are you sure? Would you remember it?"

"I'm sure he hasn't directly come to me in any dreams. I've had some strange dreams, but nothing like before," I replied, watching Mark's reaction. He was acting nervous, but I wasn't sure which topic had him on edge. Was it Henri, the dreams, my brother's experiments or the smell of vampire and blood on me? I honestly wasn't sure which topic had me more on edge either.

"What kind of dreams?" he asked quietly.

I sighed, thinking back to the recurring nightmare I'd been having. "I'm caged," I began softly. "It's like it was when Sarah had captured me. At first it's dark and cold, and I'm all alone. Then I see a light in the distance. I try to reach it when the cage disappears and I'm suddenly drowning in a pool of blood."

I stopped talking, and Mark looked at me expectantly. "What happens then?" he asked.

I swallowed, not sure if I should tell him about drinking the blood in my dreams. For some reason, I feel guilty about it. Maybe it's just a dream, and maybe not. I looked down at my hands resting in my lap, unable to look at him as I continue. "The blood gets higher around me until it covers me completely. I know I'm going to die and the only way to survive is to open my mouth and drink the blood," I said softly, still not looking up. "It's the same night after night. The dream ends when I drink."

I heard Mark's sharp intake of breath, but I still refused to look up. I felt ashamed, even though I wasn't sure how much control I had. Even in my dream, I knew it was a bad idea to drink the blood, but I still made the same decision each time.

"How long have you been having this dream?" Mark asked carefully.

"Every night since..." I trailed off, unable to continue. Every night since we'd rescued my brother. Every night since Kirk had died. Every night since I'd killed Patricia.

"Do *you* think it's the vampire?"

I shrugged, and finally looked up into Mark's eyes. He was staring at me with concern etched clearly on his face. Jared sat on my other side, patting my leg reassuringly. Mark reached out and gripped my hand in one of his own, much larger ones. He squeezed it gently and I smiled timidly back at him.

"I think I should sleep with you," Mark said seriously. I felt my face flush instantly as my thoughts drifted to a naked Mark in my bed. "I mean here, at the house, in your room. So you're not alone and I can smell for vampires."

Mark smiled, obviously noticing my flushed face and pounding heart. Part of me wanted him desperately, but then I remembered that I was mad at him. I pulled my hand out of his and crossed my arms. "How far away can you smell a vampire?" I asked and continued as he frowned at me. "If I dream about Henri, can you smell it from out here on the couch?"

Mark's frown deepened as he realized what I was getting at. "The smell on you was faint earlier. I don't think I'd notice from that far away," he replied.

I looked over at Jared, who had been sitting quietly patting my leg. He looked me directly in the eyes when he answered me. "He's right about the proximity. I didn't notice it until I was up close. Of course, if you don't want Mark in your bed, I'd be more than willing to offer my services," he added with his crooked smile.

I smiled in return and turned back to Mark, who was glaring angrily at Jared. He opened his mouth to speak, but stopped when the front door opened and my brother entered the house. He had obviously cleaned up in the lab, although his hair was still disheveled. He wore a rumpled navy t-shirt and blue jeans. I didn't notice any blood on him either as I scoured him with my eyes, but the dark clothing could easily conceal it. Justin eyed me warily as he walked toward us and sat down on the other couch.

Mark patted my other leg as he turned to face my brother. Justin shifted uneasily as he sat, his eyes darting to the werewolves on either side of me. "Izzy, can we talk?" Justin asked as he rubbed his hands together.

"Go ahead and talk," I replied testily.

"Alone?"

"No, I don't think so," I stated, watching the confusion and hurt in my brother's eyes. We used to be able to tell each other everything. There had been a time my brother was the only one to know all my secrets. Now, it seemed everyone knew my secrets, but I knew no one else's. At least with two werewolf lie detectors, I'd be able to know if my brother was telling the truth or not. It pained me to think he might actually lie to me, even if it was to protect me.

Justin sat at the edge of the couch and ran his hands over his knees, as though wiping at sweaty palms. "Okay," he said, nodding. "I hope you can understand that what I'm doing is for all of us, Izzy. It's for the future of humankind. Sometimes drastic measures must be taken to further scientific endeavors."

"So, you're experimenting on vampires?"

He took in a breath and nodded, never taking his blue eyes

from mine. "You have to trust me, Izzy. Jed trusts me. I hate what I was a part of. I started this whole thing, Izzy. It's my fault, and I have to make it right. You understand that, don't you?"

I took a deep breath and kept eye contact with my brother. "That part I understand, Justin. I know you're doing what you think you need to do to find a cure. What I don't like is having fucking vampires this close to where we sleep! Add in the fact that you weren't going to tell me about it. Vampires are more powerful than you realize. If one got loose, you'd be dead before you had a chance to call for help."

"Malcolm is with me at all times," Justin responded, but I could see the concern on his face. He was worried about the vampires too.

"Do you need them chained up here?"

Justin nodded and said, "We kill them before night falls. They may as well be dead during the day. They don't move at all until dark, and we kill them before that happens. It's as safe as possible, and it's necessary for my research."

"Not all vampires are out of it during the day. The older, more powerful ones are awake longer. Patricia was like that," I added.

Justin looked away from me at mention of Patricia. He had watched me kill Patricia, and hadn't uttered much to me on the subject. He had helped Patricia at some point, but I wasn't sure what had transpired, and Justin wasn't talking about it. As more time went on, my brother confided in me less and less. Perhaps we were just growing apart. I certainly didn't confide in him much either.

"So you're okay with all this? You don't have a problem torturing and killing for your experiments? You're okay putting your life in danger?"

"Yes, Izzy, I am. It's not like I have much choice," Justin responded tartly. His eyes, so much like my own, were rimmed with red. He hadn't been getting much sleep lately, and it showed. "Please, just trust me. And stay away from the lab. I promise we won't keep any vampires overnight."

"This is a bad idea, Justin. What if other vampires find out what's going on and follow you back here?"

"Jed assured me they are taking precautions against that."

I glanced at Mark, who nodded slightly. Justin was telling the truth, for now. "The pack is always taking care of vampires," he muttered softly.

I turned back toward my brother, watching the anxious look on his face. "I just want you to be safe," I said softly. "I'd feel better if maybe there was another werewolf in the lab with you and Malcolm."

Justin exhaled in relief and nodded eagerly. "I'll talk to Jed right away. That would be helpful, anyway. You're not mad at me, are you?" he asked fervently.

"No, Justin, I'm just worried about you," I replied, even though I was a tiny bit mad still. Mark glanced at me sharply, hearing the lie, but he wisely held his tongue. "Mark and Jared will be staying here too, so they'll be close if anything happens."

"There are only two more rooms. What about you?" Justin asked. "I thought you were moving in here."

I paused, feeling two sets of werewolf eyes on me, waiting for my answer. "I will be staying here," I replied. "I already put my things in the back room."

Justin's eyebrows shot up in surprise as he darted looks at Jared and Mark. I felt my face flush and my heart speed up once more. Maybe Mark and Jared could room together. Or, one of them could sleep on the couch. Of course, there was also the vampire dream issue. I could feel everyone staring at me, waiting for me to make a decision. Heat rose to my cheeks.

"Mark will stay in my room," I added softly, and I could feel the smugness emanating from Mark's direction. I rolled my eyes and tried to ignore him. "He can sleep on the floor."

Jared snorted loudly and reached behind me to clap Mark on the back. "Let's head back to the house and get our things," Jared said, still chuckling.

I smiled at the werewolves as they left to go gather their things. Justin made a sandwich before heading back to his laboratory, while I went to my room. The queen sized bed was along the far wall of the room, but between the large dresser and the closet, there really wasn't much room on the floor for Mark to sleep. I shuffled my clothes around in the dresser, making room for Mark to place his few belongings. I spent the rest of the time putting my toiletries away in the bathroom while I waited anxiously for the men to return.

Chapter 8

I didn't have many belongings, so it only took a half hour to organize my things in the little cottage. I went back into the living room and sat beside the fire, sipping another cup of hot chocolate when Mark and Jared returned. Jared winked at me before hurrying off to claim his bedroom and put his small box of clothes away. Mark carried a cardboard box of clothes in his arms, but he didn't move toward the bedroom. He stood in the middle of the living room, waiting for me, I realized.

I set my mug down on the coffee table and stood up. "Come on," I said as I led Mark toward the back bedroom.

I opened the bedroom door and entered with Mark on my heels. He kicked the door closed behind him and set his box down on the floor, surveying the room. I sat down on the bed and bit my lip nervously. "The bottom drawer is empty for you," I said as I pointed at the dresser. "There's also a little room in the closet too." The closet was tiny, and only contained my jackets and shoes.

Mark nodded and silently pulled the bottom dresser drawer open. He quickly moved his clothes into the drawer, then carried his bathroom belongings down the hall. I waited for him to return, unsure what to say or do. Why was I so nervous? Mark returned a minute later, closing the door gently behind him once more. He leaned against the door, arms crossed, watching me as I fiddled with my fingernails anxiously.

Several minutes passed before Mark let out a loud sigh and finally spoke, breaking the silence. "Am I really sleeping on the floor?"

I swallowed hard and looked up into his face. The look on his face was cautious, as though he was waiting for me to run away screaming. I smiled at him timidly and he moved across the room in two quick steps. He stopped in front of me and pulled me to my feet, so we were toe to toe.

"Izzy," he said softly, caressing my cheek.

"I'm still mad at you," I stated. His nearness had my heart speeding like a freight train and I could feel my body flush with desire. I tried desperately to hold onto my anger, but it was difficult with his body pressing against mine.

"Why are you mad at me?"

I blinked up at him. Was he serious? I felt my anger bubble back to the surface. "You have to ask? First, there was the whole incident with Beth. You treated me as if I did something wrong, when she stood there insulting me. Then, instead of telling me that you smell vampire on me, you run off to Jed. You should have told me first! Do you have any idea how scary it is to not know what is happening with your own body?" I added, feeling my anger grow with each word.

"I'm sorry," he said softly as he ran his hands down my arms. He put one arm around my waist and pulled me tighter against his body, angling his face toward me as though he was going to kiss me. I pulled my face back and pushed my hands against his chest, trying to give myself room.

"That's it? You say you're sorry and all is forgiven?"

Mark sighed loudly and tipped my chin up so I was looking directly into his chocolate eyes. "I took care of Beth already. She should never have said what she did to you. I was afraid you were going to punch her. She doesn't have the best control of her wolf, and

I didn't want you to get hurt. Maybe I didn't react appropriately, but I swear my only concern was your safety."

"Okay," I said softly, trying my best to let that one go. "What about the vampire and blood smell?"

"My Alpha ordered me to tell him immediately if anything like that happened. I am unable to disobey my Alpha, Izzy. It's virtually impossible now that I'm back in the Pack. I know you don't understand. It's just... a werewolf thing."

"A werewolf thing?" I muttered, not expecting a response. That wasn't the first time I'd heard something along those lines. "Whatever, Mark. Just please, promise me you won't keep secrets from me."

Mark nodded and smiled as he caressed my cheek. "I promise I won't willingly keep secrets from you," he said as he leaned forward and kissed me. I didn't like the way he had worded his promise, but I supposed it would have to do. It was probably a werewolf thing.

I returned his kiss, feeling the roughness of his facial hair tickling my skin. He moved his hands to my jacket, pushing it off my arms. The jacket caught on my shoulder holster and Mark stopped kissing me to look. He frowned at the gun under my arm and stepped back, lifting the edge of my jacket to see the Glock on my hip as well.

"Two guns?" he asked. "I thought I smelled guns, but didn't realize you were packing both. Are you planning to go into battle?" A small smile quirked the corner of Mark's lips, but I knew him well enough to know the smile was just a cover for his true feelings. He didn't like me armed to the teeth.

"No," I retorted as I shrugged my jacket back on. "I was hoping to do some target practice," I lied.

Mark cocked his head to the side, and I wondered if he sensed my lie. "If target practice is what you want, I can take you now. Or, maybe later," he added as he pulled me into his arms again and ran a hand down the back of my thigh, clearly indicating that he had other things on his mind than target practice.

My heart sped up at his touch and he smiled at me before burying his face in my neck. I warmed all over as he kissed his way across my collarbone. His hands moved up to my shoulders and he pushed my jacket down once more before quickly removing it. Next, he disconnected the shoulder holster and set my gun on the dresser. I started to help him, but he grabbed my hands and shook his head.

He removed the Glock next and set it next to the Browning, before sliding his hands under my shirt and lifting it over my head. Mark smiled and kissed me again as his hands moved around me to unclasp my bra. He flung it unceremoniously across the room, where it landed somewhere behind the bed. I used the opportunity to reach under Mark's shirt, feeling his washboard abs as I raised his shirt over his head.

Mark lifted me up suddenly and tossed me onto the bed. I giggled as he grabbed my feet and yanked my boots off. He climbed on top of the bed, straddling me as he popped the button on my jeans and slid the zipper down. My heart raced as he laid his body across mine and kissed me thoroughly once more. One hand moved to my breast, fondling me as he kissed me.

I groaned and ran my hands down his body until I reached the top of his jeans. I fumbled with the button and finally managed to unclasp it. I used both my hands to unzip his jeans and reach inside, where he was thick and hard. Mark groaned loudly as I grasped him, his kisses stopping temporarily. He leaned back and grabbed my jeans, attempting to pull them down.

The tight jeans wouldn't budge past my hips, and Mark growled in frustration. I reached down to help him, and realized the jeans were stuck on the knife holster strapped tight to my thigh. Mark wasn't able to see it, but it was preventing my jeans from sliding down. Mark moved to my feet and pulled on the jeans from the bottom. I pushed the jeans down from the top, concentrating on the place the holster was. The jeans finally moved, and Mark flung them off, where they landed with a loud thud.

Mark turned and frowned at the noise, but I sat up and began kissing my way across his chest as I tugged at the top of his jeans. He pushed me back onto the bed and removed his pants with such speed I only saw a blur of movement. He crawled back across me, naked, and fingered the lace edge of my panties. I could sense his urgency as he pulled the panties off and moved his body atop mine. He kissed my lips hard and I felt him press himself into me with a sudden ferocity that took my breath away. I stared up into his bright golden eyes and my heart stuttered as I realized it was almost the full moon, and Mark's wolf was very close to the surface.

I didn't have time to think about the moon as Mark growled suddenly and slammed his body into mine, drawing a scream of pleasure from my mouth. He moved out tantalizingly slow, only to slam himself into me again. Several more times he repeated this before his rhythm sped up; his lovemaking much more intense than it had been before. Last time he had been slow and meticulous, as we had explored each other's bodies fully. This time was raw and fierce, with an almost animalistic quality to it. He thrust himself into me quicker and harder, until I screamed my pleasure loudly. Mark sped up to lightning speeds as he came with me, a howl emanating from his throat before he collapsed on top of me.

We laid there for several minutes, breathing hard. Mark finally pulled himself off and looked down at me with his glowing yellow eyes. He kissed me once more before hurrying across the hall to the bathroom. I struggled to sit up, my muscles screaming out against any movement. The soreness would likely be worse later, but for now I was basking in the euphoria of lovemaking. I smiled as I began gathering my clothes off the floor. My bra I found wedged next to the bed, but my underpants had disappeared completely. After a fruitless search for them, I gave up and picked my jeans off the floor. My knife holster was still stuck on the pant leg, and I had to undo the clasps to remove it.

I had just managed to unhook the holster when the bedroom

door slammed shut, making me jump. My eyes jerked up to face Mark, who was glowering at me as I stood naked, holding the knife in one hand and my jeans in the other. We stared at each other for several heartbeats, neither of us saying a word, when I noticed my panties lying atop the dresser. I turned away and exchanged the knife for the panties, quickly pulling them on. Mark moved finally, throwing his clothes on in a flurry of movement before he left the bedroom without a word.

I stared at the closed door, feeling an overwhelming desire to burst in to tears. Tears wouldn't do me any good, though. I gathered up the rest of my clothes and pulled them on before turning back toward the knife sitting on the dresser. There really wasn't a debate in the matter as I strapped the knife back on and moved to the bathroom, where I cleaned up quickly. Clean and mostly calm, I walked down the short hallway to the living room. Mark had been pacing in front of the door, but he stopped when I entered. He ground his teeth together and stared at me, clearly agitated. His eyes roamed across my body, pausing on my legs as though he could see the knife fastened there. I stood at the edge of the living room, debating what to say or do. Mark was the first to break the silence.

"You promised not to wear it," Mark said simply, biting off each word.

"That was before I knew there were vampires in the next building," I retorted, as I crossed my arms under my breasts.

Mark took in a deep breath and closed his eyes, obviously trying to get his anger under control. "I will protect you, Izzy. You don't need to wear it," he said finally. He looked back at me, and his eyes were still golden. His wolf wasn't going below the surface any time soon.

"John didn't see anything wrong when he looked at it, Mark."

"John's not an expert on the mystical. He has a man coming to look at it. Couldn't you just wait?" he asked, running a hand through his thick hair.

"I could have waited, but it's not that simple anymore. The knife helps me feel safer, Mark. Don't you get that?"

Mark moved toward me in two long strides and took my face in his hands. "I should make you feel safe, Izzy."

"You do, Mark," I said as I gently pushed his hands down. "But you're not always here. I need to protect myself. I'm just a measly human. Remember, I break easily." I closed my eyes as memories of flying through the air and crashing through a wall came back to me. Without vampire blood in my system, I'd be dead right now, and the blood wouldn't be in my system forever. Would it?

"You may just be human, but you're surrounded by werewolves. I get that you need to feel safe when I'm not around. Wear a gun if need be. I'll take you out shooting more, so you're comfortable with the guns. Just, please, leave the knife here."

"You'd rather have me wearing guns?" I asked, shaking my head in disbelief. I was lucky if I hit a target 10 feet away. The knife was simple to use. Put the pointy end in the vampire and watch them burn from the inside out. I shuddered as the memory of Patricia's burning corpse came back to me. "It's just a knife, Mark."

"Sure, I'll find a knife for you, then," Mark replied. "I'm sure John has some blessed knives that would work great."

Mark wasn't going to let it go, and I was tired of arguing about it. I had only agreed not to wear it when there hadn't been any immediate threat. Vampires in the building next to me changed all that, despite everyone's assurances. "I'm keeping the knife, Mark. It's not your decision," I added sharply.

Mark backed up and glowered at me, his eyes glowing brightly. Without a word, he turned on his heel and stormed out the door. I stood there for several minutes, wondering what I had just done. I hadn't kept my promise, and I felt guilty about that part, but I wasn't going to let Mark order me around. My life, my decision. After several minutes of holding in the threatening tears, I walked back down the hallway and stopped at Jared's bedroom door. I knocked on the door, but no one answered. I knocked again louder before finally turning the knob and opening the door. Jared was lying on his bed with a set of black headphones on. He glanced up at me with yellow wolf eyes as I stepped into the room.

Jared pulled the headphones off and tossed them on the bed before moving across the room and enveloping me in a hug. I smiled and buried my face in his chest, breathing in his scent. After a few seconds, he pushed me away gently and looked down at me with his crooked smile.

"What's wrong?" he asked.

"You didn't hear?" I asked, my eyebrows rising in surprise.

"Jed gave me some serious headphones," Jared replied, pointing back to the headphones on his bed. "They cancel out just about everything. I could hear you and Mark, uh, making noises periodically, but that's about it."

I blushed and looked down, remembering how I had screamed. Mark had even howled at least once. Those were probably the noises he had heard. I took a steadying breath before looking back up at Jared, hoping my face wasn't as red as it felt. "He's mad I'm wearing that knife again," I replied honestly. I wasn't sure what Jared's opinion was on the subject, and I worried he would take Mark's side.

"Mark asked you not to wear it until he had it checked out," Jared stated thoughtfully. He rubbed at the facial hair across his chin thoughtfully as I nodded in response. "So, when you saw the vamps in the lab you strapped the knife on along with the guns. It's your security blanket."

I nodded again and looked up at his face. His eyes were still yellow, but he didn't look agitated. He looked sympathetic as he grabbed my arm and steered me down the hall to my bedroom. Jared opened my bedroom door and rushed in to grab my guns off the dresser. He thrust them into my arms, and waited while I strapped on the holsters. I quickly put jacket back on, covering the guns up, before following Jared outside.

"Where are we going?" I asked as Jared started walking through the snow.

"Target practice," he replied simply and I smiled.

The walk to the shooting range took ten minutes through the wet snow, but I found my anger had diminished considerably by the time we got there. The range was a simple affair, with just a small covered building and a row of targets spaced at varying intervals. Inside the covered area was a large locked cabinet, containing practice rounds for just about any gun imaginable.

I had been to the range a few times now with John and Mark, but never with Jared. Jared let me get bullets and ear protection while he set up new targets. He didn't say anything as he came back, letting me fumble with the Glock on my own. Mark was usually inclined to load my gun for me, and John would stand over me meticulously pointing out every detail. Jared did neither; he just stood back and watched. I loaded the gun with the practice rounds and turned toward the nearest target, casting a glance at Jared. He nodded his head and stepped back to watch me. I sighted down the gun, using the stance Mark and John had shown me with my feet planted wide. I fired off a few rounds slowly, getting a feel for the gun, but not actually making a mark in the target.

The Glock was large and heavy, and I had to use both hands to hold onto it as it kicked back with each shot. After I had unloaded the first clip, Jared finally stepped up and started teaching me. He moved my feet and shoulders slightly, making slight adjustments to my stance as I began shooting through the second clip.

My arms quickly ached after two clips with the Glock, and I set it aside to use the Browning. Jared had me practice shooting one-handed with the 9mm, alternately using my left hand and then my right. Ten minutes in, I was managing a large grouping on the target. After thirty minutes, I had closed my grouping down on the target with the Browning. Jared had me shoot one more clip with the Glock, and I managed to close my grouping in a bit tighter. I even succeeded in a few hits on the bull's-eye.

"Much better," Jared said as I put the empty Glock onto the shooting table. "I think you can finally hit the broad side of a barn."

"Ha," I said as I shook out my tired arms. My shoulders ached, but I felt good.

"How do you feel?"

I looked at him and really thought about my answer. "Better," I replied with a shrug. "I'm not the best shot, but I feel a bit more confident."

Jared smiled and shook his head. "No, I mean how do you *feel?*"

I looked at his eyes, which were back to their light brown color. Jared seemed relaxed and at ease, and I realized I felt the same way. Shooting had loosened something inside me. I grinned and nodded at him. "I feel much better. Calmer, I think."

"Good," he replied with a nod of his head as he went to retrieve the targets. He came back with the targets, and tossed all but my most recent one in the garbage, which he handed to me to keep. I folded it up in my pocket as we trekked back to the house.

We were walking in the cottage just as the sun was setting behind the trees. The fire had died in the fireplace, having been neglected for the past few hours. Jared stirred the coals and tossed in kindling until he had managed to bring the fire back to life. My stomach growled loudly, reminding me that I hadn't eaten in hours. I rifled through the refrigerator for something to munch on. There wasn't much food in the cottage, and we were still expected for dinner at the main house. I sighed and closed the fridge door.

"It's dinner time," Jared stated as I walked back into the living room.

"Yeah," I replied softly. I didn't want to go back to the main house, but Jared was a new werewolf and needed to eat. I doubted he had eaten enough today. I knew I hadn't, but if I didn't eat, I wouldn't turn into a wolf and eat someone's arm.

Justin walked into the house just as Jared and I were heading to the door. He smiled at us and I tried to ignore the fine ash that clung to his sleeves. "Dinner?" he asked and we both nodded. "Let me go wash up."

As soon as Justin had washed up, the three of us climbed in the jeep and drove back to the main house. Smells of food wafted to us as soon as we opened the front door. We followed our noses to the dining room, where Jed, Hugo and Mirabelle sat among platters of food. We joined them and filled our plates quickly. A few minutes later, Logan, Lucas, Malcolm and Leon joined us as well. I ate quickly, hardly tasting my food while everyone chatted amicably.

I darted glances at Jared, who sat beside me. Jared patted my knee reassuringly under the table, but I still couldn't help worrying as dinner passed and neither Mark nor Beth showed up. I helped clear the table when everyone was done, and volunteered for dish duty. Justin joined me, and we washed dishes side by side, as we had done when we were children, only without the fighting.

I relaxed a little, but couldn't stop the worry gnawing at me when Mark still never showed. We finished cleaning up the kitchen and put the leftovers in the fridge. I wandered around the house, looking for everyone else. I entered the large living room, where Jed was sitting with John and another man. All three turned toward me when I walked in, and I stopped in my tracks.

I started to turn around, when Jed's voice stopped me. "Isabella, please, come here."

The authority behind Jed's simple request made it clear he was demanding, not asking. I may not be a werewolf, but I knew enough not to ignore the Alpha. Suppressing a sigh, I turned back around and moved into the living room to sit down on the couch beside John. Jed stared at me, his eyes assessing, while I focused on the new person in the room. The man was older, with short, gray hair and a distinguished look about him. He was dressed immaculately in a slate gray suit that appeared tailored, with shiny black shoes and a turquoise blue tie. He turned toward me when I sat down, his pale gray eyes a match with his suit.

"Isabella, this is Declan Murphy," Jed said by way of introduction.

I nodded politely as Declan spoke in a thick, Irish accent. "I see you, Isabella," he began oddly, and I frowned at the introduction. "Quite the knife you have there."

I flinched, immediately wanting to touch the knife at my side. I resisted the urge and kept my hands folded in my lap while I studied this man more. Declan smiled at me and leaned back casually in his chair. He wasn't as old as I had first thought, despite the gray hair. While he did have an aura of knowledge about him that made him outwardly appear older, his face had only a few lines. I was hard-pressed to put an age on him. I guessed he was somewhere between 35 and 60, but couldn't pinpoint it any closer.

"Isabella, I brought Declan here to look at your knife. Do you have it on you?" John asked, and the way he asked it indicated he knew very well that I did. His tone was slightly accusatory.

I sighed and nodded, glancing back toward the newcomer. Declan smiled and said, "She has it strapped to her thigh. Powerful thing, that knife. I could feel it upon entering the house. May I hold it?"

I sat still, debating. This man was a stranger, and an odd one at that. Would he give the knife back if I handed it over? He held his smile as he watched me watch him. He knew I was assessing him, and the situation. John shifted on the couch, drawing my attention. He smiled and nodded at me reassuringly. I glanced over at Jed, who also nodded.

Despite Jed and John urging me, I still felt uneasy about this man. "Your word you will give it back?" I asked finally.

Declan placed his hand to his heart and nodded. "I give you my solemn vow, lass. I will return your knife to you."

I pulled the knife out of its sheath and Declan ducked his head down. He hurriedly pulled a pair of dark sunglasses out of his pocket and thrust them on before turning back toward me. I stared at him, suddenly unwilling to hand the knife over. Declan pulled a cloth from his pocket and held it in his waiting hand. "Who are you?" I asked, still clutching the knife.

Declan sighed loudly and moved his head so he appeared to be looking straight at me. The sunglasses were so dark I could no longer see his eyes to gauge the truth of his words. "I am a practitioner of ancient magic. It is a family calling, or curse, depending on your point of view. That knife you hold sings with magic and glows with a brightness to rival the sun. You carry something ancient and powerful, Isabella. Now, may I see it?"

Chapter 9

My heart stilled at Declan's words. The knife was magic? Could I believe something so ridiculous? I looked down at the knife I held, feeling along the intensely sharp blade. I felt the small remaining part of my naiveté die. Vampires were real. Werewolves were real. What else? Magic had been at play creating these supernatural creatures, so it only made sense that there were other magical forces in the world. Deep down I think I always suspected there was something extra special about the knife.

I stood and walked toward Declan, clutching the knife. He held his hand out, with the cloth resting on his palm. The knife pulsed as I drew closer to Declan, as though it could sense what was happening. I held the knife above his hand before slowly setting it on the cloth. Declan nodded at me before pulling the knife toward him. I backed up and sat down, never taking my eyes off the strange man.

Declan held the knife carefully for several moments without moving. Slowly, he moved his other hand over the top of the knife, while still not touching the blade with his bare hands. I found myself holding my breath, anxious and curious at the same time. I hated to admit that maybe Mark had been right about me not carrying the knife until it was inspected. I wasn't ready to say that to him though.

Declan did seemingly nothing but hold the knife for several minutes, while I tapped my leg nervously. After ten minutes, he covered the knife fully with the cloth and lowered his hands. He pulled the sunglasses off and looked at me with his steely gray eyes. He motioned toward the sheath still strapped to my side. I unhooked it from my leg and walked over to the strange man.

"Please, put the knife away," Declan said.

I uncovered the knife while Declan turned his face away. I took the knife and carefully slid it back in the sheath. Declan turned around as soon as I had replaced the knife. I returned to my seat beside John, still holding the knife in my hands.

Declan stared at me for several minutes before he finally spoke. "I do not believe that knife will harm you, so you may carry it on your side if you wish," he said simply. I sighed in relief, but he wasn't finished speaking. "You are already too linked to that knife to sever your connection."

"Connection? What does that mean?" I asked.

Declan stared at me, his eyes focused on mine intently. "Centuries ago, when the vampire plague was fully upon the world, there were those who wielded magic as a weapon against this threat. They created blades to combat the evil, and gave these blades to warriors tasked with destroying the vampires. These warriors volunteered to do whatever it took to eliminate the vampires, including submitting themselves to ancient blood magic. Each weapon was created individually and linked to the man who would wield it. Over time, some of the blades began to change the wearer, or perhaps the wearer changed the blade. Either way, as soon as the vampire threat seemed diminished, the very men who created the blades sought to destroy them. Not all blades were successfully destroyed, and several were lost. I believe the dagger you carry is one of those lost weapons."

I stared at him blankly, soaking in what he had just said. "So, this vampire threat has happened before? And some magicians made weapons to kill them? Then they destroyed the weapons?" I asked, feeling more confused than ever.

Declan flinched visibly at my words, but when he spoke it was much like that of a patient teacher. I knew the tone well. "The vampire threat upon this world has been here for centuries, but there was a dark time when the vampires spread like a disease and rose up against humankind. It was during this time, magic rose as well to counter the threat. There is always a balance needed. As the vampires were eliminated, the balance shifted too far, and the men who wore the blades began to change. Bad things happened."

"Bad things?"

"People died at the hands of these men. The magic used to forge the weapons should have been neutral, but when blood is involved, the rules change. Each blade was connected to one man only, but you have to understand something about the men chosen. They didn't have wives or children. In fact, many of these men were criminals. As such, when the weapons were created using their blood, some of their attributes were contained inside the blades."

"What about my knife?"

"I will have to research this particular knife, but it doesn't *feel* evil. Not all the men were bad, so not all the blades were bad. It's hard to know whether to blame the blades themselves, or the men wielding them," Declan shrugged, his eyes assessing me. "Perhaps both."

"And you still think it's safe for me to wear it?" I asked, feeling reluctant to hold the knife for the first time. The knife didn't feel evil to me either, but what did I know?

"The knife is linked to you now, and you aren't evil, are you Isabella?" he asked, and I shook my head immediately. "I cannot do anything about the link, so it is up to you now."

My heart pounded in my chest as his words sunk in. The knife was linked to me, like it had been to some possibly murderous man centuries ago. "You know this magic. Can't you fix it?"

Declan shook his head, his eyes shifting to the knife in my lap.

"Magic is not what it used to be. There are a few families with the gift still, but we do not possess the magic our kin of old did, or the knowledge. That time has passed, I'm afraid. The ability to sever your connection, if there ever was such a thing, is unknown to me. We are in the age of science, and magic doesn't always mesh well with that."

John leaned forward and asked the question that had been on the tip of my tongue. "Can you just destroy the knife? Wouldn't that fix things?"

"As it is, no, I don't think I can. There may still be information on how to destroy it, and I will look into the matter, but the real question remains. Should I? For that knife to show back up after centuries is... interesting," Declan finished.

"You think it means something?" John asked suddenly, his eyes darting to the knife.

Declan shrugged and sat back, seemingly relaxed. "How did you come by the knife?"

I smiled at Declan and said, "A vampire gave it to me."

Declan stared at me, blinked, and suddenly laughed. The sound caught me off guard and I jumped, as Declan's laughter rose to almost hysterical levels. "A vampire gave you a vampire-killing knife?" he asked between chortles.

I nodded and he laughed harder, grasping his sides as the absurdity of the situation overtook him. The irony wasn't lost on me, but I didn't think it was quite as funny as Declan apparently did. John looked over at me with raised eyebrows. I shrugged in response. John didn't seem to think it was very funny either.

"I also used the knife to kill the vampire who gave me the knife," I stated between Declan's giggles.

Declan's laughter ceased as he looked at me with a suddenly serious face. "You killed the vampire who gave you the knife?" he asked, and I nodded. "That may explain the knife's attachment to you."

"How strong is this attachment?" John asked sharply.

"It's difficult to say," Declan began. He gestured at me with his hand. "The knife has an aura about it, just as Isabella has an aura about her. We all do. The knife's aura is intertwined with Isabella's. I can still see the two distinct auras, but they twine around each other and blend. When I took the knife, it was as though there was a magical cord tying them together."

"After all you know, you still think it's safe for Izzy to carry it?" John asked.

Declan looked at me as he spoke. "Do you think it is safe to carry? Have you noticed anything strange about it that causes you concern?"

"It's invisible," I muttered in reply. Declan nodded and gestured for me to continue. "Sometimes it feels warm."

"That could be the magic you are feeling. Magic doesn't speak, but it does have a mind of its own. It may be communicating with you in its own way," Declan said, before turning back toward John. "For whatever reason, that knife and Isabella are linked together. I do not have the knowledge to unlink them, or even destroy the knife. I will travel home and attempt to find an answer for you, but I make no guarantees. I am sorry, but that's all I can tell you for now. Remember, that knife was forged to combat vampires, and it will do that very well. As to if it will change Isabella in the process; that remains to be seen."

"Thank you, Declan," John replied.

We followed Declan to the door, where Jed and John thanked him again. Declan shook my hand, and I felt a jolt of electricity run up my arm at his touch. He grasped my hand tighter, so I couldn't break free. "No one else should handle that knife," he whispered.

I swallowed hard and nodded, then said in a whisper to match Declan's, "What if someone already has?"

He squinted at me, still clutching my hand. "Who was this person? Did anything strange happen?"

"Mark," I replied, shaking my head. "Nothing happened. He strapped it on and it disappeared, just like it does for me."

Declan's eyebrows rose at that. "Is this Mark here?" he asked, glancing from me to Jed.

Jed nodded and replied, "Yes, he's in the barn."

Well, that answered my question about Mark's location. Declan finally released my hand and motioned at Jed to lead the way. "Please, I should meet this person before I leave."

Jed nodded and we followed him to the barn. My heart was pounding in my chest, and John kept glancing worriedly in my direction. I hadn't strapped the knife back on yet, so I held it in my sweaty palm. We entered the barn and walked past the empty cages, toward the back room. Mark walked out before we reached the room, shirtless and sweaty. My heart sped up again at the sight of him, and I wasn't sure if it was from nervousness or desire.

Mark padded toward us on bare feet, his eyes darting to me before locking onto Declan. John moved forward and introduced Declan and Mark. They shook hands and politely greeted each other. Declan turned and motioned for me to move toward him. I sighed and walked forward, my eyes on Mark.

"Isabella," Declan said softly, and I jerked my face toward his. "Hand Mark the knife, please."

I swallowed hard, suddenly worried about what the knife might do to Mark. I held the knife out and Mark reached toward it. I watched Declan's face as Mark's hand inched closer to the knife. I felt Mark grasp the knife, and I flicked my eyes up to Mark before letting him take the knife.

I realized I'd been holding my breath, and I exhaled loudly when nothing happened. Mark held the knife just like it was any regular knife. I glanced at Declan, who had his head cocked to one side as he stared at the knife in Mark's hand.

Declan pulled his glasses on and said, "Mark, please pull the knife out of its sheath."

Mark pulled the knife out, but again nothing happened that I could see. I looked at Declan, hoping to read a reaction on his face. He simply stared at the knife, his expression unreadable. He motioned with his hand, and Mark put the knife back in its sheath. Declan removed his glasses and turned his gray eyes toward me.

"The knife will not harm him," Declan said simply.

"What about anyone else?" I asked.

"I would not suggest letting anyone else touch the knife. Now, I must leave," Declan said as he hurried back the way he had come in.

Jed and John hurried after him, but I stood rooted to the spot. I had the feeling Declan wasn't telling us something. Mark still grasped the knife, and I held my hand out for Mark to hand it back to me. Mark looked at me curiously, obviously wondering what had just happened. After a brief, silent moment, he set the knife in my hand and turned away.

"Mark," I said, following him. I reached my free hand out and grabbed his arm. "Please, talk to me."

Mark stopped walking and turned toward me. "What do you want to talk about, Isabella?"

I blinked at his harsh tone. He hadn't been rude, just blunt, but it hurt nonetheless. I swallowed, not sure where to begin, when the sound of glass breaking caught my attention. I looked around Mark toward the sound, but he pushed ahead of me. He rushed into the storage room, with me close on his heels.

I stopped dead in my tracks at the sight before me. Beth stood in the middle of the room, with a pile of broken glass at her bare feet. Her hair was disheveled and blood was flowing freely down her left hand. She wore nothing but a large t-shirt. The shirt was a plain navy shirt, but I was certain I'd seen that same shirt earlier, on Mark. I felt blood rush to my face as I looked around the small room. Mark and Beth's shoes were pushed into the corner and the small couch had a rumpled blanket thrown haphazardly across it.

Mark quickly moved into the room and grabbed Beth's bleeding hand. Beth looked up at me, and our eyes met in a silent exchange. She smiled smugly at me, the look clearly saying she was enjoying my discomfort. I could hear the blood rushing in my ears and nothing else. I knew Mark was saying something, but I couldn't understand the words.

I turned on my heel and marched out of the room with my head held high. My hands were shaking with each step, but I refused to run or cry. I walked slowly, concentrating on the steps I took, so I wouldn't let my imagination get the best of me. I was probably reading too much into the situation. There was obviously a logical explanation, but the logical part of my brain wasn't working. I was jealous.

The realization stopped me in my tracks. Did I have a right to be jealous? Did a couple rolls in the hay give me a claim on Mark? I shook my head and continued out of the barn. As soon as I was out in the cool, night air, I stopped walking and fastened the knife back on my thigh. Dangerous or not, I immediately felt better with the blade strapped into place. I hurried to the back door of the house and through the kitchen, looking for Jared. I found Jared with Hugo in the small living room, playing a game of cards.

Jared smiled when I entered the room, but it quickly turned into a frown. He stood up and rushed toward me, sniffing the air around me. Hugo cleared his throat loudly, and Jared immediately stopped sniffing and straightened up. He blushed and looked at Hugo apologetically.

"It's not polite to sniff people when they enter the room, Jared," Hugo said in his deep voice. A small smile tugged at the edge of Hugo's lips as he admonished Jared.

Jared shrugged and looked back at me. "Sorry, Izzy," he said softly. "Sometimes scents get the better of me. Are you okay?"

"I just want to go back to the cottage," I replied. "Is Justin still here?"

Jared shook his head. "Justin went back to the lab with Malcolm. They left the jeep here for us though."

It was after dark, so my brother shouldn't be working on any vampires in the lab. I wondered what other experiments he was working on. I let the thought go. No use worrying about something I couldn't control. "Let's go," I said, turning toward the door.

"Only if Mark is with you," Hugo boomed before we had taken two steps.

"What?" I asked, looking at Hugo.

"Jared is in Mark's charge at the cottage," Hugo replied.

Jared rolled his eyes and looked at Hugo. "I'm fine. I've been with Izzy all day, and nothing has happened."

"The full moon is two days away. Tomorrow will be much worse for you, and while you're sleeping who knows what could happen. Someone needs to be close by to keep an eye on you. Mark already agreed, since he's staying at the cottage too. So, where is he?"

"Hugo, really, I'm fine. I'm sure Mark will be there later," Jared replied with a quick glance at me.

"Either you have one of us supervising you, or you go in the cage," Hugo replied, standing up. "Those are your options until the full moon."

"Mark's in the barn," I said softly before turning back to Jared. "I'll go ahead to the house. I'll see you there later."

Jared stared at me, his expression worried. I smiled weakly at him and he shook his head. He could see right through me. I turned toward the door and Jared added, "Take the jeep, at least."

I shook my head, not turning around. "No, I think I'd rather walk," I replied as I hurried out of the house before anyone could stop me.

Walking back to the cottage would take longer, but the walk would clear my head. I decided to take the path Mark had led me on the first time. With the almost full moon glowing down on the snow, it was fairly easy to see my path without a flashlight. I hurried through the snow, which crunched loudly under my feet. Within minutes, I reached the edge of the trees, and my visibility diminished greatly. I still plowed through, but I was quickly regretting my decision to take this path.

I breathed easier when the path led me to the small graveyard, and my visibility increased slightly. My mind wandered over everything that had happened in the past weeks. I tried to force myself to think about the Mark and Beth situation, but instead thoughts of Kirk's dead body kept flashing in my mind. I walked to the edge of the graveyard, seeking out the telltale signs of a fresh grave. The only marker on the grave was a flat stone with Kirk's name on roughly etched on it. I stopped briefly and brushed snow from the smooth stone. No flowers had been placed on his grave, and I felt a pang of guilt. His mother would never know of his death. His sister would spend years wondering what had become of her brother. No one would place flowers on his grave.

I choked back tears and stood up, vowing to find some flowers for Kirk's grave. I stumbled back through the graveyard, found the other pathway easily, and began trekking down the trail. The temperature had dropped significantly with the setting sun and I found myself shivering and wishing I had just taken the jeep, but I had needed the walk.

The walk took longer than I had remembered it taking before, but I eventually reached the edge of the clearing. I stopped, admiring the view of pristine white snow and the small cottage in the distance. The view was serene, like something out of a painting. I was about to walk out, when I heard the sound of a vehicle. Still hidden by the trees, I watched as the jeep stopped in front of the cottage. Two people got out, but even though I couldn't see them well, I knew by the body shapes that it was Jared and Mark.

I stepped back into the forest, not ready to face Mark yet. The walk obviously hadn't cleared my head enough. I backtracked down the path, where I had spotted a boulder that was mostly free of snow. I sat down on the cold boulder and pulled my legs in, listening to the quiet of the forest. I knew I didn't have much time before someone came looking for me, but I wanted to relish the few moments I did have of peace.

I closed my eyes and took several long, deep breaths until my heartbeat had slowed. "Isabella," a voice said softly. I opened my eyes and looked around, waiting for the speaker to step forward. It hadn't been Mark's voice, or Jared's, I was sure of that. "Isabella," the voice said again, like a whisper on the wind.

By the third time the voice said my name, I was sure I knew who it was. The strange accent was unmistakable. "Henri?" I called softly. A minute passed as I held my breath, listening, but no reply came. I tried calling out again, but this time I closed my eyes and concentrated on speaking his name in my mind. "Henri?"

"Isabella," Henri said, his voice faint in my head. "Please."

He didn't say any more, so I tried again. "Henri?" I called out. I waited with my eyes closed, hoping for another response.

The knife on my thigh suddenly grew warm, seeming to pulse with energy. I touched the hilt with my hand, caressing it. "Help me," Henri pleaded, his voice slightly louder this time.

"Henri, where are you? What's wrong?" I asked.

The knife on my side stopped pulsing and eventually the warmth seemed to seep away, until the knife felt just like any regular knife. Henri didn't speak again, and I figured he was gone from my mind. I wasn't sure what had just happened, but I was worried about Henri. It seemed silly to be worried about a vampire, but I couldn't help it. If a vampire like Henri was reaching out to me asking for help, he was probably in big trouble.

I sighed as I stood up, my hand straying to the knife at my side. What had Declan said about the knife communicating with me? Was that what the warm pulsing was? If so, what was the knife trying to say? Maybe it was just responding to Henri speaking to me. Or maybe it was a warning.

The strange encounter filled my mind as I made my way back down the path. I hadn't made it to the clearing when Mark suddenly appeared before me. I stopped in my tracks and stared at him, my heart pounding in surprise. It was dark under the canopy of trees, but I could see well enough to know he was wearing a light gray t-shirt and jeans. Werewolves didn't seem to need jackets. Jared moved around Mark and came up beside me, throwing an arm casually around my shoulders.

I ignored both of the men and continued down the path. Jared dropped his arm and followed closely beside me. Both men were silent, and the only sounds were my own footsteps in the snow. On my right, I could see Jared glancing at me worriedly. Mark moved up on the other side of me and I quickened my pace. The men had no trouble keeping up with my short strides. My irritation had not diminished on my walk, and I found Mark's presence aggravating. I resisted the urge to lash out at him in anger, and trudged as fast as I could through the frozen snow.

The fire was already going in the cottage, but it hadn't warmed the room up yet. I kicked my boots off at the door and moved to my bedroom without a word. I rifled through my drawers, attempting to find something suitable to wear to bed. I needed to ask Mirabelle if she had some sweatpants I could borrow.

Mostly, I had been wearing oversized t-shirts to bed, but the thought brought up memories of Beth. The top drawer of my dresser was filled with the under garments Vanessa had brought me, which included mostly sheer or lace items. I pulled several items out, staring at them. I growled in frustration. Finding clothes to wear to bed shouldn't be difficult! I shoved the lingerie back in the drawer and rifled through the drawers again until I found a soft pair of shorts and a tank top. I dressed quickly, turned off the bedroom light, and slipped under the covers. Mark could sleep wherever he damn well felt like sleeping. I closed my eyes and drifted off to sleep.

Chapter 18

I hadn't been asleep long when the sound of my bedroom door opening woke me up. I opened my eyes and peeked at Mark as he tiptoed into the room. Feigning sleep, I rolled over as quietly as possible. I heard him rustle around and finally shut the bedroom door, enveloping the room in darkness once more. The bed was a queen size, and I was right in the middle of it. Mark moved the blanket, and I felt the bed shift as he climbed in.

"Can you scoot over a little?" he asked softly. I ignored him, and continued to pretend I was asleep. That farce apparently didn't work on werewolves. "Izzy, I know you're awake. Would you share the bed, please?"

"Fine," I snapped, as I scooted to the opposite edge of the bed.

Mark shifted, presumably taking up more space on the bed. I kept my back to him and closed my eyes. The blankets moved, and Mark's hand was suddenly on my bare arm. "Izzy," he said softly.

"I'm trying to sleep," I said testily as I pushed his hand off my arm.

Mark growled, and I felt the little hairs on the back of my neck raise. I flipped over on my back and faced him. The room was too dark to see his features, just a rough outline of his face above me. "Izzy,"

Mark said my name as he snaked his hand across my stomach, lifting my shirt. I felt the stirrings of desire, but quickly squashed them.

"Don't touch me!" I yelled, pushing his hand back.

Mark sat back as though burned. The bedroom door suddenly opened, and I looked up to see Jared. He stood in the doorway, in just a pair of boxer shorts. His eyes glowed bright yellow as he stared at us. The sound of his growl grew in volume with each passing second. "Get away from her," he said gruffly, his chest moving rapidly in time to his quickened breaths.

Mark jumped out of bed and was across the room in the blink of an eye. "Calm down, Jared," he said, pushing Jared out into the hallway.

Damn werewolves! I rolled out of bed and hurried after the men. They stood in the middle of the hall, toe to toe, with Mark towering over Jared by several inches. Jared growled loudly, and I shivered as Mark roared in response. Justin's bedroom door opened, and he peered out into the hall. He wore a pair of shorts and a rumpled blue t-shirt. He'd obviously been asleep, but he looked wide-awake now as he assessed the scene in the hallway. We exchanged worried glances as Mark moved Jared backward into the living room.

"Jared, get control. You need to calm down," Mark ordered loudly as Jared's growls grew in intensity.

I crept down the hallway until I could see both men again. The fireplace dimly lit the room, but Jared's eyes glowed clearly. Jared turned toward me, and I knew that beseeching look he gave me. I stepped into the room slowly, keeping eye contact with Jared. Justin tried to follow me, but I pushed him behind me gently. The knife was in place on my side, and I could feel it pulsing gently against my thigh.

"Jared, it's alright. I'm fine. I'm safe," I said as calmly as I could manage, despite my pounding heart. "Everything is okay."

Jared stared at me, his chest heaving with his breaths. Mark had his hands on Jared's arms, holding him in place tightly. "You yelled," Jared said slowly, as though it hurt to speak. He heaved a loud breath again, and the muscles in his chest and arms twitched.

I walked closer, and Mark cast me a worried glance with glowing eyes of his own. If Jared didn't calm down soon, he'd turn into a werewolf. "Jared, I know I yelled. Mark didn't do anything, though. I'm just mad at him, that's all." Jared growled as his body jerked against Mark's hold. The muscles in Mark's arms rippled with the exertion of holding the other man. "Look at me, Jared," I implored.

Jared jerked his face back toward me, his wild eyes seeking mine. He stared at me, and I kept steady eye contact as I edged closer. When I was beside Mark, I stopped walking and reached out to touch Jared's arm. I could see Mark tense out of the corner of my eye, but he didn't say anything. Jared's eyes jerked toward my hand, then back to my face. I touched his arm tenderly as I made soft shushing noises, as though I was soothing a wild animal. Perhaps I was, I thought absently.

Jared kept his eyes on mine, and I watched in fascination as the glowing yellow slowly diminished. Mark relaxed visibly beside me, and I stepped under his arm so I was sandwiched between the two werewolves. Jared kept his eyes locked on mine as I reached both my hands out and ran them across his biceps. His muscles flexed at my touch, and I moved my hands across his chest. I found myself marveling at the sculpted perfection of his body, my hands tracing across his chest and abdomen. His body had been almost too thin during his captivity, but he had built muscle back onto his body in the past weeks. I ran my hands across his stomach, feeling him flex his muscles under my fingertips.

Mark moved behind me, pressing his body against my back. He growled and breathed hot air on my ear. "Izzy, what are you doing?" he whispered.

I stopped moving my hands and stared up at Jared's face. His eyes were back to normal, but he was looking at me with a frown. What was I doing? Jared meant a lot to me, but I usually thought of him as more of a brother. I felt warm, as though my whole body was flushing.

I lowered my hands and turned around, so I was facing Mark. Desire surged through me as I looked at him. His brown hair was longer than usual, brushing into his eyes. He was wearing nothing but a pair of boxer briefs, and I found my eyes suddenly transfixed. I backed up into Jared, and I could feel how happy he was to be there. My body tingled and I was quickly losing the ability to think straight as I ran my eyes up and down Mark's chiseled body.

"I'm mad at you," I whispered, even as I reached out and ran my hands across Mark's chest and down the thin trail of dark hair that disappeared into the top of his boxer briefs.

Mark closed the space between us, and took my hands in his. "Not here, Izzy," he growled as he held my hands clasped in his strong ones.

I stood on my tiptoes and kissed him, running my tongue across his lips. He let go of my hands and pulled my body close to his. I was on fire! Every inch of me burned with an overwhelming desire. I needed him now. I moved my hands down his stomach and reached inside his briefs. Mark's hand grabbed mine before I got further. He pushed me back gently and turned me around, his hands clasping my hands together as he began walking me down the hallway.

I pulled against him, catching sight of my brother staring at me wide-eyed. What was I doing? "Mark, let go of me," I said testily, feeling the anger suddenly return.

Mark freed my hands and I pushed him back. "I almost forgot!" I screamed, and Mark's eyes widened in surprise. He shared confused looks with Jared and Justin. "I saw you and Beth," I sobbed, feeling a sudden rush of tears. The tears choked me as I attempted to stifle them.

"Izzy, are you feeling all right?" Jared asked behind me.

I shook my head in confusion. I shivered suddenly, no longer feeling as though I was burning up. "I'm not sure," I said softly. Was I feverish? I looked over at Jared, and I breathed a sigh of relief that I no longer felt the overwhelming urge to run my hands over his half-naked body. There was no denying Jared was attractive, but I couldn't see myself with him in that manner. There was also the question of Mark. I really didn't know what to do with him. I glanced at him, and desire and anger still warred within me at the sight of him.

"Izzy, I think we should talk," Mark said slowly as he grasped my hand. He pulled me back into the living room and settled me onto one of the couches while he put another log on the fire. Jared sat down beside me and I leaned into him, resting my head on his shoulder. He patted my leg reassuringly and I felt instantly calmed. Justin skirted the edge of the room, pacing back and forth and darting me worried glances.

As soon as the fire was blazing, Mark turned back toward me. He sighed loudly and moved to the couch across from us, sitting down on the edge as though he would jump up at any moment. "Justin, I think it'd be best if you go to bed," Mark said without taking his eyes off me.

"I don't think I should leave my sister alone with you two," Justin said as he stopped pacing. He puffed his chest out and stared down at the two men, with his hands on his hips. I smiled at the gesture, but we all knew there was nothing Justin could do against two werewolves. Even had Mark and Jared been human, my brother wouldn't have been much of a match. Justin had always been more interested in the mind than the body, and while he was in good shape, he could hardly compete with the two muscle-bound men.

"Justin, you can go ahead and go to bed. I'm sure you need your sleep so you can get back to saving the world," I said with a smile.

Justin stared at me, weighing my words, before he nodded and padded toward me. He leaned over and kissed the top of my head, whispering a soft good night before turning toward the two men. "If either of you hurt her, I will make you regret it," Justin muttered angrily before spinning on his heel and returning to his bedroom.

As soon as Justin's bedroom door clicked shut, Mark turned

toward me and spoke. "Izzy, are you feeling okay? You're acting very strangely."

I sat up and looked at Mark. "I feel fine now," I replied.

"Now? As in you weren't feeling fine before?"

"I don't know," I muttered. I felt as though I had been through a marathon. No, it was worse than that. I was confused, angry, tired and felt like I had been through a long, emotional battle. My mind went of its own accord to Sarah, and the torture I had endured at her hands. I swallowed hard, trying to erase the thought of her. Still, I could feel the sting of her whip on my skin.

My body flushed again, and I felt warmth spread across my skin. I closed my eyes and tried to cease the memories that were flooding back to me. Jared shifted on the couch, and I flinched as though I had been stung. What was wrong with me?

"Maybe you should just go to bed," Jared said softly beside me. I leaned back against his shoulder and he put a comforting arm around me. "We can do this in the morning."

"He's not sleeping in my bed," I murmured quietly to Jared. I kept my eyes closed, not looking at either man as I snuggled against Jared.

Jared leaned back into the couch, pulling me with him. I settled in closer, resting my head against his chest as I curled the rest of my body onto the couch. "He's supposed to, Izzy. Remember, he needs to keep an eye out for vampires," Jared replied.

"Why doesn't he just go sleep with Beth?" I retorted, finally opening my eyes to glare at Mark. "Again," I added.

Mark jerked back as though he'd been punched, his eyes widening in either anger or surprise. Jared's arms tightened around me and I could feel his body vibrate.

"What?" Mark asked. "I haven't slept with Beth."

"No, you just had sex with her."

"Izzy, I have done no such thing," Mark said sharply.

Jared whispered in my ear, "He's telling the truth."

"Then why was she wearing your t-shirt, and nothing else?" I asked, sitting up angrily. "What happened? Did we interrupt you before you got the chance?"

Mark closed his eyes and ran a hand through his hair. When he opened his eyes, his expression was patient and kind. It irritated me, since I was ready to be angry with him. "Izzy, there is absolutely nothing going on between Beth and me. I needed to go for a run to clear my head, and Beth asked if she could accompany me. We changed into werewolves, Izzy. We had just gotten back to the barn and changed back to human form when you and the wizard showed up. Beth put my shirt on because she couldn't find her own."

I stared at him, taking in his words. My face burned in embarrassment. I glanced quickly at Jared, who nodded in the affirmative. Mark was indeed speaking the truth. "She couldn't find her clothes," I muttered, shaking my head. Beth had laid a trap, and I had stepped right into it. The woman was more conniving than I had realized. She had probably broken the glass on purpose, so I would find her like that. "Damn it."

"Well, now that that's settled, let's go to bed," Jared said gruffly.

I smiled and turned my face toward his. He had a five o'clock shadow and a grin plastered on his face. I scooted toward him and kissed him on his rough cheek. My knife dug into my thigh and pulsed, radiating warmth across my body. I ran my hand across Jared's chest and moved my mouth to his, kissing him passionately.

Jared tensed, and I moved my mouth down his chest, laying gentle kisses across his body. Arms were around my waist, pulling me from behind. I was suddenly dangling several inches off the ground, with strong hands around my waist. I wriggled until the hands lowered me back to the ground and I turned around. Mark held me tight, pressing my arms to my sides.

"What are you doing? Are you trying to drive me mad?" Mark growled. "I get you're mad about Beth, but nothing happened. Get over your jealousy issues!"

Everything snapped back into place as my anger suddenly returned. "Jealousy issues!" I shouted, pushing my hands futilely against Mark's chest. "I'm done! I'm going to bed! You can sleep on the couch!"

Mark let go of my arms and I stormed out of the room. Fire was racing down my thigh, emanating from the knife. I slammed my bedroom door behind me and climbed into bed. The knife throbbed and pulsed against my leg. Maybe it wasn't safe to be wearing the knife after all. Was the magic in the knife making me crazy? I felt completely unhinged, and not myself at all. I pulled the covers off and unstrapped the knife. The burning sensation was instantly gone, and I felt suddenly calm. I pushed the knife under my pillow and curled up in my blankets, feeling blissful sleep overtake me as soon as I closed my eyes.

Chapter 11

Morning light filtering in through the curtains woke me the next morning. I stretched, feeling sore muscles all over my body. What had I done to be so sore? The blankets tangled around my legs, and I rolled onto my back in an attempt to untangle myself. That's when I realized I was completely naked. I lifted up the blankets to double-check and sure enough, I wore nothing under the sheets. I distinctly remembered going to bed with clothes on.

I rolled over and caught my breath. A man was lying beside me with his bare back to me and his sandy brown hair tousled from sleep. A quick peek under the covers revealed that he, too, was naked. Heart pounding in my chest, I looked around the room in panic. The room was simple with no definitive decorations, except a painting of a seascape. A large dresser with a mirror atop it rested against one wall, and a computer desk with a black laptop on it sat on the other side of the bed. Two windows on adjoining walls indicated I was in a corner bedroom.

I carefully edged out of the bed and looked around the floor for my clothes. My shorts were under the bed and my tank top was lying atop the dresser on the other side of the room. I had no idea where my panties were, but I quickly pulled on my shorts. My boots were lying on the floor by the bedroom door. I debated walking across the room, not wanting to wake the man in the bed, but I had no other way of retrieving my clothes.

As quietly as possible, I tiptoed around the bed, my eyes glued to the man in the bed. Seeing his face only confirmed my suspicions about his identity, and I felt my heart flutter in panic. My hands shook as I snagged my top off the dresser and pulled it on. What had I done?

I turned my back on the man and pulled my boots on. All the while, I pursed my lips tightly together to hold in the panic that was building. I would not cry. I would not panic. I would pull on my boots and get the hell out of the room as quickly as possible. Then, when I was alone, I could figure out what the hell was going on, and possibly scream.

"Going somewhere, beautiful?" the man asked behind me.

I stiffened and shoved my foot into the boot unceremoniously before turning around. Lucas had flung the blanket off, revealing his naked body. Muscles rippled as he stood up and walked toward me, a smile plastered on his face. He was definitely happy to see me, while I was choking on panic. I didn't like Lucas, so how had I wound up naked in his bed?

"I'm leaving," I managed to squeak out as Lucas closed the distance between us. I backed up further, until I was pressed against the bedroom door.

Lucas leaned into me, pressing his body against mine. "Why? I thought we could have breakfast in bed?" he added as he ran a finger down my arm.

"You thought wrong," I said, shoving him roughly away from me. He barely budged, cocking his head at me. "Get away from me."

Lucas chuckled and pulled me toward him. "Oh, now you're playing hard to get," he mused as he moved his mouth to my neck and began kissing me.

I could feel the tears welling in my eyes, but I squashed the emotion down and concentrated on anger instead. "Get the fuck off of me!" I said angrily, pushing at him again.

Lucas stopped kissing me and stepped back, a frown creasing his brows. "Izzy, what's wrong?"

"What's wrong? What's wrong? What the fuck am I doing here, Lucas? What the hell happened?" I asked. My hands shook uncontrollably and my eyesight began to blur with unshed tears. I didn't want to cry, but I couldn't seem to hold in the emotions. "How did I get here?"

Lucas backed up further and held his hands up. He kept eye contact with me as he spoke. "Izzy, you came here to me last night," he said slowly. "You walked here in the snow from the cottage and right into my room. I asked you what was going on, and you said you couldn't stop thinking about me. That's when you took your shirt off."

"I did what?" I asked incredulously. No, that didn't sound like me at all. I ran my hand down my thigh, searching for my knife, but it wasn't there. Then I remembered I had taken it off and put it under my pillow just before going to sleep. The knife had been burning my skin, and making me act strangely. Maybe putting it under my pillow hadn't been enough to stop the strange magic inside the knife.

"We made love all night long," Lucas said softly, reaching toward me. I flinched away from him, and he dropped his hand. "You were insatiable. You kept begging me for more. The things you asked me to do..." he trailed off, shaking his head.

"I don't want to hear any more," I said as the first tear trickled down my face. "Just, stay away from me."

I felt behind me until my hand grasped the door handle. My whole body trembled with panic. I had to get out of there. I turned the knob and ran out of the room without a backwards glance. The room I had been in was the corner room on the top floor of Jed's house. I stumbled down the stairs, taking them two at a time and falling down half of them. I didn't pause as I raced through the house and out the front door into the cold morning.

The sky was clear of clouds for the first time in days, and the sun peaking over the horizon indicated today would be a beautiful day. Icy snow crunched under my boots as I ran down the path toward the cottage. My footprints from the night before were clearly visible on a separate path. I frowned at them, wondering why I had taken a different route through the snow. By my best guess, the path was a direct route.

I ignored the prints and followed the more used path that was mostly free of snow and made travel much quicker. Running when I could, I made good time past the graveyard and through the forest. I stopped at the edge of the clearing, breathing hard as I stared at the cottage. Mark was hurrying through the snow, presumably following my footsteps from the previous night. I stayed where I was until Mark was out of sight, then I raced through the snow to the cottage.

Jared jumped up as soon as I opened the door, and ran toward me. He was fully dressed in jeans and a black t-shirt and smelled freshly showered as he put his arms around me. I shivered into him as he led me toward the already roaring fire. I turned in his arms, letting him hold me from behind as I warmed myself. He sniffed loudly in my ear, and I swallowed hard, wondering what he would smell on me. My heart thudded loudly in my chest.

"Where have you been?" he asked softly as he sniffed along my body.

"Jared, please stop smelling me," I implored. Please don't ask me any more questions, I thought.

He stopped sniffing me and squeezed me tightly in a hug. "Izzy, where have you been?" he asked again.

A tear ran down my cheek, followed quickly by another. Once I let the first few tears free, the flood began. I turned in his arms and sobbed loudly into his chest. Clutching his shirt in handfuls, I held on as though he was a lifeline. He hugged me tight and stroked my hair until my sobs slowed, and finally subsided. I didn't say anything as I sniffled and pulled away, looking for a tissue. Not finding one, I walked to the bathroom and cleaned myself up, not daring to look at myself in the mirror as I blew my nose on a tissue.

When I came out of the bathroom, Mark and Jared were both there, staring at me expectantly. I glanced at Mark's face, then quickly looked away. I couldn't face him. Hurriedly, I shuffled toward my bedroom. To my dismay, both men followed on my heels. I ignored them and looked around my room. My sheets were on the floor along with both pillows. My knife was lying in the middle of the bed, but everything else looked normal.

"When we woke up and realized you weren't here, we pulled your pillows and sheets off," Jared said by way of explanation. "Mark followed your scent out the back door."

I moved to the sliding glass door, where you could visibly see my footprints in the snow. "When did you realize I was gone?" I asked softly, still staring out the window.

"About thirty minutes ago," Mark replied. "I don't know how we didn't hear you leave."

I didn't either. Compared to a werewolf, I was rather noisy. Even compared to regular humans, I was less than stealthy. "I need to shower and get dressed," I said, not turning around.

"Izzy, why did you leave the house in the middle of the night?" Mark asked. "Where did you go?"

"Didn't you follow my tracks?"

"Jared called and said you were back here, so I turned around and came back," Mark replied.

Mark didn't know yet that I had been at the main house, although my tracks had obviously led straight there. He wouldn't know why I'd gone there yet, or whom I'd spent the evening with. A shower was in order, quickly. I wasn't sure what Jared had smelled on me, but I didn't want Mark getting close enough until I had showered any trace of Lucas from my skin. The last thing I needed was Mark smelling another man on me, especially Lucas. I turned and looked over my shoulder. Both men stood in the doorway, eyeing me warily.

"Let me shower, please," I said.

They nodded and backed out of the room, closing the door behind them. I sighed in relief to be alone for a few minutes. I gathered clothes quickly and stopped, staring at the knife still sitting on my bed. After a moment's debate, I grabbed it and put it on top of the dresser. I opened the bedroom door and peered out; making sure the coast was clear before I scurried down the hallway to the bathroom.

As soon as I was in the bathroom, I set my clothes down and turned toward the mirror. My dyed brown hair was disheveled and there were large, dark circles under my eyes. I felt exhausted, as though I had run a marathon and only slept for an hour. Perhaps I had, I thought ruefully. I carefully stripped and stepped into the shower, wincing at the hot water pulsing on my skin. Pale bruises splattered my skin, making me wonder what had happened.

I closed my eyes and stood under the water, trying to drum up memories of the previous night. They came in patches, almost like a dream. I remember trekking through the snow and heading straight for Jed's house. Why, I didn't know. I sighed and grabbed the shampoo, scrubbing my hair as small glimpses of memory came back.

I pushed open the bedroom door, flicked on the light, then shut the door quietly behind me. A man sat up in bed, looking at me curiously. I took my shirt off and flung it onto the dresser, before kicking my shorts off as well. Desire raced through my body. I slipped my panties down slowly, teasingly, before tossing them toward the man.

The shampoo bottle slipped from my hand as the memory ended. What the hell? I remembered it now, but it was more like seeing a movie through someone else's eyes. I didn't want to remember any more, but the next memory came quickly behind the first.

The man grasped my hands hard, pressing me against the wall as he slammed his body into mine, drawing moans from my mouth. "Harder," my voice whispered.

"I don't want to hurt you," the man replied.

"You can't hurt me," my voice responded. "Now, fuck me hard!"

The memory left, thankfully, and I dropped to my knees in the shower. It was my memory, I knew, but it wasn't me. It couldn't be me. I let out a loud, racking sob. What had I done? Guilt overwhelmed me, choking me. I felt unclean, as though I had been invaded body and soul. I grabbed the soap and scrubbed my body, covering myself in a thick lather before rinsing off. The soap ran clean, but I still felt dirty. I soaped up again and cranked the water up to the highest heat, until the water scorched my skin.

I tried not to notice the bruises that littered my skin. Already they were pale, healing quickly. Despite the fact that my body was healing quickly, I still ached. Every muscle in my body hurt, and now I knew why. I scrubbed myself clean as tears ran down my face unchecked. My mind raced as I tried to make sense of what happened. Had I been drugged? Was it a vampire? Was it my knife? Was it some other sort of magic? Those were the logical questions, but it was the other thoughts that had me sobbing. Maybe I had done it consciously. Was a part of me so afraid to commit to someone again, that I rebelled and sought out the one man I knew was a last resort?

I hunched down in the tub portion of the shower, letting the hot water pour over me. Pulling my knees to my chest, I sobbed. Mark would never forgive this, not with Lucas. No matter that Mark and I had no formal agreement; there was still an unspoken commitment. I had broken a trust. I thought of how I had come on to Jared right in front of Mark. I had felt strange, reckless, but I had thought it was the knife. That's why I had taken it off.

I continued to sob in the tub as the water turned cold. Memories trickled in, making the sobs come harder and louder. I did my best to ignore the memories, but they overwhelmed me, flooding my mind with flashbacks. With each memory, I cried harder, feeling an overwhelming sense of guilt and confusion.

The bathroom door opened and the curtain pulled back, but I didn't look up. I curled my body in tighter and clutched my legs as the water turned off. Someone draped a towel around me and lifted me out of the tub. I raised my head and looked up at Mark's strong jaw. His eyes were kind as he looked down at me, but I quickly looked away, tucking my head against his chest. If he knew, he wouldn't be looking at me with such kindness in his eyes.

Mark carried me down the hall and settled me onto my bed. He pulled the blankets up around me as he simultaneously removed the damp towel from my body. I curled around the sheets, tucking them closer around me. Mark ran the towel through my wet hair, drying it. I hated his kindness, and it only made me sob harder, but my eyes were dry of tears.

I felt someone crawl across the bed and lie down beside me. I opened my eyes to see Jared lying next to me, staring at me with golden-ringed eyes. Mark moved the towel away, and I felt the bed move as he settled down behind me. He moved in close until his body was touching mine, and I resisted the urge to flinch away. Jared moved in closer in front of me as Mark wrapped an arm around my waist.

Neither of the men spoke as my dry sobs finally subsided to sniffles. Mark stroked my hair gently and pulled the blankets tight around me. Jared kept eye contact with me, his eyes silently speaking volumes. He was here for me, for whatever it was that was happening. I finally closed my eyes, lulled to sleep by Mark gently caressing my hair and the exhaustion of crying. For now, I was safe and protected. Eventually, I'd have to return to the real world and face what had happened. What had happened? The thought plagued me as I drifted off to sleep.

Chapter 12

Time seemed to flow oddly while I slept. I had no idea how much time had passed. Day, night, it was all the same to me. I knew people had come and gone, but I refused to wake up fully. I had heard people speaking around me, although I have no idea what was said. I slept the sleep of the dead. It was similar to that of a coma, but I had chosen this sleep. I didn't want to be awake and face the world. Strange things had happened to me, and my mind and body had had enough. I was done.

It wasn't that I necessarily wanted to die. It was more that I was tired of the strange, supernatural things that kept happening. Depression gripped me and pulled me down into slumber. I was lost between the real world and this new, paranormal world. Before my brother had disappeared on that fated mission, the world had been so much simpler to me. Teaching high school, having a glass of wine with friends and ogling the P.E. teacher had been the norm for me. Vampires and werewolves had been the stuff of fairy tales. Of course, that wasn't true. The world hadn't changed at all, only my perception of it had. I longed for those days of ignorance again. Only, I couldn't un-see what I had seen. I had tasted the forbidden fruit, and now I was living with the consequences.

When my body had finally had enough, I woke to a darkened room. The curtains were thrown open, revealing night outside. The only light was coming from the moon glinting off the remnants of snow on the ground. I sat up, staring at the small amount of snow on the ground visible out the sliding glass door. Last time I had been awake, there had been close to a foot of icy snow. Now, there was only a small smattering of snow. The sun must have melted it during the day.

"You're awake," Justin said, and I jumped, turning in my bed.

Justin lay on a small mattress on the floor of my bedroom. I frowned down at him as I clutched the blankets around me. I wore a thick sweatshirt and sweatpants, and I had to wonder where they had come from and who had dressed me. The sweats felt wonderfully soft and cozy, but I certainly didn't remember putting them on. I didn't even own sweatpants. Justin got up and flicked on the bedroom light. The light was blinding, and I winced as my eyes adjusted.

"What time is it?" I asked, my voice raspy, as I shielded my eyes to look at my brother. He was wearing gray sweat pants and a navy t-shirt. Dark circles were visible under his eyes, and it looked like he hadn't slept in quite some time.

"It's after midnight," Justin replied, picking up a cell phone resting on the dresser. He typed something into the phone before setting it down and looking back at me. "Are you hungry? You've been asleep for a long time."

I shrugged, not really feeling hungry. "I guess I should eat something. I am thirsty," I added as I crawled out of bed. I felt a sudden fullness in my bladder, and scurried out of the room toward the bathroom. I could hear Justin following me, but I shut the bathroom door quickly behind me.

After relieving myself, I took a look in the mirror. I looked worse than ever, I thought. My hair was matted, and it took several minutes to brush the tangles out. I took time to brush my teeth and make myself presentable. Even after washing my face, I still felt incredibly tired. Justin was in the kitchen making sandwiches when I came out of the bathroom. He handed me a large glass of water, which I drained quickly. I refilled the glass and sat down at the table, drinking the second glass slower this time.

Justin plopped a plate full of peanut butter and jelly sandwiches in front of me. I grinned and looked up at him. He shrugged and sat down opposite me, leaning back in his chair. He never had been much for cooking. I picked up the first sandwich and began eating, taking my time. The moment I swallowed the first bite, I realized how ravenous I was. Still, I took slow bites, drinking down every few bites with a sip of water. It was strange how delicious a simple peanut butter and strawberry jelly sandwich could taste

I ate two sandwiches and had picked up the third, when Justin finally spoke. "Are you okay, Izzy?" he asked softly.

I looked up at his face, wondering at the meaning behind his words. His brows were drawn in worry, and he was wringing his hands on his shirt. I shrugged and took another bite, chewing slowly as I thought of a response. Was I okay? I honestly didn't know. I was doing my best to think of nothing but the taste of the sandwich.

"You've been asleep for two days," Justin said softly, and I jerked my head up to look at him.

I swallowed the food in my mouth and drank several gulps of water before responding. "Two days? What? That can't be right. Are you sure?" I stammered, my words coming out in a rush. How could I have possibly slept for so long?

"You fell asleep the morning before yesterday. Dr. Humphry was here checking on you, but no one really knew what was wrong with you. Mark and Jared kept talking about your knife and someone named Declan. I'm not sure, because they didn't exactly share any information with me. They also said something about vampires."

"They didn't tell you?"

"No, that's just what I overheard. And there was something else about that werewolf Lucas." Justin shrugged, but his words had my heart pounding in my chest.

"What about Lucas?" I asked slowly, watching my brother for his reaction.

Justin frowned and leaned across the table toward me. "I don't know," he said slowly. "They wouldn't tell me much."

"But Mark and Jared both mentioned Lucas's name?" I asked, feeling the panic rising in my chest.

Justin nodded, "Yes, they both did, a few times. Neither of them seemed happy with Lucas either. I heard Mark attacked him shortly after you went to sleep yesterday, and John had to pull him off. Jared said he would have killed Lucas if he had the chance, but when I asked him why, Jared wouldn't say any more. Logan took his brother and went to meet some of the other werewolves to change for the full moon further from here."

"Where are Jared and Mark now?" I asked, glancing around at the seemingly empty house.

"It's Jared's first full moon. He's locked up in the barn," Justin replied. "Mark volunteered to guard the barn with John. He said he didn't trust himself in wolf form, whatever that means."

I sat back, dropping the remnants of my third sandwich back on the plate. My appetite was completely gone, and I felt exhausted once more. Mark knew about Lucas, that much was obvious. How would I face him? I finished the last of my glass of water and got up, intending to head back to bed. Justin put my plate in the sink and followed me back to my bedroom.

"I'm not leaving you alone," Justin said before I had a chance to ask.

I stopped in the bedroom doorway and closed my eyes. "Justin, I just need to be alone," I said softly.

"It's a full moon, Izzy. There are werewolves all over the woods, and I was asked to keep an eye on you and make sure you didn't leave the house if you woke up. Dr. Humphry will be over in the morning to check on you," Justin added as an afterthought.

"So, you're going to sleep on a mattress on the floor?" I asked, opening my eyes to look at Justin. He nodded his head and pushed past me into the bedroom. Giving in, I followed him back into my bedroom and crawled back in bed.

Justin sat down on his bed, watching me as I curled up in the blankets. "Izzy, what happened? No one is telling me anything, and I'm worried sick about you."

I laid my head down and stared at my brother. Concern was clearly etched on his face, but I didn't know if I could utter the words that seemed stuck in my throat. I didn't even know what to tell him, since I truly didn't know what had happened. What could I say? "I don't know what to tell you," I responded slowly, watching Justin's reaction.

"Izzy, I'm your brother, and I love you no matter what. My mind has made up all sorts of terrors over the last few days. Please, just talk to me. I'm afraid you're going to go to sleep again and not wake back up," he added softly.

"Justin, I..." I stopped, swallowing hard. "I don't know what happened, but you don't need to worry about me."

"You're really not a very good liar," Justin said with a small smile on his face. "And I will always worry about you."

I smiled weakly in return, knowing he was probably right about my lying skills. "You don't want to know, Justin. Please, trust me on this."

Justin shook his head, his smile vanishing as he crawled across his bed toward me. He grabbed my hands in his and stared at me. "Izzy, what happened with Lucas? Why did Mark try to tear him apart?" I closed my eyes, unable to respond. How could I explain to my brother, or anyone else, what I didn't understand myself?

"I don't know what happened, Justin. Please, can we talk about this later? I'm really tired," I replied.

"How can you be tired after sleeping for two days?" Justin asked, but I just shrugged in response. I didn't know why either, but I could feel sleep beckoning to me. "Okay, just make sure you don't leave this room without telling me. And wake up in the morning."

I smiled and looked at my brother. He was worried, but he accepted what I was saying. He let go of my hands and rolled across the mattress to turn off the bedroom light. The room wasn't completely dark, with the moon's light filtering in, but I found it comforting. I settled back in and closed my eyes.

"Justin?" I asked softly.

"Yeah, Iz?"

"Do you know where my knife is?" I asked, as a sudden worry gripped me. I wasn't sure if I wanted the knife close to me or far away, but I needed to know it was safe.

"It's on the dresser," he replied slowly. "Do you want it?"

"No," I replied sharply, settling back into my pillows. I pulled the blankets tighter and closed my eyes. Sleep came slowly, and with it came a new dream.

At first I thought it was the same dream, but there was no cage. I was lying in blood, my body covered in the warm, sticky wetness. Panic gripped me and I flung my arms out, worried I would drown in the blood. After a couple seconds I realized the blood was just a small amount on a cement floor. I sat up and looked down at myself. Except for the blood coating my body, I was naked. The room was concrete and empty, except for a man chained against the far wall.

I stared at the man, marveling at his perfectly chiseled body, despite the fact he was obviously a prisoner. Slowly, I crawled toward him. The man was naked and chained awkwardly with his upper body off the ground and his feet splayed in front of him. I stared at the chains, seeing the strange mechanism he was attached to. The device looked medieval, with chains, cranks and wheels. I eyed it, wondering what it did as I moved to the man's feet. Manacles enclosed his ankles, with chains running loosely from each leg to the other end of the mechanism. He tipped his head up to look at me, his brilliant blue eyes flashing with surprise.

I sucked in a breath as realization coursed through me. "Henri?" I asked in bewilderment.

Henri nodded his head, his eyes taking me in. "Do we dream?" he asked softly.

I frowned, wondering what he was talking about. Then, I remembered. Yes, this was a dream. I was at the cottage, in bed. "Yes, this is a dream," I replied softly. "Take these chains off."

Henri smiled weakly at me and shook his head. "I have not the strength, even here in my realm," he said, closing his eyes as though he was incredibly tired.

I crawled toward him, carefully avoiding the strange contraption attached to his arms and legs. I touched his chest, and he opened his eyes to stare at me. "Henri, where are we?" I asked. "What is this place?"

Henri looked around the room, as though seeing it for the first time. He shrugged his shoulders as far as he could and crooked a smile. "It seems we are in the torture room," he said softly, turning his face toward mine. "I am happy I finally reached you."

"You've been trying to speak to me?" I asked, and he nodded. "I thought I heard you a few days ago, saying my name, but then you were gone."

"Too weak," he said, taking a deep breath. "Help me."

I swallowed hard, staring at this man who had seemed like a god before. Now, he was weak and apparently being tortured. The room started dimming, and my eyes fluttered. I was waking up, I realized quickly. I closed my eyes, willing myself to stay just a few minutes longer. When I opened my eyes, I was still kneeling on the cold floor beside Henri.

"Henri, I'm waking up. How can I help you?"

Henri turned his head slightly, and I noticed his hair was long enough to brush his shoulders. He blinked several times, as though he was having difficulties staying awake. Or perhaps he was having difficulties staying in the dream. Either way, it seemed odd for the man who called himself the Master of Dreams. "Please," he pleaded softly.

I looked down at my body, still coated in sticky, drying blood. Gingerly, I scooted closer to Henri, until I had positioned myself right beside him. I knew what he wanted. He opened his eyes, revealing startling black orbs staring back at me. I had a moment of panic at the sight, but it didn't stop me. I leaned forward, pressing my chest against Henri's as I pulled my hair back and angled my neck toward his mouth, until I felt his lips against my soft skin. Pain erupted in my neck as Henri bit down suddenly. Blood flowed rapidly from my body to his mouth. Part of me was worried about sharing blood with a vampire, while the other part argued that this was just a dream. But then, things seemed different where the Master of Dreams was concerned. I still hadn't fully learned what that meant.

Henri only drank for a few moments, before I felt myself being pulled away and back to reality. He released me and I stared into his black eyes. "Save me," he implored, just before I woke up.

I blinked and pressed my hand to my neck automatically, startled to feel wetness there. Justin sat over me, holding a blood-drenched towel in his hand. I pushed myself into a sitting position and took the towel from my brother, pressing it to my neck. His eyes were wide and bright blood covered his hands and arms. Blood coated my shirt as well and there was a large patch on my bed.

The front door banged open loudly and I heard footsteps pounding down the hallway. Hugo flung the bedroom door open and rushed in, followed quickly by Mirabelle. The doctor hurried to my side and pulled the towel from my neck, inspecting the wound. She dug through the medical bag she carried, and pulled out antiseptic swabs.

Hugo came around the bed and looked at my neck, his eyes growing wide. "That's a vampire bite," he stated.

I stared at him, not sure what to say. This didn't usually

happen when Henri drank my blood in dreams. He would drink and I'd wake up as though nothing had happened. There had been a few instances though, I recalled, that waking had been difficult. Henri hadn't been himself though, chained up and weak as he was. The Master of Dreams didn't seem very in control of his dream world.

"There was no vampire in this room," Justin said. "I think I would have known."

Hugo glanced at Justin, but his words were for me. "No vampire can get in this house without an invitation."

"I didn't invite any vampires in," I replied, wincing as Mirabelle cleaned the bite wound with alcohol. I wrinkled my nose at the antiseptic smell. "It was a dream."

Mirabelle's hands stopped briefly before she continued with her work. Justin and Hugo looked at me wide-eyed, as though seeing me for the first time. "Damn," Hugo said as he flopped down on my bed. "It's that other vamp, isn't it? It's the slimy bastard that almost killed you in a dream before."

I didn't think Henri was slimy, but I nodded all the same. "Yes, it was the same vampire."

Hugo moved in close to me, sniffing the air. He climbed onto the bed, breathing loudly as he tried to catch the scent. "There," he said, smiling. He sat back, nodding to himself as Mirabelle bandaged my wound. "I have his scent now. I can track that reeking corpse if he ever shows up in person."

"How can a vampire do this in a dream?" Justin asked, his confusion and worry evident in the creased brows and the way he clutched the bloody towel in his hands.

"I've only heard of a few instances of people waking up, bleeding from apparent bite wounds. Some vamps are said to have extra powers. Not sure if that's true or not," Hugo added, shrugging. "It would appear some of these stories are true. Not a good thing, I think."

"He's the Master of Dreams," I whispered, more to myself.

"Master of Dreams?" Hugo asked, frowning at me. "Is that what he calls himself? Cocky little blood-sucker, isn't he?"

I nodded, not sure if I should have said that or not. I felt strangely protective of Henri. He had never harmed me. In fact, he had helped me on more than one occasion. He had given me his blood, strengthening me, when Patricia was killing me. This time, I had been the one to offer blood to help him. That probably wasn't something I should share with the werewolves though.

"There you are," Mirabelle said, breaking the awkward silence as she closed up her medical bag. "The wound was already healing when I got here. I imagine it'll be completely healed in an hour or so."

"She was fine when I got up to make breakfast. I came back in a couple minutes later to check on her and she was bleeding everywhere," Justin said, his eyes still wide. "Blood was pouring from her neck and soaking the sheets, but she wouldn't wake up. I was only gone a few minutes, I swear."

"It's morning?" I asked, glancing around. Sunlight brightened the room, and I realized with a start that it was no longer night. It felt as though I had only slept for a few minutes.

"You were sleeping peacefully when I got up," Justin replied.

"Stay awake," Mirabelle admonished, looking at me sternly. "Shower, eat a good breakfast and rest, but don't sleep. Hugo and I will go speak with Jed, but I imagine he'll want someone to stay with you at all times from now on. Mark should have been here."

"Good thing Justin called us," Hugo added with a smile.

Mirabella pursed her lips, turned and left the room, anger evident on her face. Hugo followed slowly, clapping Justin on the shoulder as he walked by. Justin smiled weakly at the bigger man. His smile slipped the moment Hugo was out of sight, and he turned toward me with a worried frown on his face.

"Justin," I began, climbing out of bed. "I am okay."

"None of this is okay, Izzy," Justin replied, wringing his hands on his shirt. He looked down, taking in the blood covering his hands and shirt. He sighed loudly and looked back up at me. "This is all my fault."

"Justin, you can't blame yourself," I began, but Justin cut me off.

"Yes, I can blame myself, because it is my fault. You're mixed up with werewolves and vampires because of me, and my stupid ambition. If I hadn't left..."

"Justin, stop," I said, harsher than I had intended. I smiled and tried again, gentler. "Justin, the vampires were already here. They were just waiting for an opportunity. At least we know what's happening. What about all those clueless humans out there being given the vaccine? They don't even know that they're following vampire orders. They're being manipulated and controlled, and don't have a clue."

"Sometimes I think it'd be better to be ignorant," Justin replied, his words echoing my thoughts from earlier.

"I know," I said softly as I climbed off my bed and grabbed my brother in a firm hug. "So, you were making breakfast?"

Justin chuckled and shook his head. "We have those packets of oatmeal. I was warming up hot water."

I laughed and shook my head. "That works for me. Let's get cleaned up first," I said, holding up my blood-covered hands. I glanced back over my shoulder at my bed. Somehow, I doubted the blood would come out.

"Don't worry about the bed right now," Justin said, reading my thoughts. I nodded and followed him out of the room.

We cleaned the blood off our hands and changed clothes before returning to the kitchen. I had found another pair of sweats in my dresser and had pulled those on with a t-shirt and burgundy sweatshirt. Justin warmed up hot water and we ate packets of fruit flavored oatmeal. Breakfast at the main house was usually as much of an ordeal as dinner was, but I didn't want to be around a bunch of werewolves the night after a full moon. The simple breakfast with my brother was perfect, but over too soon.

We had barely cleaned our bowls when the front door opened. I sighed and turned toward the door, wondering who it was. Jared hurried into the house and straight toward me, a grin plastered on his face. He scooped me up in a hug, lifting me off the ground. I hugged him back tightly as he lowered me back down. He stood back, eyeing me closely.

"Damn it, Izzy. You need to quit scaring me," Jared said, his eyes running over the bandage on my neck. "First you sleep like the dead, then you get bit by the dead. What's next?" he asked. He obviously already knew about the dream bite, and he wasn't happy about it despite his playful banter.

"Henri's not dead," I retorted.

"Henri," Mark sneered as he walked in, slamming the front door behind him. "Walking corpses don't deserve names."

I swallowed hard and peeked around Jared to look at Mark. His eyes were wolf gold and he looked like he hadn't shaved in a week. He wore dark denim jeans and a black button-up shirt. He glanced at me briefly before stalking through the house to my bedroom. I shivered and looked up at Jared, who looked freshly showered and clean-shaven. He was dressed simply in jeans and a plain gray hoodie sweatshirt.

Mark came back in a moment later, clenching his jaw tightly in anger. He stopped at the edge of the hallway, his golden eyes riveted on the ground. "Jared, you'll stay with her?" Mark asked without raising his head.

Jared nodded and put an arm around my shoulder. "She won't leave my sight," he responded.

"Good," Mark said as he stalked toward the front door.

"Mark, wait," I said, pulling myself from Jared's arms. I rushed to the door, but didn't know what to say when I got there. Mark had stopped before the door, with his back still toward me. I reached out and touched his arm, urging him to turn toward me.

Mark turned partway and stared down at me with his wolf eyes. He opened his mouth to speak then closed it, shaking his head. "I can't be here right now," he said gruffly. He looked past me to Jared, nodded once, and walked out the door, slamming it behind him hard enough to make the windows shake.

Jared moved quietly behind me and slipped his arms around my shoulders, hugging me from behind. "Mark's just upset, Izzy. He didn't change with the rest of us last night, and it's taking its toll. I don't know how he could withstand changing on a full moon. It's difficult, to say the least. He's going to go run as a wolf for a while. Jed has something for him to do to take his mind off things. Don't worry," he added, mussing my hair.

I pulled away and sat down on the couch. I knew Jared was trying to make me feel better, but I wasn't in the mood to talk. Jared followed me to the couch and sat down close beside me. Justin shoved another log on the fire and sat down on the couch opposite us. I looked up at my brother, as he bounced his leg anxiously.

"You need to go work," I stated, looking at Justin pointedly.

He stopped shaking his leg and smiled at me. "No, it's fine. Why don't we play a game of cards or something?" he asked, standing up.

"Jared is here with me, Justin. I'm fine. Go work." I smiled at him and added, "Don't you need to go save the world or something?"

"Ha ha," he replied, shaking his head. He sighed loudly, wringing his hands on his shirt in nervousness. "Are you sure? I don't want to leave you."

"Yes, Justin, I'm sure. Your brotherly duties are finished for the day. Jared will keep me safe," I added.

"Don't let her sleep," Justin said pointedly before he hurried to put his shoes on. He grabbed his coat and pulled it on as he moved toward the door. His anxiety showed, but I wasn't sure if it was because of me or because he wanted to get back to work. He turned and looked back at me, with one hand on the doorknob. "I love you, sis. Try and stay out of trouble while I'm gone."

I grinned and nodded. "Love you too," I replied as Justin scurried out the door to his lab.

"So, what shall we do?" Jared asked. I looked up at him as he wiggled his eyebrows at me. "How about a game of strip poker?"

Chapter 13

Jared and I played card and board games most of the day. No games included the stripping of clothes, despite what Jared suggested. After I lost an epic game of Monopoly, I finally called it quits. We had spent the day sitting before the fire, alone. Justin had come in briefly around noon to check on me and grab lunch. He had come back in time for dinner, before returning to his lab once more.

By the time Jared and I had cleaned up after our spaghetti dinner, I was feeling exhausted. Neither of us had brought up any touchy subjects as we attempted to keep the conversations light. We laughed so much my sides hurt, but I still caught the worried looks Jared gave me when he thought I wasn't looking.

"I need to clean up my bed," I said as I dried my hands on a towel.

Jared looked at me sharply and darted a look down the hallway. "I think your bed is ruined, Izzy."

I sighed and leaned back against the refrigerator. "Probably," I agreed, tossing the towel onto the counter. "Still, I do have to sleep somewhere. You're not planning on trying to keep me awake all night, are you?"

Jared shrugged and looked away from me, toward the front

door. When he turned back he had a smile on his face, but I could tell it was forced. "Of course not," he muttered. "I'll be right back."

I watched Jared as he grabbed the cell phone off the counter and walked down the hallway to my bedroom. He was probably calling Jed or Mark to ask them what he should do. It was obvious Jared was my babysitter, but I didn't mind. Jared came back in a minute later, his face serious.

"What does the boss say?" I asked.

Jared smiled halfheartedly and shrugged. "Jed just told me to stick close to you and inform him immediately if I smell vampires or anything out of the ordinary. It was a short conversation," he muttered.

"Where's Mark?"

The smile slipped from Jared's face and he shook his head. "He's still in wolf form," he said slowly. "The newer wolf, Leon, is with him."

I remembered Leon, who had been a lone wolf until just recently when he petitioned Jed for acceptance into his pack. My heart sped up as I asked, "Is he coming back?"

"They went for a long run," Jared replied slowly. "Pack business. They'll be back in a couple days."

I nodded and walked past Jared, hurrying down the hallway. Pack business meant I wasn't going to get any information, and I may as well quit asking. "I'm going to take a shower. I think this should be healed by now," I added, pointing to the bandage on my neck.

I walked into my bedroom and tried to ignore the blood-soaked bed. My knife sat on top of my dresser, but I resisted the urge to grab it. I pulled open my drawers and rifled through them, trying to find something suitable to wear to bed. It was definitely time to wash some clothes since I seemed to be quickly running out. I grabbed one of the longer plain t-shirts Mirabelle had bought me and clean underwear.

Jared stood in my doorway, watching me warily. "Izzy," he

began, "what happened with Lucas?"

My heart stopped beating for a second, and when it resumed it was loud and fast. I had spent all day hoping to avoid the topic, and here Jared was bringing it up. "Jared, please, I don't want to talk about it."

"Lucas said you came to his room," Jared said quietly. I stared down at the ground, unable to make eye contact with Jared. "Did he... did he force himself on you?"

"No," I muttered simply. "Like you said, I came to his room."

"You wanted to go to his room?"

"No."

"Izzy?"

I sighed and looked up at Jared. He didn't look accusatory, just worried. "I woke up in his bed. At first, I didn't remember anything."

"At first?"

"Yes, at first. I remember most of it now. It was all me, Jared. You can't be mad at Lucas for something I did."

"But it wasn't really you, was it?" Jared urged. "Just like when you kissed me. It had to have been that damn vampire."

"Maybe I wanted to kiss you! Maybe subconsciously I wanted to have sex with Lucas. Besides, I thought you werewolves could smell vampires. Isn't that what you wolves do? Smell things! Did you smell Henri on me?" I asked

Jared shook his head, and I felt the small glimmer of hope I'd been holding on to die. No matter what I said, I had been secretly hoping my actions had been because of a vampire. Not necessarily Henri, but a vampire nonetheless. "No, we didn't smell vampire. We asked Lucas too. He said you smelled like lavender, blood and sex, but not vampire."

"So you can't blame Henri."

"We can blame whoever and whatever we damn well feel like blaming!" Jared retorted angrily. "I know this wasn't you, Isabella. You can't stand Lucas! Whether it was vampires or your knife, or some other sort of weird magic, it doesn't matter. You didn't do this! Don't you dare blame yourself!"

"I can blame whoever I want!" I retorted as I pushed past Jared and hurried toward the bathroom, slamming the door behind me.

As soon as I set down my pile of clothes, I leaned toward the mirror and peered at my reflection. My face was splotchy and red, with big dark circles under my eyes. I peeled the bandage off my neck with one swift move. Dried blood caked my neck, but a quick swipe of a wet towel revealed perfect skin beneath. Apparently, I was healing as quickly as Mirabelle had expected.

The hot shower was relaxing this time, and I savored every moment of peaceful solitude. When the bathroom was full of steam, I finally got out and dried off. I needed to sleep. I could feel Henri's presence, as though he was pressing gently at the back of my mind. He wanted to speak to me, and to do that I needed to sleep. Maybe Henri would have an idea about what had happened to me.

I toweled off and put the t-shirt and underwear on. The shirt barely covered my butt, but it would have to do since the only alternative was to prance around in lingerie. After what had happened the other day, I was definitely not going to do that. I wiped the steam off the mirror and stared at my reflection, not recognizing the woman looking back at me. Isabella Howerton the schoolteacher was gone forever, but I didn't know the woman who replaced her. I pulled open drawers, looking aimlessly for something I couldn't put my finger on. Then my hand touched the scissors, and I pulled them out. For so long, my beautiful blonde hair had been my pride and joy. I'd allowed Vanessa to dye my hair brown, but I'd drawn the line at cutting it.

Henri pushed at my mind again, and I shivered at the sensation. This was something I hadn't experienced before. I looked back at my reflection, grabbed a handful of hair, and cut. Halfway through, I realized this was probably a desperate cry for help. I laughed at myself, feeling like a stupid teenager rebelling against her parents. Who was I rebelling against? Was it Mark, the werewolves, my brother, or none of them? Perhaps I was just rebelling against the way my life was going. The sensation of pressure in my head returned, doubling me over against the sink. I lowered the scissors, looking at my half-cut hair. Vibrations rippled across my body. It felt as though I had stepped into a low current electrical fence. I waited for the strange sensations to leave before I hacked my way through the rest of my hair as quickly as possible.

When I was done, I felt lighter and more carefree. I had needed this. It was a way of controlling something, I knew. In school, I had taken plenty of psychology classes in preparation to become a teacher, and I recognized the signs right away. Startlingly, I didn't care. I giggled as I stared at my reflection, snipping off random stray pieces until my hair was a strange, choppy cut. Hair cutting had never been my forte, but this didn't look bad. I set down the scissors and ran a hand through my hair, which stopped well above my shoulders. As soon as I had cleaned up the hair, I opened the bathroom door.

Jared stood in the hallway, anxiously waiting for me. His eyes widened when he saw me, and his jaw dropped open in surprise. "What the fuck did you do to your hair?" he blurted out.

"Wow, Jared, thanks," I muttered in reply, a little hurt. Maybe it didn't look as good as I thought. Was it too late to get Vanessa to come fix it?

Jared closed his mouth, cocked his head to the side, and grinned. "Sorry, you just took me by surprise. I love it, by the way. Very sexy," he added. His eyes trailed down my body to my bare legs. "Very sexy, indeed." Jared was obviously back in good spirits, or at least putting on a good show.

"I'm going to bed," I stated bluntly, crossing my arms. "I'll grab some blankets and sleep on the couch."

Jared shook his head. "No, you won't. You'll sleep in my bed," Jared said as he steered me toward his bedroom. I debated on arguing, but I didn't really want to sleep on the couch.

The bedroom was similar to mine, but with no sliding glass door. I crawled into bed and slid to the far side, leaving room for Jared. He shut the door and flicked the light off before climbing in beside me. The bed bounced as he shifted, getting comfortable. He breathed in loudly, and sneezed.

"Bless you," I muttered, closing my eyes.

"I thought I smelled something," Jared whispered. He moved around and I heard him sniffing at my neck.

"Go to sleep."

Jared didn't reply, and I felt myself falling quickly to sleep. Henri was waiting for me, and I felt my dream-self racing towards him. Coldness greeted me, and I knew I was back in the dungeon with Henri. I opened my eyes and looked around. Once again, I was naked and covered in blood. I stood and walked toward Henri, examining the ancient device that chained him once again. The contraption was the same, but it had shifted so Henri was now suspended horizontally a foot above the floor, his arms and legs pulled taut, like a medieval stretching device. No part of his body touched the ground, and the manacles around his wrists and ankles dug into his skin, leaving angry red welts.

"Henri," I said softly as I moved toward his face.

He opened his eyes and turned his head toward me. Blue eyes greeted me, and he smiled feebly. "There you are," he rasped.

"I could feel you," I replied, touching my head, "in here."

This time he smiled wider, revealing sharp fangs. "Our bond has improved slightly," he responded.

"You're still weak." It was a statement, not a question, but he nodded in response anyway. "I don't know how long we have. Last time, I woke up bleeding all over my bed. I don't think a repeat would be a good idea. I have enough to deal with, without adding almost bleeding to death to the list."

"I am sorry about that, Isabella. You were pulled from me too quickly, or I could have prevented that from happening." He closed his eyes and laid his head back. He was silent for several minutes, breathing slowly. "We need to share blood."

"I figured you'd say that."

Henri chuckled and looked back at me. "Ah, it is good to speak to you. It is good to speak with anyone, actually."

"You're alone?"

"Except for my torturers, yes, and they're not much for conversation."

"Who are these torturers?" I asked, moving closer to Henri. I touched his chest, feeling the taught muscles as the device stretched him above the floor.

Henri stared at me intently, his eyes changing from blue to black in the blink of an eye. "The wolf is trying to wake you," he commented. "We must hurry."

"Jared," I said softly, frowning. "What do you need me to do? Can I get you out of this contraption?"

He shook his head. "No, it is a dream, and will do no good. If I was at full strength, this could not hold me in dream or waking. There is no time to lose. Bite me," he said.

I frowned, thinking of his sharp teeth. "Is this my dream or yours?" I asked, feeling along my teeth with my tongue. There was no way I could just bite him.

"The dream is shared," he replied, which didn't really answer my question.

"Can I change things?"

"Try," was all he said.

Maybe he didn't know either. I closed my eyes and concentrated, picturing a knife in my hands. I opened one eye and looked at my hand, but no knife appeared. I closed my eyes again, this time concentrating on my teeth, imagining them sharper, like Henri's were. Pain pulsed in my mouth, and I ran my tongue along my teeth. Yes, my canine teeth definitely felt sharper.

I wasn't sure how long it would last, so I moved quickly around Henri so I could reach his neck with my mouth. Could I do this? I brushed his blond hair aside and pressed my mouth to his neck, tasting the saltiness of his skin.

"Higher," he whispered, and I moved my mouth up. "Right there."

It's just a dream, I told myself. I took a deep breath and bit down hard, feeling my teeth tear into his skin. Blood seeped slowly into my mouth, and I found I had to bite down harder to coax more blood out. I tried not to breath or think about what I was doing as I swallowed the blood down. With each gulp, I felt my strength increase, and the repulsion of drinking blood diminish. Henri was sharing his power. I moved my wrist and pressed it to Henri's mouth. He grunted and bit down, drawing a startled gasp from me.

I stopped drinking and licked my lips, staring at the teeth marks on Henri's neck. Imprints of my human teeth marred his skin, along with two distinct holes where my fake fangs had penetrated his skin. I ran my tongue along my teeth, but the fangs had disappeared the moment I stopped concentrating on them.

"Izzy, wake up!" Jared shouted, and I jumped, looking around the bare room.

Henri stopped drinking and kissed my wrist. "Thank you, sweetness," Henri said, smiling up at me. "I feel better already, but not strong enough. Dream blood only lasts for a short time. I need you to come to me."

"Where are you?"

He grinned as his eyes returned to their startling blue. "We are connected strong enough now that you should be able to find me, if you hurry. Leave right away, before your wolf returns."

"My wolf?" I asked, frowning.

Henri ignored me as he continued. "When you are close, I will guide you to my location. I must conserve what little strength I have, but you need to come quickly."

I nodded, ready to wake when a thought popped into my head. "Strange things have been happening to me lately. The wolves think its vampire related."

"I have done nothing but seek you out," Henri responded immediately. "We don't have time for questions right now, Isabella. Help me."

"Why should I help you?" I didn't know why I asked it. The pull toward Henri was strong, as though I could close my eyes and point right toward him no matter where he was. Still, a small part of my brain was screaming at me to run away and never return.

Henri stared at me before replying, "Trust me; our paths are aligned at the moment."

I had trusted vampires before, and it hadn't ended well. Maybe the Lucas incident had nothing to do with him, but that didn't mean he was completely trustworthy. Would this be any different? Was Henri any different? Jed had warned me against trusting vampires, and last time he had proven himself right. "That's not really an answer, Henri. You are a vampire after all, and my experience with vampires isn't a good one."

"I am calling in your debt to me," Henri said sternly, and I felt his words echo in my mind.

"Yes, of course," I replied, nodding earnestly. "I'll come for you right away."

"Izzy!" Jared shouted again.

I woke up, sputtering. "What the heck?" Water covered my face and chest.

Jared sat over me with an empty glass in his hands. "You wouldn't wake up," Jared said, the panic clear in his voice. "I was just about to call Jed."

"No, don't do that!" I responded, climbing hastily out of bed. "I have to go."

"What? Go where? What are you talking about?"

"I have to go," I said again as I hurried out of the room.

Jared followed on my heels as I rushed to my bedroom and flicked on the light. I pulled open my dresser, flinging clothes out in my haste. "I'm changing," I stated, looking pointedly at Jared.

"You're not leaving my sight until I know what the hell you're going on about!"

Ignoring Jared, I pulled my shirt off and grabbed the black bra that matched my underwear. Next, I pulled on a low cut black top that conformed to my curves. I finished the outfit with tight black jeans and my knee-high black boots.

"Izzy, what the hell are you doing?" Jared asked as he followed me around the bedroom.

"I told you, I have to go."

"Where?"

I paused, looking at him for the first time. His eyes were frantic and yellow-ringed. I shrugged and pointed, knowing only that I could feel Henri in the direction my arm faced. He followed my arm and shook his head in confusion. I turned and grabbed a black jacket out of the closet, feeling very stealthy in my ensemble.

"Let me call Jed," Jared said slowly.

"No!" I yelled. "Jared, you can't tell Jed. You can't tell anyone. I have to do this alone."

"The hell you are!" Jared shouted back, startling me. I had never seen Jared so agitated before, and it caught me off guard. "Tell me what the fuck is going on right now, or I pick up this phone and you have a dozen werewolves tying you down. Don't think I won't do it, Izzy. I'm stronger and faster than you."

I stared at Jared in shock, my mouth hanging open. My jacket was dangling from one arm, and I slowly pulled it on the rest of the way while I contemplated what I was going to say next. I decided to just go with the truth, and damn the consequences. "I'm going to rescue Henri," I said with a shrug.

"The vampire?"

"Yes, Jared, the vampire," I responded, pushing past him.

Jared grabbed my arm, stopping me from leaving the bedroom. "That vampire has almost killed you twice, and you're going to rescue him?" I nodded as I tried to shake his hand off my arm unsuccessfully. "Who are you rescuing him from? *Why* does he even need rescuing? He's a vampire!"

"I don't know who has him. I'm not even precisely sure where he is, but I am going anyway. He saved my life, Jared, and I owe him a debt. Patricia had almost killed me, draining me of blood. I had lost consciousness, and that's when Henri came to me. He saved me, giving me the strength to kill Patricia. If not for him, I'd either be dead or under Patricia's control right now." I took a deep breath and stopped pulling against Jared's solid grip. "You'd be dead too," I added.

Jared ground his teeth together and let out a roar of frustration, releasing my arm. He paced back and forth, glaring at me angrily with his yellow wolf eyes. "Fine," he finally said, nodding his head. "Let me change."

"Change?" I asked, confused.

"You don't think I'm going to let you go alone, do you? As I see it, you have two choices. Either I come with you, or I tie you up and call the Pack. You can't sneak past me, Izzy," he added pointedly.

It was my turn to groan, but I knew he was right. The pack would never let me go after Henri. I nodded my assent and Jared hurried back to his bedroom. I stood before the dresser, staring down at my knife as I debated my next course of action. The knife called to me, but I wasn't sure if I should take it or not. What if the knife was making me crazy? If vampires hadn't been responsible for my night with Lucas, then perhaps the knife was.

Jared came back in, dressed in dark jeans and a baggie black hoodie. A backpack slung casually across one shoulder. He grinned, and I was happy to see his eyes were back to normal. He handed my guns to me, and I had to remove my jacket to strap them in place. After securing my guns, I put my jacket back on and left the room. I wandered into the living room and waited impatiently for Jared. Several minutes later he joined me.

"What took you so long?"

"Just wanted to make sure I packed extra supplies."

"Supplies?"

"Ammo," Jared replied bluntly as he walked toward the door.

It was sometime after midnight when we left, and I wondered if anyone was at the main house monitoring the surveillance videos. If they were, I doubted we'd get far. Jared climbed in the driver's seat of the jeep and backed out, leaving the headlights off. He drove toward a secondary access road, away from the main house. It would take us longer to reach the main road, but at least we wouldn't be driving right by the house.

I stared out the windows as we drove along the bumpy road. Most of the snow had melted, but the moon was still bright overhead. Today wasn't a true full moon, but I had listened to enough talk amongst the werewolves to know that the pull of the moon was strong leading up to the full moon. Usually, after changing for the full moon, the werewolves had more control and the urges diminished. New wolves, of course, were the exception to this.

I glanced worriedly at Jared, thinking that maybe it wasn't the smartest idea to run off with a new werewolf. He had good control, and seemed to listen to me, but I couldn't help but remember Mark's story about Beth's brother. I hoped Jared's control was better than that. If it wasn't, I'd be the one dealing with the consequences.

After about thirty minutes, we finally reached the main road. I had worried Jed would have werewolves blocking the road, but it appeared no one had seen us. Jared idled at the junction, looking at me. He was waiting for me to tell him to turn around, or that I'd changed my mind, but that wasn't going to happen. I lifted my arm and pointed down the road. Jared sighed loudly, flicked on the headlights, and pulled out onto the road.

Chapter 14

We drove to the freeway, using it as a guide to our destination. At first, I had just a vague idea of where Henri was. As time went on, and we drew closer, my connection to Henri grew stronger. After we left the freeway, and entered the city, driving became more difficult. We wandered down dead end roads and paths that took us in opposite directions. I could still pinpoint where Henri was, but the roads didn't necessarily line up with what I was feeling.

Jared turned us onto a long stretch of road that appeared to head in the direction we needed. It was still dark out, making it hard to recognize landmarks, but I had the strange sensation I had been on that particular road before. Bright lights were visible down the road, illuminating a large hotel. I gasped in surprise, recognizing the hotel immediately.

"That's the hotel Mark and I were held in," I whispered.

Jared cut his eyes toward me, and slowed his progress down the road. "Is that where this vampire is?"

I shrugged, my eyes glued on the hotel. "He's in that direction, and he's close."

"I don't like it, Izzy," he muttered as he drove past the hotel entrance. "That's too much of a coincidence."

I felt the pull from Henri, and I opened my mind toward him. "Henri?" I asked, whispering it aloud while I thought it in my mind.

"You're close," Henri's voice answered in my mind.

"I've been here before," I replied.

There was silence, and I wasn't sure if Henri had heard me or was purposely not answering. Finally, he spoke again. "There is a road that runs behind the hotel, but does not connect to it. There are houses on that road. Find the house numbered 210."

"Go that way," I pointed for Jared, turning him down a side road. When we reached the next road, I led Jared again. "We're looking for house 210," I said.

"What if this is a trap?" Jared asked as he turned onto the quiet residential street.

"Henri, is it safe?" I asked.

"Yes," he responded. "When you find the house, park and go to the back door. There is a key under a rock on the porch. Let yourself in and go to the basement."

"Henri says it's safe," I replied.

Jared snorted, but continued driving slowly. "You know, if he set the trap of course he'd say it was safe."

"Henri didn't set a trap," I muttered, pointing at the correct house number. "Here it is. We enter in through the back door."

We stopped in front of the house, staring at number 210. The street was empty, most likely due to the early hour. No animals barked and there were no lights on in any of the houses. It didn't look like anyone had been to the house in months, and it was in serious disrepair. The blue paint was chipped and several roofing shingles had broken off and were lying in the dead grass. There was a small sign in the window indicating the house was for rent, along with an unreadable phone number.

Jared opened his door and sped around to my door, holding it closed while he breathed in any scents on the air. When he deemed it safe, he quietly opened my door and let me out. He continued to sniff the air as we walked around the side of the house. "I don't smell anything," he said softly.

I nodded and continued toward the back of the house, my hand resting on the butt of the gun on my hip. We reached the corner of the house, and Jared held his hand up for me to wait. He pulled his gun out and peered around the corner, smelling the air as he did. He moved quietly, disappearing into the darkness. I hurried up to the corner and looked around for Jared, straining my senses. The hotel was too close for comfort, with only the large back portion of the parking lot separating the houses on this street from the hotel itself. I wasn't surprised at the state of the house. I doubted many people wanted to live in such close proximity to the fancy hotel, with its bright lights and constant traffic.

Jared returned a moment later and motioned for me to follow him. The back door of the house was old, but sturdy. I looked around the ground for the rock Henri had mentioned. Finally, I spotted it and picked it up, finding the key hidden in a crevice on the bottom. I pulled the key out and moved to the door, but Jared hurried in front of me, holding out his hand insistently. Choose your battles, I thought to myself, as I handed him the key. He inserted it carefully, as though waiting for it to blow up, and turned the handle.

The door creaked open and I followed on Jared's heels as we entered the house. He held up a hand, motioning me to wait again while he moved through the house silently, gun in hand. I waited for him to return, straining to hear his footsteps. Silence was all I heard, but Jared quickly returned and pulled me into the house behind him.

"I can smell vampire, but it's very faint. I don't think anyone has been in this house in quite some time," Jared said softly in my ear. "What are we doing here?"

"I'm not really sure. Henri just said we need to go to the basement," I whispered back.

Jared nodded and took my hand, leading me through the dark house. I followed closely, unable to see anything beyond Jared's form.

He pulled me through the house and opened a door. I leaned over him, struggling to see beyond him. Jared fumbled around, and finally flicked on a light, illuminating a set of stairs going down.

Jared took the lead once more as I stumbled behind him. He walked slowly, sniffing the stagnant air with each step. The basement was a standard affair of concrete floor and walls, with no windows. We wandered around the basement, but there was nothing and no one there. Jared shrugged, looking back at me.

"Henri?" I whispered in my mind, pushing my thoughts out to the vampire. "There's nothing in the basement."

Henri responded immediately, his mental voice sounding anxious. "Open the door beneath the stairs," he said.

I turned around and noticed the door. It looked like there was a small closet beneath the stairs. My hand was on the handle, ready to turn, when Jared suddenly raced up beside me. He elbowed me out of the way and flung the door open, holding his gun up. The closet was small and contained one shelf full of water bottles, flashlights, blankets and canned food. A rich-looking crimson rug on the floor was the only other thing in the small space. Jared shot me a look and pushed the rug aside with his foot, revealing a wooden trap door beneath it. He squatted down on the ground and heaved the door open with one hand, the gun still gripped in his other.

I grabbed a flashlight off the shelf and flicked the light on, shining it down into the hole. There was no ladder visible, but the ground beneath didn't look far. Jared leaned his head into the hole, smelling and looking. He sat back up and looked at me, his face grim.

"I don't like it," he said softly.

"Do you smell anything?"

He sighed and shook his head. "It's like the house. There's a faint vampire scent, but I don't think anyone has been here in quite some time. Of course, I'm new at this whole scent tracking thing." He shrugged and half-smiled.

I nodded, debating the wisdom of what we were doing. I only

had Henri's instructions to go by, but he wasn't very forthcoming with details. "Henri, we found the trap door."

"Good, wait for daylight and then enter. Follow the tunnel until you reach the third passageway to the right. Take this and continue to go down. There will be many paths here, and you will have to use our connection to find me. Be careful here. I'm not sure who will be awake still. There are also human guards. I suggest stealth," he added.

I sat down and looked at Jared. "You can shut that for now," I said, nodding my head toward the trap door. "We wait for daytime."

"Then what?" Jared asked as he closed the door and sat down on the floor across from me.

"We take the third tunnel on the right and I have to use my connection to Henri to find him. He says there are humans and vampires down there, and who knows what else."

"Great," Jared responded as he removed his backpack and sat back.

"Anything else in the bag?" I asked curiously.

"Just vampire killing supplies."

I rolled my eyes and smiled in spite of myself. Of course Jared would just pack ammo. Although, I'd been secretly hoping he'd packed coffee and chocolate.

"We probably have an hour or two until sunup. Might as well get some sleep." Jared muttered as he leaned his head back against the doorframe and closed his eyes.

"Sleep? How can you possibly sleep?" I asked. I felt anxious, afraid to close my eyes in case a vampire suddenly popped out of the hole. Jared seemed surprisingly at ease, but it could purely be a show for my benefit.

Jared grinned, his eyes still closed. "In the military you learn to sleep and eat when you can," he replied. "Don't worry; I'll wake if anything weird comes our way."

"Thanks, that's very reassuring," I muttered dryly.

Jared grinned wider. "Grab a blanket and nap. We may need our energy," he added, the smile slipping.

I stood and grabbed one of the blankets off the shelf, wrapping it around my shoulders as I sat back down. Despite Jared's reassurance, I was scared. I curled my legs up and leaned against the doorframe opposite Jared. Doubt crept into my mind as I closed my eyes. I was immensely thankful Jared had come with me. Now that I was here, I couldn't imagine trying to rescue Henri on my own. What had I been thinking?

I closed my eyes and eventually drifted off into a fitful sleep. Henri beckoned to me, pulling me to him in my sleep. I tried to fight against him, afraid to fall into too deep a sleep. I knew Jared would probably wake if anything happened, but I wasn't sure if I'd wake up. Henri pulled at my mind, tugging me closer until I opened my eyes to the same dream once more.

"Henri," I muttered irritably.

"Not happy to see me?" he asked.

I stood up, taking note of myself. For once, I wasn't naked. Instead, I wore the outfit I was currently wearing. I reached a hand up, feeling my short hair as well. Henri was strung up as he had been last time, suspended a couple feet from the floor. I walked toward him, my arms crossed over my chest.

"I just closed my eyes to take a nap while we wait for sunrise," I said, stopping beside him and staring down at his startling blue eyes.

"We?" he asked, frowning. "You brought a wolf with you."

"Jared wouldn't let me leave without him. It was either I bring him, or he'd tie me up. Not much I can do against a werewolf," I added, shrugging.

"A silver blade would work well."

I glared at Henri angrily, grinding my teeth together. "I won't hurt any of the werewolves, especially Jared. He's here to help," I added pointedly.

"He's here to help you, not me, my sweet," Henri responded. He smiled up at me suddenly, his blue eyes twinkling. "I welcome the assistance though, of course."

"Sure," I responded, not really believing him. "So, is there a plan?"

"All will be well as soon as you find me," he said, suddenly flinching in pain.

I jerked back, watching in horror as the strange mechanism cranked over and the chains moved of their own accord. Henri groaned as his body stretched, pulled taught as the chains stretched his body in two different directions. Blood streamed from his wrists and ankles as the manacles cut into his skin.

"Henri?" I asked worriedly. "What's happening?"

"She doesn't like me retreating here while she tortures me," Henri replied through gritted teeth.

At first, I didn't understand what he was talking about, but then the room flickered around me, as though I was only partway in the dream. I saw flashes of the room Jared and I were in, then I was suddenly back in the dream with Henri. He screamed in pain as blood blossomed across his chest, and the dream flickered again.

"Henri, what can I do?" I asked as I rushed back to Henri's side.

His eyes were wild with pain as he cried out. Blood poured from his neck as a deep gash suddenly appeared. I tried to control the dream, imagining everything from bandages to towels, but nothing happened. I pressed my hand against the wound, trying to stop the flow. The room flickered again and I woke with a start.

Jared jerked up, the gun in his hand as he looked for the source that had awakened him. He looked at the trap door, still closed, then back at me. "What's wrong?" he asked in a whisper. He was still on alert, ready to react at a moment's notice.

I shook my head and curled the blanket back around me. "Henri is being tortured," I whispered, not trusting my voice.

"Tortured? How do you know?"

"A dream," I responded. Jared frowned at me in confusion, not understanding. "Henri can speak to me in dreams. I think I saw where he was, and what was happening to him. He said someone was torturing him. I couldn't see the person, but I could see what was happening to his body. I think it was too much for him, and I lost the connection."

"Lost the connection?" Jared asked, the frown deepening.

I closed my eyes, trying to feel Henri. He was still there, but he was blocking me somehow. All I got was a general sense of where he was. I opened my eyes and looked back at Jared. "I don't really understand it myself. It wasn't like this with Patricia."

"Damn vampires," Jared muttered as he put his gun back. "We still have a while yet till sunrise, and I don't particularly want to interrupt some vampire's torture session. Better to go when the vamps are out for the day."

I nodded in agreement and leaned back, trying to fall back asleep. Jared's breathing slowed and I imagined he was asleep again. I settled back, but sleep never truly came. I flitted in and out of a light doze. Henri didn't pull me back into a dream, but I got impressions from him occasionally. He was in pain, and he was growing weaker. I wasn't sure what would happen if I didn't rescue him soon. Finally, Henri's torture ended and he spoke to me again.

"Sunrise. Come," he said.

Chapter 15

"Jared," I said, kicking Jared's leg gently.

He opened his eyes and stared at me, his hand automatically seeking his gun. "Time to go?" he asked quietly, his eyes darting to the trap door.

I nodded and stood up, putting the blanket back on the shelf. I shoved a flashlight into the top of my boot and grabbed a second one to carry. Jared didn't take a flashlight, but he was a werewolf and could probably see far better than I could. He moved to the trap door and pulled it open, leaning over it to look around. Effortlessly, he lowered himself into the hole and held up a hand for me to wait.

Jared hurried down the tunnel and I had counted only to twenty when he returned and rushed off down the opposite direction. He came back thirty seconds later and stopped below me. He put his gun up and stood below the hole with his arms wide, ready to catch me. I lowered my body into the hole and Jared grabbed my legs, pulling me gently to the ground. I flicked on my flashlight and shined it around the tunnel.

The tunnel was dirt and wood, and went in both directions. There was nothing to distinguish the tunnel directions. I looked up at the ceiling, but it was seamless wooden planks. I imagined the trap door would be virtually invisible when closed. I pointed with my light down the tunnel that headed toward the hotel, and Henri. Jared took my flashlight and flicked the light off, immersing us in darkness. A faint amount of light came from the opening above our heads.

"Let me be your eyes," Jared whispered in my ear. His hand gripped mine and he tugged me gently behind him.

I didn't like fumbling down the small, dark tunnel, but it was probably the best course of action. We didn't need to alert anyone ahead of time that we were there. I gripped the back of Jared's shirt as he moved silently ahead of me. The floor was dirt and thankfully muffled my steps as I stumbled behind Jared. Of course, vampires and werewolves could probably hear my footsteps anyway, no matter how quiet I tried to be.

Jared stopped suddenly, and I held my breath, waiting. We stood there for a moment in the darkness, before he cautiously took a step forward, leading me behind him once more. I couldn't see anything as Jared led us further down the tunnel, and away from the small amount of light that had filtered from the trap door. After several minutes, Jared stopped us again, before quickly pulling me behind him. He moved faster, and I struggled to keep up in the darkness.

Jared stopped for the third time and pressed me against the wall. He moved his body close to mine until I felt the roughness of his facial hair against my cheek. We stood like that for several beats, with my heart pounding loudly in my chest. "Stay here," he whispered lightly in my ear.

He moved away suddenly, and I held my breath, counting silently in my head as I pressed my body against the tunnel. After five minutes, I began to worry. Another five minutes passed of silence before I felt a body press against mine. My heart sped up in panic since I was unable to see a thing. The person pressed his body against mine, and I recognized Jared's light woodsy scent as he moved his face against mine.

"We're at the third tunnel, but it branches off quite a bit. I found one that seems to lead downward, but the place reeks of vampires. Stay close and keep quiet," Jared breathed as he took my hand and pulled me behind him.

We moved slowly down the tunnel, and after about five minutes, I noticed I could see a faint light ahead. Jared slowed down further, stepping lightly. We stopped at a junction of tunnels, and Jared pointed toward one that sloped downward. I nodded my head, feeling Henri in the direction of that tunnel. We moved to the tunnel, walking much slower as the floor changed from dirt to wood, and finally to stone. I shivered in my jacket as we walked slowly downward. Fluorescent lights hung from the low ceiling, spaced out so the light faintly illuminated the entire tunnel.

The tunnel branched off several times, and I pointed the way silently for Jared. With each step, my connection to Henri grew stronger. At first, I could just sense his direction, but as I drew closer, I began sensing his feelings, as well as his thoughts. He was injured worse than I had initially thought, and whatever torture he had endured had greatly weakened him. Foremost, he hungered for blood.

I shook off his emotions as Jared pulled me to a stop. The tunnel separated again, and I pointed down the tunnel ahead of us. Jared suddenly backed me up several steps and pressed me against the wall. He held up his hand, pointed to his ear, and then to the tunnel on our right. He pursed his lips, listening intently, before holding up two fingers.

I swallowed hard, figuring he meant there were two people down that tunnel. The juncture was well lit, and we would be visible to anyone looking in our direction. Jared stood still, breathing silently. My heart pounded loudly in my chest, and I hoped whoever was down the tunnel couldn't hear it. After an excruciating wait, Jared finally grabbed my hand and pulled me across the juncture.

Jared sped up, pulling me faster behind him. The heels of my boots clicked loudly on the stones, but Jared didn't seem to care as he hurried me along behind him. We reached another juncture and Jared paused once more, cocking his head to the side as he listened for anything down the side tunnels.

We continued at this pace for several minutes, with me pointing the way at each juncture. I had no idea how long we had traveled, when the tunnel we were in suddenly opened to reveal a large room. Jared stopped me at the edge of the dimly lit room while he ventured forward. He peered around the room and quickly came back for me, pulling me close so he could whisper in my ear.

"There's a door on the far side of this room, and I can hear and smell people on the other side. I think we're in some sort of dungeon. Is the vampire close?" he asked, and I nodded my head. "There are people talking, but I don't know if they're human or vampire. If we shoot our guns, the sound will echo and we could have more people on us than we can handle. I'm going to rush in fast. I'll try and take care of whoever is down there, while you find that vampire."

"Okay," I whispered in response, my heart pounding in my chest.

I followed Jared through the room to the far side. The room we were in was empty, but cages lined the wall. The walls and floor were concrete here, and there was a large drain hole in the middle of the room. Even in the dim fluorescent lights, dried blood was still visible on the floors and wall.

Jared stopped at the door and paused, taking a deep breath before he slowly pulled the door open. No one immediately rushed out to greet us, so we swiftly rushed through the door, letting it close quietly behind us. Jared walked calmly down the hallway, with me on his heels. I could see two men at the end of the hall, dressed in black suits with guns visible. The men turned when we came closer, both reaching automatically for their guns.

Jared didn't waste any time as he raced down the hallway at speeds I had never witnessed before. The werewolf was a blur of movement. The two men were on the ground in seconds, never managing to pull their guns out. At any other time, I'd be ogling at Jared's amazing abilities, but I felt Henri close by, calling to me. I hurried down the hall, but Jared rushed out of view ahead of me. I heard a commotion, but I had to trust that Jared could handle whatever it was.

The hallway led into another large room with cells lining the walls. Some of the cells were full, with men and women inside, while others were empty except for blood. The center of this room also had a large drain, with a water hose coiled on the floor nearby. I peeked in the cells as I hurried through the room, but I knew Henri wasn't in them. The room from my dreams looked different, and I could feel him further away.

The vast room branched in three more directions, and I could hear a commotion coming from the right. Based on the noise and the bodies in the hallway, I guessed Jared was that direction. Henri, on the other hand, was down the center hallway. I debated briefly on waiting for Jared to clear a safe path, but the pull of Henri urged me forward. He was hurting and needed me quickly.

I moved as quietly as was humanly possible down the tunnel, my hand on my gun. I heard a noise ahead, as of someone walking across the stone floor. Pausing briefly, I pulled the Glock out of its holster. Despite Jared's warning, I wasn't going down the tunnel unarmed. Jared was a werewolf, after all, and I was just human. I continued walking, being careful to step as lightly as possible. I was almost at the end of the tunnel when a man stepped into view, a gun raised in my direction. I stopped, staring down the barrel with my heart pounding in my chest.

"Drop the gun," the man said, pointing at my hand with his gun.

My heartbeat sped up a notch as I stared down the barrel of a gun. I slowly lowered the gun to the ground, carefully keeping my jacket closed so the man wouldn't see the other gun. I stood back up and held my hands out to my side, trying to look as unassuming as possible. My hands shook as I took slow steps toward the man with the gun. The man looked comfortable with the gun, but uncomfortable in the suit he wore. The dark suit hung on him awkwardly and I guessed it was more a uniform than anything he would have chosen himself. His facial hair looked two days old, and his black hair was unkempt and greasy.

"Please, don't shoot," I said in a sweet voice. The man didn't bat an eye as he kept the gun trained on my chest. "Please," I said again, as I walked toward him, batting my eyelashes and swaying my hips provocatively.

The man's eyes roamed quickly down my body before returning to my face. "What are you doing down here?" he asked, the gun never wavering.

I reached the end of the tunnel and surveyed the room behind the gunman. The room was small, equipped with a small table and two chairs. A single door stood opposite the hallway, and I could feel Henri behind it. He was close. I looked back at the man and forced a smile as I slowly lowered my arms to my sides.

"Guess I got lost," I said with a shrug.

"Are you alone?"

"Do you see anyone else?" I responded.

"Tell him you're here to play," Henri's voice sounded in my head. "Tell him Sarah sent you."

I swallowed hard at hearing Sarah's name, wondering if it was the same sadistic Sarah I knew and loathed. I forced myself to smile at the man again. "Sarah sent me to play. Am I in the right place?"

"With a gun?"

"I just do what I'm told," I responded, and I could see a flicker in the man's eyes that said he clearly understood. "You know how it is."

The man narrowed his beady eyes at me before holstering his gun. "You won't mind if I search you first?"

"Let him search you," Henri said again in my head. "His name is Barry, but he likes to be called Dmitri. He's a vampire wannabe. Play with him."

"I have another gun on me," I said as Dmitri closed in. He stopped, staring at me as I spread my arms wide. "I figured you'd want to know first. Not that I know how to use it," I added with a small shrug.

He nodded and smiled weakly back at me as he took the Browning from its holster and shoved it in the back of his pants. Then he grabbed me, backing me into the wall as he ran his hands across my breasts and under my arms. His hands groped down my body and moved to the inside of my thighs. I swallowed down the anger as I tried to play along, keeping the smile plastered on my face as he fondled me. He finally moved on, his hands running down my legs.

After he reached my boots, he turned me around roughly so I faced the wall. He began his search over, starting from the bottom and slowly coming back up. He traced his hands around my butt, grabbing me as he moved in close. "So, you're one of Sarah's playthings?" he whispered, his face so close to mine I could smell coffee on his breath.

"Say yes," Henri commanded in my mind. "He's suspicious. Play along or he will kill you."

"Oh yeah, I am," I said seductively, looking over my shoulder at him. "You must be Dmitri."

He grinned when I said his name and nodded eagerly. He pressed his body against mine, and I could feel his hardness pressing against my back. "What are you going to do to the prisoner?" he asked. He continued his search of my body as his hands slowly moved up underneath my shirt. His fingers lifted my bra up until he was cupping my bare breasts with both hands.

"Hmm, I haven't decided yet," I whispered seductively. "Want to give me some ideas?"

The man who called himself Dmitri began kissing my neck as he moved his body against mine. My heart thudded in my chest with fear. Jared hadn't returned, but I couldn't worry about him yet. I had to get past this creep first. I turned around so I was facing Dmitri. He angrily tried to turn me back to face the wall, but I shoved him with both hands. He stumbled backward, his eyes glinting with anger as he reached for his gun. I quickly pulled off my jacket and began raising my shirt. Dmitri stood still, watching me as I pulled my shirt off and sauntered toward him. His hand moved away from his gun as he watched me.

"I have an idea," I rasped as I twirled my shirt in my hands. "Do you want to play?" Dmitri nodded his head eagerly, and I pointed toward the small table.

Dmitri hurried to the table and undid his belt, slipping the gun holster off and tossing it away. I paused, watching the gun slide across the floor away from the man. "He has a knife in the top of his right boot," Henri whispered.

I hurried across the room, pushing Dmitri down on the small table. He grinned and sat up, reaching toward me with eager hands. I swung my shirt and flicked it across his chest playfully. "My game," I said quickly.

I pushed him back on the table and spread his legs wide so I could step between them. He grinned up at me as I flicked the shirt playfully at him. How in the hell was I going to get out of this? Dmitri had already undone the top button on his pants in his haste, and was waiting for me to make the next move.

"Shirt off," I commanded as I ran my hands down his legs.

Dmitri complied, sitting up slightly so he could pull his shirt off over his head. I trailed my hands down his legs until I reached his boots. Sure enough, in the top of his right boot sat a knife. There was no time to waste. I grasped the knife and stood up. Dmitri pulled the shirt off his head and tossed it across the room before reaching down to unzip his pants. With my left hand, I traced my hand across Dmitri's chest. His chest was pale and covered in thick, black hair, which I twirled around my fingers. I leaned in across Dmitri's body, keeping my right hand and the knife behind my back. He grinned up at me and reached his hands toward me, grasping my breasts hard. I cried out in pain, but this only urged him on as he sat up and tucked one hand into the top of my jeans. He pulled me closer and moved his mouth toward my neck once more.

I didn't waste any more time as I angled the knife in my hands. Dmitri was distracted trying to put a hand down my jeans. I pulled myself closer, which only excited Dmitri further. I took a deep breath, pulled my arm back, and plunged the knife upward into his chest, pushing with all my strength. The knife slipped in beneath his breastbone with a sickening sound. Blood blossomed from the wound as I pulled it out and struck him a second time. Dmitri shuddered, clutching his chest as he stared at me in shock. I pulled the knife out and stepped back, watching as Dmitri fell to the ground. I studied him as he crawled across the floor slowly, obviously seeking out his gun. I walked past him and kicked his gun across the room before turning back toward him. He rolled onto his side and looked up at me, his hand reaching toward me as though imploring me to save him.

Guilt washed over me briefly. This man was human, not vampire. He would have killed me though, I reminded myself. I could feel Henri pushing at me, urging me to hurry. I stepped toward Dmitri and knelt down over him. He looked up at me with a mixture of horror and surprise on his face as I plunged the knife down a third and final time. I kept eye contact and watched his eyes until the light left and he drew his last breath.

"That's my girl," Henri whispered in my mind, clearly pleased.

I smiled as I wiped the knife off automatically before putting it into the top of my own boots. I retrieved my shirt first and pulled it back on. Then I scoured the ground until I found both my guns, putting them back into place, with my jacket settled on top. A set of keys hung from a peg beside the locked door. I snagged the key ring and rifled through several keys before finally unlocking the large, metal door.

The door opened silently into a concrete room that sloped

down in the middle, where blood pooled around a drain hole that obviously wasn't draining properly. Henri was chained as I had remembered in my dreams, hanging on the far end of the room from the strange medieval contraption. I walked toward him, avoiding the large amount of blood in the center of the room. Henri looked different than he had in my dreams. Dried blood crisscrossed his thin, pale body. He turned his face toward me, and I gasped in surprise at the dark circles under his eyes and his overall gaunt appearance.

"How do I get you down?" I asked as I walked around the chains, looking for a lever or switch of some kind.

Henri's voice was weak and raspy as he responded, "There's a release lever on the floor."

I looked around, finally finding a handle at the bottom of the chain pulley. I grabbed it, pulled, and the chains on one side released, dropping Henri's left side to the ground with a loud thud. He groaned and I quickly found the second lever, releasing it the same way. As soon as Henri was on the ground, I hurried toward him with the keys in hand. One key stood out on the ring and looked as medieval as the device attached to Henri. I inserted the key and quickly unlocked the manacles from Henri's wrists and ankles.

I knelt beside him and caressed his face until he opened his eyes and looked up at me. His blue eyes flashed to black before my eyes and he opened his mouth wide, revealing sharp fangs. It was obvious what he wanted. This wasn't a dream though. If I shared my blood with him now, it would surely solidify the connection between us.

"Isabella, please," he muttered, imploring.

What had I expected to happen saving a vampire? I moved my wrist to his mouth, but he shook his head and gently tugged me toward him until I was lying across his chest. He ran a finger across my neck and I moved closer, until his mouth pressed against my neck. I felt immediate pain as he bit into my neck. This was definitely not a dream anymore. I cringed at the pain, my body pulling away from him automatically.

Henri held me tight, sucking blood from my neck effortlessly. I tried to squirm away, but Henri's vampire strength held me easily. Panic had my heart pumping faster, which probably just sped Henri's drinking. After a couple minutes, the pain subsided and I drifted from calm to euphoric. I smiled and relaxed into Henri as he drank.

"There we are," Henri said in my mind.

Henri loosened his grip around me, but continued to drink. I closed my eyes, feeling as though I was floating on a cloud. There were no worries. There was no pain. Henri held me, caressing my arms gently. I sighed in pleasure, feeling warmth spread through my body. His dream bites had been good, but this bite had me reeling. This was better than chocolate. I was on cloud nine and I didn't ever want to come down.

"What the hell?" Jared said, startling me and causing me to jerk reflexively.

I opened my eyes and looked blearily across the room. Jared stalked toward me, but I had no time to react as Henri suddenly pulled away from me, flipped me over, and settled me on the cold concrete floor. The world spun around me as I attempted to roll onto my side. Henri stood in one fluid movement and turned toward the werewolf. Jared held his gun in front of him, pointed at Henri's chest. I stared up at them, struggling to make my body rise.

"No," I squeaked, and Jared's eyes flickered to mine briefly before returning to the vampire.

Jared wrinkled his nose. "I know your scent. You're Henri," he stated.

"I am," Henri replied, his voice strong and deep. "Put your gun away, wolf."

"Not gonna happen."

"Put your gun away, or die."

"Jared, Henri, stop," I squeaked as I rolled over and struggled to my knees. My arms wouldn't respond properly, and I toppled back to the floor.

"I need to give her blood," Henri stated.

"No," Jared replied bluntly.

"Isabella needs my blood. Unless you want her to die," Henri added, and Jared glanced back at me.

I stared up at them, taking in their words but not truly understanding them. The room suddenly seemed so dark and cold. I shivered and tried to wipe away the wetness I felt on my neck. I needed to sleep. Yes, sleep would help me. I closed my eyes and curled into a ball, surrendering to the darkness.

Suddenly, arms were around me, sitting me up. I opened my eyes and stared at Henri's beautiful face. His skin was pale perfection as he smiled at me, pressing his wrist against my mouth. Something tickled my lips, and I licked them, tasting salty blood. I tried to spit it out, but Henri pressed his wrist to my mouth tighter, forcing me to drink. I swallowed, and immediately felt more alert. His blood flowed into my mouth, rejuvenating me. I grabbed his wrist, coaxing blood from it with my tongue as I drank eagerly. This was what my body needed, and it quickly became what I wanted as I swallowed the blood down.

Henri pulled his wrist away from my mouth, and I sat up fully, looking around as I licked the lingering traces of blood from my mouth. Henri cradled me in his bare arms, smiling at me. The circles were gone from under his eyes, and his face looked fuller and healthier. I sat back, examining him. His body already looked healthier, instead of gaunt. The muscles across his body rippled as he moved, but he still didn't quite look himself. There was slimness to him that I'd never seen before, as though he'd lost a great deal of weight.

"Izzy," Jared said softly, and I looked around the room until my eyes landed on Jared. He stood with his gun still in hand, aimed at Henri's back.

"Jared, you can put the gun away. Henri won't hurt you," I

added, darting a meaningful look at Henri.

"Of course I will not harm the wolf, if that is your wish," Henri replied, placing a hand on his bare chest.

"I wasn't worried about him harming *me,*" Jared replied testily, still not lowering his gun.

Henri turned toward Jared, a smile on his handsome face. "Isabella will not come to harm by my hand."

"You bit her. That's harm in my book," Jared responded.

"She offered herself to me. She could have refused, and I would have found blood elsewhere. What we have is a mutual sharing, wolf. I could offer the same to you," Henri added, smiling wider and flashing his clean white fangs at Jared.

I rolled my eyes and stood up, moving between the two men before Jared shot Henri. Jared immediately lowered his gun and glowered at me. "Jared, let's get out of here," I said simply.

"Fine," Jared replied testily. "We rescued the damn vampire, so now we can go."

Henri moved behind me, and I could feel his presence like a warm embrace. "I am not quite at full strength, and it is daytime. Speed would be wise," Henri rumbled, his mouth beside my ear.

I looked over my shoulder at Henri and he closed the distance, pressing his naked body against my back. My heart sped up at his closeness, all thoughts leaving my mind. Jared growled across the room, but I ignored him as Henri moved his lips across my cheek, seeking my mouth. I turned my face toward his until our lips met. He kissed me softly as one of his hands wrapped around my waist, pulling me against his hardness. I moaned in pleasure and turned my body around to face him.

"Let's go!" Jared growled, yanking on my arm.

I broke away from Henri's kiss, smiling giddily. "Jared, stop it."

"What the hell, Izzy? This is not the time or place to make out with a vampire. Actually there is never a time or place to make out with a vampire."

I rolled my eyes and pulled my arm out of Jared's grip. "Oh, you want to join in?" I laughed.

"What are you doing to her?" Jared growled at Henri as he moved in closer.

Henri shrugged and responded calmly, "It is just a side effect of the blood. The Rapture will diminish soon."

"Rapture?" I asked, frowning at the emphasis Henri had put on the word. What did that mean? I turned back toward Jared and gasped in surprise. His eyes glowed bright yellow and sweat dotted his brow. My heart sped up in worry, and I reached out to take Jared's hand. "Jared, focus on me."

"I'm fine," he responded, biting off each word.

"We should go, Isabella," Henri said, taking my free hand and pulling me from the room.

I stumbled behind him, casting worried glances over my shoulder at Jared taking up the rear. Sometimes I forgot that Jared was a very new werewolf, and that could be a very dangerous thing to forget. Of course, there were bigger worries on my mind, like vampires. I shook my head, trying to clear it as I followed the naked vampire out of the dungeon.

Chapter 16

Henri led us back the way we had come in, moving swiftly past Dmitri's corpse on the ground. I stared at his naked back, marveling at how strong his body looked already. Jared wasn't incredibly tall, probably somewhere around 5'10, but Henri towered a good foot above him. Mark wasn't even that tall, I mused, and immediately banished the thought as I stumbled. Henri stopped, waiting for me to regain my balance. I glanced behind me to see what had caused me to stumble, and realized it was Dmitri's outstretched foot. Even in death, the man was still fighting against me. I shuddered and looked away, my eyes making contact with Jared's briefly. His eyes asked a thousand questions I didn't want to answer.

I turned back toward Henri and took his offered hand, smiling at the confidence he had despite his nakedness. Somehow, I doubted anything could faze the man. Jared stayed close behind me with his gun gripped tightly in his hand as we hurried down the hallway. I wasn't sure what would happen after we made it back to the surface. I had fulfilled my agreement to Henri, but now that I was with him, I didn't want to leave his side. That didn't seem right though. The thought flitted across my mind quickly. I had only planned to rescue Henri and return to the safety of the werewolves.

We stopped at the end of one of the long hallways, and Henri suddenly veered to the right. "That's not the way," Jared seethed in my ear. I nodded, knowing he was right.

Henri had taken several steps before stopping and looking back at us. He sighed loudly, seeing us still standing in the main hallway. "We need to go this way first," Henri said patiently.

"Why?" Jared asked.

"There are things I need to take care of," Henri replied with a shrug of his broad shoulders.

"Well, then, you go take care of them. I'm sure you know the way out. Izzy and I will be going now," Jared stated, grabbing my arm and pulling me down the hallway.

Henri grasped my other arm, and I felt a tingle run down my arm, like electricity. "I need my belongings, and I'd like to take care of a few nuisances."

"Nuisances," Jared muttered, pulling my arm free of Henri's grasp. "Listen to me, you bloodsucking demon, I don't give a fuck what you think you need to take care of. It isn't safe down here, and you know it. Weren't you just saying we needed to hurry? Where's the urgency?"

"We need to hurry while the other vampires are still asleep," Henri responded exasperatedly. He sighed loudly and put his hands on his hips, only emphasizing the fact that he was completely naked and drawing my eyes downward. Perhaps he did it on purpose.

Jared narrowed his eyes at Henri and shifted his gun hand, raising it slightly. "Why is it the other vamps are asleep, but you seem just fine?"

I had heard that older vampires could stay up longer, while younger ones were down for the day. I was sure Jared knew this too, so why was he asking? Henri smiled at Jared, flaunting his fangs purposely. "I am much older than most of the vampires here. Unlike with humans, the older a vampire is, the more strength and power he attains."

"Then how did a bunch of baby vamps capture you, if you're so much older and more powerful?"

Henri chuckled and shook his head before responding. "Touché, wolf. Even the strongest can be outnumbered, or betrayed," he added the last word pointedly.

"Is that what happened?" I asked, reaching out toward Henri until I touched his arm. "You were betrayed?"

Henri's blue eyes turned toward mine, and he smiled at me in what I took for confirmation. "I will explain all later, but now is not the time, as the wolf continually points out. Even if the vampires are sleeping, human servants are still about. We need to hurry while I am awake for the day."

"We're still not going with you," Jared retorted, pulling me away from Henri.

"Not even for a chance to kill Sarah?" Henri asked, and I sucked in a breath.

I looked over at Jared, who had gone completely still. Henri had mentioned Sarah before, but I hadn't been sure he was actually speaking of the same Sarah. Jared glanced at me, and I read the eagerness there warring with his duty to protect me. I pulled my gun out, smiled at Jared and nodded. We hadn't spoken more about our torture at the hands of Sarah, but we hadn't needed to. The experience had bonded us together tightly, and we both shared a common goal where Sarah was concerned.

I wasn't sure how my brother would respond to her demise though. Justin still held the belief that he could somehow fix Sarah. I had confidence in my brother's abilities, but I wasn't sure it was possible to cure vampirism. And if it was possible, what would that mean to a person like Sarah? She wasn't the person she once was, or maybe we'd never known her well enough to begin with. How much did vampirism truly change a person? I glanced at Henri, wondering what made him different.

Jared moved up beside me and touched my arm that held the

gun. "Sarah's mine," he stated simply, lowering my hand gently. I stared at him, fighting the urge to argue with him. We had both endured her torture, but mine had been a few days only. How long had Jared been Sarah's plaything? Long enough to watch Sarah turn Jin crazy and change one of his best friends into a shell of a man. Jared had definitely earned the right to Sarah. I nodded once in acceptance and holstered my gun.

Jared turned back toward Henri, frowning at the vampire. "Sarah is here?"

Henri smiled wide and said, "Oh, yes, wolf, she is here. Sarah has bloodied more bodies in this dungeon than any before her."

"And she's asleep?"

Henri shrugged his shoulders at this. "It's hard to say. As the day goes on, more and more vamps will go down. She is strong, but not very old."

"Then why don't we just wait until everyone is asleep?" I asked, thinking that seemed like the most logical course. If all the vampires were down, couldn't we just walk around with wooden stakes in our hands seeking out the coffins? Life was never that simple though, and I doubted it would work like that.

"Waiting for them to sleep would be helpful, if we knew when they slept, where they slept, and if I could stay alert long enough," Henri responded. "If I had more blood, perhaps I could guarantee my services longer."

"We could just leave you behind," Jared retorted.

"You don't know how to find Sarah," Henri responded calmly back. "Face it, wolf, our paths are aligned. Besides, I doubt Isabella would leave me now. Not after everything you've done to rescue me."

I opened my mouth to argue, but I realized Henri was right. I would go with him, wherever he asked me to go. Jared looked at me sharply, a deep frown creasing his forehead as he realized Henri was right. "Alright, leech; we'll play this your way for now."

Henri smiled at me and I automatically smiled back. He

turned on his heel and led the way down the side hallway, with us following closely behind him. Jared and Henri both moved silently, while I tripped over the uneven ground as it changed from concrete to stone. I kept my hand on the gun at my side, ready for anything, although I doubted I needed it. The vampire and werewolf were both more than capable of handling anything that jumped out at us.

A set of stairs met us at the end of a long, empty hallway. Henri paused briefly before bolting up the steps in a blur of movement. Jared pushed me against the wall, shielding me with his body as he focused his eyes in the direction Henri had gone. I held my breath, waiting for whatever danger was nearby to pass. After several minutes, Henri sauntered into view and motioned for us to follow. Jared stayed close to me as I hurried after Henri, who smiled down at me with red lips.

There were two dead bodies at the top of the stairs, one with his head turned around backwards, and the other with two bright puncture marks in his neck. The landing branched out in three directions, and Henri led us confidently to the right. I gingerly stepped over the dead men before following the vampire. He opened the first door in the hallway and entered. Jared kept me behind him as he peeked into the room, surveying the situation quickly. Then he unceremoniously yanked me into the room and shut the door behind us.

The room was fairly large and filled with boxes, chests and two large cabinets. Henri was rifling through a box, tossing clothes onto the floor behind him. He finally stopped, holding a pair of jeans up to himself. Satisfied, he pulled the jeans on and zipped them up carefully. He then stooped to tear through the boxes again. He came up with a long-sleeved black buttoned shirt that he threw on without buttoning. A large chest on the floor was filled with shoes of varying styles and sizes. Henri rifled through them, until he finally found a pair in his size. He frowned at the neon orange Nike shoes in his hand. After a moment's debate, he sighed loudly and pulled the shoes on.

"I take it these aren't your clothes?" Jared chuckled quietly, pointing at Henri's shoes.

Henri glared at him and shook his head sharply. "No, but they will suffice for now," he said, walking toward me just as silently as ever. "My other belongings should be here somewhere."

"While I appreciate you putting clothes on, what other belongings do you need?"

"You will see," Henri remarked as he opened the door and led us down the hallway. He opened the next few doors, peering in quickly before closing them and moving on to the next. We followed in his wake, Jared keeping an eye on our surroundings as we moved to the end of the corridor and turned around.

We walked down the opposite hallway, following Henri as he continued looking in rooms for his mysterious belongings. By the time we reached the last room, Henri was visibly irritated and had begun slamming doors until several broke off their hinges and hung haphazardly. I winced at the noises he was making, sure it would alert more guards, but Henri didn't seem to care. He moved to the main corridor and hurried down it, while we rushed to follow him. The passage ended at a second set of stairs leading up, which Henri raced up at vampire speed.

In my haste to keep up, I stumbled on the second step, scraping my shin on the stone. I winced loudly, and Jared stopped beside me to check out my scraped leg. Henri had already disappeared, and my leg would heal. I shook Jared off and pointed up the stairs in the direction Henri had gone. Jared nodded silently and helped me to my feet.

When we reached the landing, Henri was nowhere in sight. Three poorly lit corridors were visible at the top of the stairs. Jared cocked his head to one side, using his werewolf hearing to our advantage. He suddenly grabbed my arm, turned me back the opposite direction, and pushed me down the stairs in front of him. I was halfway down the stairs when I realized Jared wasn't with me. The stairwell was empty except for me, and silent as a tomb.

I stopped between steps, unsure of my next move when I heard a loud thud coming from the direction I had just left. Jared had been trying to get me to safety, but I wasn't about to leave him behind. My hand strayed to the Glock on my side. If something was hurting a werewolf, I'd definitely need a gun in hand. As quietly as possible, I pulled the gun from its holster and turned toward the noise.

I rushed back up the stairs and stopped at the landing, peering around the corner. On my right, there was an empty hallway. I peered down the left hall and sucked in a breath. Jared was lying on his back on the floor at the far end of the corridor. He moaned and rolled over, and I breathed easier knowing he was all right. I turned my focus on the reason Jared was lying on the ground. A man with his back to me stalked toward Jared slowly. Blood dripped from one of his hands onto the floor. My eyes darted back to Jared, who was struggling to rise. I wasted no time. The man hadn't turned to look at me, and that would be his mistake. I sighted my gun as I had been taught, planted my feet, and fired off several consecutive rounds.

The man turned toward me, his eyes black and wild in his pale face. He screeched and I squeezed the trigger, firing off more rounds into the center of his body. The vampire moved toward me, and I backed into the wall as the gun clicked empty. Jared finally rose, and raced toward the man, but the vampire dropped to his knees. His body began to smoke where the blessed bullets had penetrated into his body. The vampire struggled to remove the bullets, clawing at his own body in frustration. He shrieked suddenly, a high keening wail that had me quivering, as his body burned from the inside out and he toppled to the ground in a pile of ash.

I lowered the gun and crouched beside the wall, my arms shaking. Someone was bound to have heard the gunshots, and Henri still wasn't in sight. Jared stepped in front of me, and I looked up at his glowing yellow eyes. He was panting hard, but seemed to be controlling himself for now. He grasped my arms, pulling me to my feet. I could feel Henri nearby, and I turned down the right hallway toward him. Jared moved up beside me, breathing loudly.

I had used all the ammo up in the Glock, and holstered it with shaking hands. There was probably more ammo in Jared's pack, and I did have another gun, but I wasn't sure if my hands would stop shaking long enough to use it. I didn't have a chance to think more on the subject, when the third door down the hallway opened and Henri appeared. His clothes were immaculate, but fresh blood dripped from his chin to the floor. He licked his lips and carefully wiped his mouth off, savoring every last drop of blood before striding toward me. His strong hands wrapped around my arms, drawing me toward him.

I stumbled behind Henri as he hauled me down the next corridor, taking the twisting paths as though he knew exactly where he was going. Henri took long strides, but my shorter legs couldn't keep up and I soon found myself jogging to stay beside him. He glanced at me once, but didn't slow down or loosen his grip on my arm. Jared took the rear again, not saying a word as we wound through the maze of paths, although his eyes spoke volumes.

We took several more turns and climbed another set of stairs, which ended in a large, white door. Henri stopped before the door and put his ear to it before opening. Satisfied no one was beyond it, he led us through the door and down a short hallway. The hall ended in a stairwell and elevator. He opened the stairwell door and led us upwards.

I recognized the stairwell immediately. If it wasn't the same one Mark and I had been in, it looked exactly like it. My heart pounded in my chest as I remembered our escape through the hotel. If we'd known about all the underground tunnels, perhaps Mark and I could have escaped without being caught on camera. But we didn't know our way around, like Henri seemed to.

Henri silently led us upward higher and higher, until we reached the last door opening onto the roof. He opened the door and led us out, but not onto the roof. The door opened to a long, dark corridor. A second metal door on our right had a small sign indicating roof access. Henri led us past this and down the narrow hallway to the very end, where another, smaller elevator stood.

Henri opened the elevator and we climbed in. He finally released my arm and turned toward the control panel. The elevator controls had regular buttons and a second panel, which Henri pressed his palm to. The panel blinked and flashed, and a keypad lit up on the screen. Henri typed in a flurry of numbers, and the elevator moved down one floor. I waited for the door to open, but instead the back wall of the elevator opened, revealing a small entryway.

Henri strolled out casually and walked to the only door visible. I followed slowly, with Jared hovering close beside me. The floors were rich burgundy carpeting and the walls were cream with gold accents. Henri walked to the single door and pressed his hand to a panel on the wall. Once again a keypad lit up, and he entered a flurry of numbers. The door slid aside and he walked in, flicking on the light. Jared pulled me behind him as we followed Henri inside the luxurious apartment.

The foyer was burgundy, gold and cream as well, and stepped down into a large sunken living room with plush couches in matching colors. Darkly tinted windows lined the room, allowing a view of the outside without any harmful sunlight peeking in. Henri waltzed through the apartment and disappeared into another room. I walked to the bank of windows and stared outside.

We were obviously in the top floor of the hotel, facing west. Jared strode up behind me and glanced out the window. He shuddered visibly and turned around, tugging me away from the window. I chuckled and let him lead me into the sunken living room space. Figuring danger had passed for now, I sat down on one of the couches.

After a moment of indecision, Jared holstered his gun and sat down uneasily beside me. "We should get out of here," Jared whispered beside me. He bounced his leg anxiously as his eyes darted back toward the still open door.

I smiled and leaned back against the couch, feeling surprisingly at ease. "Henri, where are we?" I asked, raising my voice slightly.

Henri strolled back into the room a moment later, a frown on his face. He quickly replaced it with a smile as he walked toward the front door and shut it. Jared winced as the door closed, but didn't comment. "We are in one of my apartments," Henri answered as he strolled toward me.

I blinked at that, feeling the truth of his words. "This is the hotel Mark and I were held under," I said slowly.

"Yes," Henri replied shortly as he sat down beside me, his leg brushing against mine.

"Did you know about that?"

Henri took a deep breath and stared at me with his gorgeous blue eyes. I found myself mesmerized by his strong, defined jaw and his piercing blue eyes. He smiled and ran a hand through his hair, pushing it back from his face as though to give me a better view of his perfection. "This place was mine, but it has been overrun by Petrivian's men," Henri responded.

"He didn't answer the question," Jared muttered beside me, but Henri continued speaking over Jared.

"Luckily, they never got my access codes, so we are quite safe here. I doubt they even know of this place. We can rest here and I can replenish my strength and find my belongings," he added testily.

"What belongings?" I asked, wondering again what he was so concerned about. I doubted it was anything as mundane as shoes.

"Nothing you need to worry about, for now. Just some things I'd rather Petrivian not have," he responded quickly. I frowned back at him. He was avoiding the question again, and it was getting irritating. I opened my mouth to speak my mind on the subject, but he spoke before I could. "I'll explain later."

"What about Sarah?" Jared asked beside me, his leg

continuing to bounce.

"She is staying in one of the hotel rooms," he replied.

"Which one?"

"I do not know. Most likely one of the suites."

"Most likely? How do you know she's in a room, or even here at all?"

"She told me as much," Henri countered with an edge to his voice.

Jared laughed mirthlessly, shaking his head. "And of course, I should just trust you."

"I endured torture at her hands as well, wolf. Her demise would please me greatly. In this, you should trust me. We are of a similar mind on the subject of Sarah."

"Hmm, I still don't like this. I think Isabella and I should leave now. You're obviously fine in your fancy apartment. You don't need our help!" Jared said, standing up.

Part of me agreed with Jared and I started to stand with him, but Henri grasped my arm. I felt him in my mind, like a gentle caress. I looked at him and smiled, feeling a strange warmth spread across my body. Slowly, I sat back down and Henri put his arm around my shoulders. I snuggled against him, enjoying the feel of his strong arms around me. Why would I want to go anywhere, when I could stay in Henri's arms?

"If you wish to leave, go ahead," Henri stated. "There are mostly just humans awake and I could give you directions out of here. You might make it. Your revenge on Sarah would have to wait, but if you're so insistent on leaving, go ahead."

"Fine. Come on, Izzy."

I looked up at Jared and opened my mouth to respond. Whatever words had come to mind disappeared and I stared at Jared with my mouth hanging open and no words coming out. I tried again, but Henri answered for me. "Izzy is staying with me. Aren't you Isabella?" Henri asked, and I found myself nodding my head eagerly.

"I'm not going anywhere without Izzy," Jared retorted angrily.

"Well, then, make yourself comfortable," Henri responded. "The kitchen is that way." Henri pointed behind us, toward a half wall near the windows. "There should be some food in there."

"Stop the vampire mind games and manipulation. You've trapped us in here," Jared growled.

"I have done no such thing. As I said before, you are free to leave. Whether you like it or not, we are on the same side. You will see that in time, as Isabella does," Henri added, looking up at Jared calmly.

"I won't side with a vampire."

"Isabella's brother works on a way to stop Petrivian's vaccine, does he not?"

"How do you know that?" Jared asked skeptically.

Henri shrugged and said, "I know a great many things. I have been watching Petrivian for some time, just as he has been watching me. Not all vampires want the same thing, wolf. I, for one, do not want the general public as mindless zombies for one vampire."

Jared laughed humorlessly and shook his head. "Unless that vampire is you?" he asked.

"Not even then," Henri responded politely. "There are others who share my beliefs. The world was much better before Petrivian came out of his cave in Romania. When I get my belongings, we can take care of your little pest, Sarah, and I will show you what I have in mind. You need me, more than you realize."

"And you need me too?" Jared asked dubiously.

Henri glanced at me, smiled, then looked back at Jared. "I need Isabella's brother to continue doing what he's doing."

"And?" Jared urged.

Henri chuckled and stood up, facing Jared toe to toe. "I also need the wolves. Who better to fight vampires, than the ones immune to the vaccine?"

"My Alpha will never agree to siding with a vampire."

"We shall see," Henri said with a shrug as he reached a hand out to me, ignoring Jared scowling at his back.

I took Henri's outstretched hand, letting him pull me to my feet. He tucked me in close to his body and I placed a hand on his bare chest where the shirt gaped open. The blood he had taken in had already made a huge difference on him, making his muscles look fuller, tighter. I moved in closer and looked up at Henri's vivid eyes. He smiled widely, but I didn't notice the fangs as he leaned his face toward mine and placed a gentle kiss on my lips. I sighed as he pulled away, not wanting the kiss to end. Henri grinned wider as he placed a hand at the small of my back and steered me toward the kitchen area he had indicated. I let him lead me out of the living room, my thoughts solely on the tall man beside me. Everything would be all right with Henri by my side.

Chapter 17

The kitchen had a small amount of canned food and random items in the cupboards, while the refrigerator was completely empty. Jared put a couple cans of chili in a pan and started heating it while I found bowls and spoons. Henri hovered around me as though he was afraid to leave my side, but I found his presence strangely comforting. Jared did his best to pretend Henri didn't exist as he warmed food up. The two men danced around each other in the kitchen, both studiously avoiding the other. Jared poured the heated chili into bowls and moved into the adjoining dining room. I followed, with Henri on my heels.

"Crackers would be good," Jared commented as he took his first tentative bite. "Cornbread would be even better."

I nodded in agreement, and Henri suddenly leapt to his feet and disappeared into the kitchen. He came back a moment later with a box of crackers, setting them down before me. I grinned and opened the first sleeve of crackers, nibbling a bite first to check for freshness. Satisfied, I crumbled several into my chili before sliding the crackers across the table to Jared. Jared stared at the crackers, then at Henri, and very pointedly ignored them as he took another large bite of chili.

"I thought you wanted crackers," I commented.

Jared sniffed loudly and took another bite, his eyes focused on the bowl of food in front of him. "The crackers reek of vampire," he stated between bites.

"Jared," I began, but Henri touched me on the arm, stopping me. I sighed and continued eating my chili, surprised at how ravenous I was.

We ate in silence and Jared offered to clean up after we had scraped our bowls clean. I was sure it was just an excuse to be away from Henri, but I relented and followed Henri on a tour through the rest of the apartment while Jared lingered in the kitchen. There wasn't much more to see, except a large bathroom with both a vast whirlpool tub and a shower, and a single bedroom. Henri led me by the hand around the bedroom, which was almost as large as the living room. A vast king sized bed was the central focal point of the room, complete with matching gold and red comforter and pillows. The headboard was a dark cherry wood, which matched the tall dresser along one wall. A large walk-in closet took up the other side of the room. There was no other decoration in the room, but it wasn't needed. The bed decorated the room all on its own.

"The day grows long and I must rest now," Henri said softly as he moved toward the bed, tugging me behind him.

"Oh, right," I replied, forgetting that vampires slept during the day.

Henri stopped beside the bed and pulled me toward him, kissing me fiercely. My breath caught at the passion behind the kiss, and I found myself falling towards him as he explored my mouth with his tongue. He moved his mouth away from my own, kissing his way down my chin as I leaned my head back, eyes closed. His lips paused on my neck, while one hand moved to the back of my head, holding me in place.

"A small drink before sleep," Henri murmured.

I wasn't sure if he was asking me, or telling me, but I nodded all the same. Henri pulled me closer, his other hand wrapping around my waist, as he moved his mouth back to my neck. This time his bite was like it had been in those earlier dreams, and I felt an overwhelming sense of euphoria as though I was floating on a cloud. He only drank for a moment before he pulled away with a tender kiss on my neck. He moved his hand from behind my head, and held his wrist up to his own mouth, biting down. Blood welled on his wrist as he held it before me. The thought of drinking his blood repulsed and excited me at the same time. I tried not to think about it as I pulled his wrist to my lips and sucked at the blood pooling there.

Henri moved behind me as I drank, tracing his free hand around my body. He pulled me back against him suddenly, until I could feel his hardness against my back. I kept drinking as his hand trailing across my stomach sensuously. Slowly, he lifted my shirt until his fingertips tickled the edge of my bra. A loud crashing noise had me opening my eyes in surprise. Jared stood in the doorway, his golden eyes locked on me while he gripped a broken mug. Henri either didn't see him or didn't care, as he moved his hand under my bra to grab my breast.

Jared growled and I pushed Henri's wrist away from my mouth, licking the blood from my lips. "Jared, calm down," I said. Henri's fingers pinched my nipple, drawing a gasp from me and another loud growl from Jared. "Henri, stop."

Henri's fingers stopped, but he didn't move as he spoke. "Go back to the other room, wolf," Henri ordered.

Jared growled loudly and dropped to the floor on his hands and knees, the broken mug scattering across the floor in a multitude of pieces. I pulled away from Henri and ran to Jared, taking his face in my hands so I could force him to look at me. "Jared, calm down. Look at me. Everything is fine," I chanted. "Jared, please, calm down."

After several minutes, Jared seemed to relax, although his eyes still glowed brightly and sweat stood out on his forehead. He stood slowly and glared at Henri. "You've taken enough blood from her, demon. Keep your hands to yourself!" he yelled, pointing a finger at

Henri.

"Are you offering your blood to me instead, wolf?" Henri responded softly. "If that is the case, then I gladly accept."

Jared growled, a low, rumbling sound, and I felt the hair on the back of my neck stand on end. "Stop it!" I shouted, standing between the two men. A fight between them would not end well. "Henri, go rest," I bid. "I need to help Jared calm down."

"Do not leave the apartment," Henri ordered, his voice echoing in my mind even as he spoke aloud. "And do not let the wolf enter this room, under any circumstances. Do whatever it takes, Isabella."

I nodded but didn't turn to look at the vampire as I pushed Jared out of the room, closing the bedroom door behind us. Jared took me by the arm, pulling me toward the door. I stumbled behind him, unable to break free of his strong grip. We reached the front door and I hit Jared on the arm, finally causing him to stop and look at me, although his grip on my arm remained.

"I can't leave," I said.

"I don't care what he says, Izzy. It was stupid to come here in the first place. We should have left as soon as we rescued him. We shouldn't have even come here at all! I should have just tied you up back at the cottage!" he shouted.

"I'm not leaving, Jared. I want you to stay, but if you can't, I understand."

Jared growled and grabbed the door handle, but the door wouldn't budge. He yanked on it, putting his immense werewolf strength to use, but the door was solid steel and didn't move. He finally released my arm as he stalked to the control panel, examining it and letting out a stream of curses. "He's locked us in," Jared muttered, slamming his hands against the wall. "Damn it!"

Jared turned, leaning his back against the wall, his yellow eyes sighting on Henri's bedroom door. He took several deep breaths before pushing off from the wall and walking purposely toward the bedroom door. I followed closely, feeling an overwhelming urge to stop him.

"Jared, no," I pleaded, grasping his shirt, but he didn't stop.

Jared reached the door and raised his arm to open it. The Browning was suddenly in my hand, without thought. I flicked the safety off and Jared stopped, looking over his shoulder at me, his eyes widening in surprise. "Izzy, what are you doing?" he asked carefully.

"You can't go in there," I responded, holding the gun aimed at Jared's chest. "If you try, I *will* shoot you."

Time seemed to stop as I held the gun leveled at Jared's chest. I didn't want to hurt him, but I knew I had to stop him from entering that room. If he went in there, something bad would happen. Jared slowly turned toward me, holding his hands out to his sides. He stared at me, his yellow eyes analyzing me. "Okay, Izzy, you win," he finally said. "I won't go in there."

I nodded, but didn't lower my gun until Jared moved away from the door. As soon as he was in the living room, I felt better. A weight lifted from my shoulders, and I holstered the gun before following Jared into the living room. "You can't go in there. You can't hurt him, Jared. I...we need him."

"Well, we do need the code to the doors," Jared muttered with a glance at the front door.

"We need him for more than that," I responded testily as I stretched out on one of the couches. "I know you don't understand, Jared, but you're just going to have to trust me on this. I need Henri. He and I are... connected. Please, promise me you won't try to hurt him."

Jared didn't respond as he stretched out on another couch and put his hands behind his head. He was silent for a long time, staring up at the ceiling. Finally, he just said, "Why?"

I shrugged, even though he wasn't looking at me. "It would hurt me if you hurt him," I said softly, although I don't know where the words came from. I hadn't thought the words before they came out. The rest of my words came out the same way, as though pulled from my mouth by an invisible string. "We are connected through unbreakable bonds. Blood to blood and we are joined."

Jared sat up, staring at me. "Why do you say that?"

"I don't know," I responded thoughtfully. "It just kind of came out. It's true though. I can feel it."

Jared leaned back down, but I could feel his eyes on me. He wasn't happy. I rolled over on the couch, putting my back toward Jared. The couch was soft and comfortable, and sleep pulled me under, even though it was the middle of the day. No dreams followed me, probably because Henri didn't need to speak to me in dreams when I was just in the other room. I slept soundly, not a care in the world.

Sometime later, I awoke with a jolt. Darkness had descended completely, making it virtually impossible to discern anything more than general shapes. I wasn't sure what had woken me, but I sat up confused. What was I still doing here? Jared was right. We should leave. Was revenge on Sarah worth the risk we were taking?

"Isabella," Henri whispered in my mind, his voice pressing around me like a dark shadow. I felt his presence encompassing me. Henri wanted me.

I rolled slowly off the couch, knowing I needed to be quiet. My eyes adjusted quickly to the darkness as I made my way through the living room. Jared snored softly from the other couch, looking peaceful and very vulnerable in his sleep. I tiptoed around the sofa, feeling my way toward Henri's room. I could feel him pulling me, guiding me through the dark. The door opened before I got to it, and Henri reached out to me. I grasped his hand, letting him pull me into the room and shut the door softly behind me. A row of candles across the headboard lit the room in a faint light and emitted a gentle aroma of vanilla and spices.

"Let the wolf sleep," Henri whispered softly in my ear as he tugged me toward him.

"I'm surprised he didn't hear me get up," I replied, grinning. "Wolf hearing is pretty amazing."

Henri smiled and tilted my chin up, placing a kiss along my jaw line. "He is having a wonderful dream. He'll wake soon enough," Henri responded between kisses.

Dreams? Wasn't Henri the Master of Dreams? "You're doing something to him?" I asked, frowning as I pulled away from him.

"Sweet Isabella, I am letting him have the best sleep he has had in a long time. No troublesome nightmares plague him. He will awake rested and happy. Do not worry," he added, pulling me close again.

I braced my hands against his bare chest, noticing for the first time that he was wearing only a pair of long, black pants. His hands moved to the jacket I still wore, slipping it from my shoulders. He smiled at the gun holster before pulling it off as well and setting it on the large dresser. I stood silently, letting him remove the belt and second holster with the empty Glock.

My thoughts drifted back to Jared. I knew he had difficulty sleeping and was plagued by nightmares, but I didn't like the idea of Henri playing with his mind. "I thought wolves were immune to vampires," I said as the thought popped into my head.

Henri set my Glock on the dresser with the Browning and looked at me. His eyes turned from brilliant blue to black orbs in a blink, and I gasped in surprise. Dread filled my body and I backed up, away from the fearful creature before me. Henri moved in a blur, his hands encircling my waist. I closed my eyes, ready for whatever terror the vampire was about to inflict on me. A finger touched my chin, urging my face upward. I raised my head, but kept my eyes shut tight.

"Isabella," Henri whispered my name. "Isabella."

I opened my eyes, and found myself staring straight into an abyss. Blackness surrounded me, pressing around me and snuffing out the light. Nothing could survive here. This was death, I thought briefly.

"Surrender," Death whispered in response.

"No," I answered, struggling to turn away but unable to move my body.

"Surrender," Death spoke again, but this time it was a command.

"Please!" I cried, feeling hot tears course down my cheeks.

"Surrender," Death urged. "Surrender!"

I couldn't fight it, I knew. Death was inevitable. I fell, hurtling through the darkness with a sureness that I would never return from the gloom. I blinked my eyes as light returned. Henri held me in his arms, his blue eyes staring down at me with an unreadable expression. All thought and indecision evaporated as Henri pulled me into his arms and kissed me as though we were kissing our last kiss and he wanted it to last forever. His hands traced along my shirt, lifting it up. I raised my arms up, knowing what he wanted and allowing him to pull the shirt over my head. He invaded my mind, pressing his wants and needs into me until we were in sync, wanting the same things. There was no questioning it. There was no fear. He picked me up, carrying me to the bed as though I weighed nothing.

Henri tossed me onto the bed among plush pillows and grabbed my feet, pulling my clothes off swiftly. Within moments, both of us were naked on the luxurious bed. Henri moved his impressive physique over me, kissing his way across my body from the bottom to the top. He gently nipped at my skin, drawing small dots of blood from my flesh that quickly healed back up. His wrist was at my mouth, pressing warm blood across my lips. I opened my mouth and automatically drank the blood that flowed there, swallowing it down as though it were the most expensive wine and I couldn't waste a single drop. Simultaneously, he ran his hand across my body, spreading my legs. There was a sharp pain in my inner thigh, but thoughtless pleasure overtook me and I ignored the piercing sting.

I felt Henri in my mind again, pressing his thoughts into my head effortlessly as we shared blood. He removed his wrist from my mouth and began kissing me in earnest while his hands traversed my body. I explored him in turn, feeling the hard muscles of his chest and stomach, reaching lower and lower. He glowed with power and strength and he moved his body away, leaning back so I could view his entire glorious form. I marveled at his flawlessness. His skin was pale and free of imperfections. The muscles that had looked weak just hours before were full and strong. He grinned wickedly before moving over me once more, and thrusting himself into me fully.

Our lovemaking was long and magnificent, with Henri using his vampire strength to its fullness. He whispered in my mind, and drew my thoughts from me, connecting us in ways I'd never experienced before. We were one. My thoughts mingled with Henri's, until I didn't know which thoughts were my own or his. The world spun around me, and somewhere deep inside I knew I'd never be the same after this.

When we were both fully satisfied, we lay back on the bed breathing hard. "I can feel you in here," I whispered between breaths, tapping my head. I didn't need to say it aloud, but I wanted to. It somehow made it more real.

Henri rolled over and looked at me, propping himself up on one arm. He grinned and pressed a quick kiss to my forehead. "That is because I am the Master of Dreams," he responded.

"I thought that just meant you could enter my dreams, or pull me into yours."

"No, it is so much more than that. At full power, I can create a world in your mind so realistic that you would have no way of discerning dream from reality. I could enter your mind and make you do things..." he stopped, grinning at me. "I could make you do pleasant things."

"Only in my dreams?"

"In a dream state," he replied carefully.

I closed my eyes against Henri's intense blue eyes. There was something I wanted to ask him, but the words wouldn't come to mind.

It was like trying to remember a dream after waking up, and his intense stare made it difficult to concentrate. Thoughts flitted across my mind quickly. I wanted to ask about darkness and death, dreams and reality, but the more I thought about it, the more the thought flitted away like trying to grasp smoke with my bare hands.

When I finally spoke, it was still with my eyes shut. "Why is it so different now, with you?" I struggled to ask. Why was I having such difficulties concentrating?

"Are you alright, Isabella?" Henri asked, ignoring my question as he stroked my cheek.

I opened my eyes and peered at him. "I can't seem to form a proper question," I muttered in response. Henri stared down at me and I pulled my eyes away from his face, so I was staring at his chest. "Have you made me do things?" I blurted out quickly, my heart pounding in my chest.

"Why do you ask such a question?"

I shrugged and closed my eyes once more. Concentrating seemed easier when I wasn't looking at Henri's piercing eyes. There were a thousand things I wanted to ask him, but I felt him in my mind, pushing the questions away before I had a chance to articulate them. That should frustrate me, but I couldn't draw any anger towards him. The only emotion that came to mind with Henri was an unquenchable desire. The desire wasn't just sexual, but more than that. I desired to please him in everything, and what I was going to ask wouldn't please him. My thoughts drifted to Mark and the pain I had caused him. "Before I came here, to find you, I did something I wouldn't have done normally," I said softly, choking on the words that didn't want to slip out of my mouth.

"You want to know if I caused you to do this thing?" Henri asked. I nodded, still not looking up at him. Tears filled my eyes, even though they were clenched tightly closed.

"Please, Henri, I have to know."

Henri's hand caressed my cheek and he tipped my face up

until I finally opened my eyes to look at him. "I have been weak," he responded softly. "Nights I spent being tortured by Sarah, and her methods are... well, you know of her methods. The dream world is my realm, and I find that I retreated to it quite frequently while at her hands. The power I possess in this moment is a fraction of what I was able to hold while under Sarah's care. It is possible, since I was seeking you out, that I accidentally pulled you into a dream state, despite my limited powers. Perhaps if you tell me what happened, I could answer your question better."

I swallowed hard, wondering if this was the answer all along. It hadn't been my knife, but Henri after all. And here I was, in his bed. That was probably a bad idea, and not at all like me. Normally, I didn't go sleeping around, and here I had slept with three different men in the span of a month! Henri lifted my head again and I met his eyes. "I was reckless," I began softly. "I did things and said things I don't think I normally would have." Sort of like now. Would I have slept with Henri under normal circumstances if he was just a human? I didn't do casual sex normally, but this wasn't normal and I wasn't so sure it was casual either. And then there was Mark...

"What did you do?" Henri pushed, interrupting my thoughts.

"I slept with someone I wouldn't have normally," I responded testily, pulling away from him. I wouldn't have normally slept with a vampire either, would I? "Are you manipulating me?"

He reached out and pulled me toward him. His hand trailed across my breast, sending a shiver down my body. "Are you saying you didn't like having sex with me? Do you not want to share my bed, and my power?"

I looked up at his face, opened my mouth to respond, and felt the words die on my tongue. What had I been about to say? "Of course not," I responded with a smile. "But that other man..."

"Do you think the incident with this other man happened in a dream state?"

"It was like I was drugged. I woke up the next morning in his bed, and eventually I remembered what happened, but it was like someone else was controlling my body. The things I asked him to do to me..." I trailed off, shuddering at the memory.

Henri sat up and grasped my head between his hands. "Remember," he whispered softly, and I felt a rush of memories course through me. I shied away from them, but Henri pulled them from me effortlessly. Once again, I saw myself walking through the snow to the main house. The memories sped up, as though we were watching them on fast forward. I took my clothes off for Lucas, and urged him to hurt me, to tie me up, and to fuck me. I didn't ask for lovemaking, I had asked for something far different; something brutal and animalistic that was very unlike me. The memory finally finished, and I collapsed on the bed in tears. Henri had pulled more memories from me that I had suppressed.

"My sweet, Isabella," Henri murmured, stroking my hair gently. "It is very possible the fault is mine, and I take full responsibility for that. I assure you, it was not a willing thing that happened. I believe it was an unintentional transference, due to Sarah's torture. I must have pulled you in."

"I don't understand," I muttered into the bed.

"What I saw you do looked like one of Sarah's games. During her torture, I would escape to my dream world, but there was always an echo of the real world to it. I would feel her whip sting, even if I couldn't see it. As my power diminished, my hold on the dream world diminished with it. That is why when you came to me in my dreams, you would still see the torture room. I couldn't hold onto the dreams as before. I am so sorry for any distress it caused you, my dear. Now that I am back at my full power, it won't happen accidentally again."

I nodded at his remarks and sat up, wiping the tears from my face. I couldn't drum up any anger toward Henri. Everything that had happened was because of Sarah once again. I would make her pay. Feeling at ease, I climbed out of bed and got dressed. I had all my clothes back on, and the two guns strapped back into place. I was ready to take on Sarah. Henri moved up behind me, wrapped his arms around my waist. I marveled at how strong he appeared after seeming so weak before. The blood had done him good, I thought absently.

Henri nibbled at my ear and whispered softly, "Vampires roam the night, and you'd be best to equip yourself against them. Your wolf has more ammunition in his pack, and your Glock is empty."

"How do you know my Glock is empty?"

"I pay attention to everything, Isabella. Let's go wake up the little wolf," he added, turning toward the door.

Wolf? Oh, yes, Jared. Henri had put him into a dream. That wasn't right. He shouldn't do that to Jared. I opened my mouth to speak my mind to Henri, but he turned those beautiful blue eyes toward me. All thought left me as I stared at my handsome lover. What was I thinking about again? The thought floated away as quickly as it had appeared. I turned and followed Henri toward the living room, eager to help him with anything he needed.

Chapter 18

Jared woke from his dream agitated and growling, rushing toward me the moment I stepped into the living room. He sniffed the air around me loudly, burrowing his face against my neck. I pushed him away irritably as I followed Henri, anxious to see what he was doing. A low, steady growl emanated from Jared as he shadowed me.

"Jared, calm down. Can't have you wolfing out in the living room," I muttered absently, my eyes fixated on Henri's every move.

Henri had walked to the front door and entered his code, opening the door. He peered out and motioned for us to follow him. I hurried to his side and Jared followed behind me silently. We stopped in the entryway, and Henri turned toward Jared.

"Isabella needs more ammo," he commanded.

Jared grimaced and shook his head, but he swung the bag out and began searching through it. He pulled out an extra clip for my Glock, and traded me for my empty one. I inserted the new clip as Jared reloaded the other clip and handed it back to me so I'd have the spare with me. My clothes didn't really supply a place for extra clips, so I stuffed it into the top of my boot next to the knife I had taken.

"We are going to the roof," Henri told us quietly as he led us out to the elevator. "The plan is to make it there and back before they realize we're here."

"What's on the roof?" I asked.

"I put a few safeguards in place," Henri replied with a small smile. "Let's hope the one on the roof hasn't been disturbed. It will make things infinitely easier."

"What is it?" Jared asked suspiciously as Henri punched in his code to the elevator.

The doors slid shut and we rose to the top floor. "Remote security surveillance," Henri replied. "With it, we can find my belongings and get out unnoticed."

The elevator door slid open, thankfully revealing no one. Henri entered a series of codes into the elevator once more to prevent anyone from using it. We walked down the hall and stopped at the windowless door for the roof. Henri went first, opening the door cautiously and looking around before motioning us to follow him.

This portion of the roof was large and thankfully empty of vampires. It was mostly flat, with metal vents spaced around the building. We followed Henri around the roof, until he stopped at one of the larger vents. He yanked the grate off and reached his hand inside, pulling out a black box. Henri grinned, flashing his fangs in triumph, as he opened the box briefly to peer inside. Satisfied, he closed the lid and led us back to the door. We had almost made it there when Jared growled and pushed his body in front of mine.

We all stopped, staring at the roof access door as it opened and a vampire walked out. His eyes widened at the sight of the three of us and the lit cigarette dropped from his mouth. He turned around to head back through the door, but Henri moved faster, grabbing his arm and tossing him back across the roof. The vampire slid across the roof but quickly jumped to his feet. Jared raced after the vampire and grabbed him from behind, holding him in place. Henri handed the heavy box to me before moving with blurring speed to stand before the other vampire.

Jared growled, struggling to maintain human form and fight

the strong vampire at the same time. Henri reached a hand out toward the other vampire and pulled back. It took a moment for me to comprehend what had happened. The vampire dropped to the ground, a look of horror and surprise on his face. In Henri's hand, he held the vampire's bloodied heart. Henri crushed the heart as though he was squeezing a tomato, until it burst into a pile of juicy, red meat. The vampire keeled over, dead at his feet. Henri tossed the heart to the ground and stalked back toward me.

"Is he dead?" I asked, my eyes still glued on the vampire. I didn't know much about vampires, but I assumed a demolished heart would mean death.

"Yes," Henri responded curtly as he stalked past me.

"He isn't turning to ash."

"Wait for it," Henri responded casually over his shoulder.

I watched the vampire as his body seemed to disintegrate before my eyes, as though he was going through rapid decomposition. It took a minute, but soon there was nothing left but a pile of dirt and ash. I was still staring at the body when Henri spoke from behind me. "Our bodies turn to replenish the earth. If we are killed by fire or holy means, we burn quicker, but the death is still the same. It is part of the circle of life. We vampires are at the very top of the food chain. The only way to put ourselves back into the cycle, is through our death."

"You're not the top of the food chain," Jared muttered under his breath as he walked up beside me.

Henri chuckled but said nothing in response to Jared's remark. We walked cautiously back into the building, but didn't run into any more vampires as we returned to Henri's room. Jared grumbled under his breath the whole way, but he wasn't going to try running through a hotel full of vampires during the night.

Henri opened the box as soon as we were in the living room. He pulled out a small laptop computer and plugged the wires into a strange floor panel beside one of the couches. I sat down beside him so I could see what he was doing as he booted up the computer. Jared paced behind us, not wanting to sit down near Henri, but still wanting to see what Henri was doing.

After a few minutes, the computer booted up and I smiled in realization. Henri's computer was hooked up to the surveillance in the hotel, and showed several small black and white surveillance cameras. The smile on my face slipped as I realized the enormity of the hotel, as more and more tiny pictures appeared on the screen. My heart thudded faster in my chest as I tried to count the vast number of vampires roaming through it. There were far too many for the three of us to handle.

Henri clicked through several screens, working his way from the upper floors of the hotel first. It was easy, even in black and white, to spot the difference between the regular hotel patrons and the vampires. The vampires moved differently, and their skin seemed to glow eerily on the video. I watched in fascination as Henri clicked through the videos one by one, obviously looking for something.

Jared retreated to the kitchen after some time and came back with a bowl of canned fruit for each of us for breakfast. I smiled in appreciation as I dug in, feeling suddenly ravenous. I devoured the contents of the bowl and walked back into the kitchen to scavenge for more food. Jared followed me and we scraped up an odd breakfast of crackers, peanut butter, and fruit. Jared was quiet, but I felt his eyes on me as we munched on our strange breakfast at the dining room table.

"What?" I finally asked as I devoured my second can of fruit.

Jared chewed his food slowly as he looked at me. He swallowed, took a drink of water, and sighed dramatically. "I don't know what to say to you," he said.

"Just say what's on your mind," I supplied as I piled peanut butter on a cracker.

"You don't want to know what's on my mind."

"Jared, just say it."

He leaned back in his chair and stared at me with wolf eyes. It startled me, since his eyes had been normal just moments before. "You had sex with him," he stated bluntly.

I felt myself blush. "With Henri? Yes," I replied.

"You had sex with a vampire, Izzy. You shared blood with him," he continued, growing louder and more animated with each word. "Do you know what you're doing, or has he mind-fucked you so much that you can't tell right from wrong?"

"He hasn't done anything to me, Jared," I retorted.

Jared stood up, banging his hands on the table and yelling, "What about Mark?"

"What about him, Jared? He left, remember?"

"Left? Izzy, he needed some space, so Jed sent him off on business. He didn't leave you," Jared replied, his voice returning to a more normal volume. He straightened up and stared down at me, the look on his face unreadable. "This isn't you, Izzy."

"This isn't the old me, Jared, it's the new me."

"The new you? So the new you is a vampire whore?"

I blanched, taken aback by his words. Tears welled in my eyes. What was Jared talking about? I really hadn't changed much, I had thought. So, I had sex with a vampire. I'd also had sex with a werewolf. Two, actually. I was just trying to become more... more....

"Powerful," Henri supplied in my head. I smiled as warmth spread across my body. Yes, I was becoming more powerful. I wouldn't be anyone's pawn again. "No, you are my queen," Henri added.

I looked up at Jared with a smile on my face. "The new me is strong and powerful, Jared."

Jared nodded and backed up, his eyes sad for some reason. "At what cost?" he muttered so softly I barely heard him. With that remark, he turned and walked away.

I returned to watch Henri flip through the monitors as I munched on crackers coated in peanut butter. Henri's vampire eyes flitted across the monitors quickly, searching for his mysterious belongings. Jared returned to his silent pacing behind the couch while I curled up beside Henri as I ate. I wasn't paying much attention to the monitor when Jared sucked in a loud breath. My eyes immediately darted to the screen.

Sarah was walking down a hallway, headed toward the elevator with Jin at her side. "Follow her," Jared ordered, leaning over the couch to point at Sarah's form on the screen.

"She is of no consequence at the moment," Henri replied as he flipped screens and Sarah disappeared from view.

"No consequence? That bitch is the only reason we're still here!" Jared growled angrily, slamming his fist on the back of the couch and making me jump.

Henri turned calmly toward Jared and said, "I will look for her later. For now, there are more important things to find."

"Such as?" Jared asked.

"My belongings," Henri replied as he turned back toward the screen.

Jared growled and stormed away, only to come back a few minutes later to stare at the screen once more. Henri wrapped one arm around me, pulling me against his chest. I settled myself there against his hard body, trying to get comfortable. The monitor screens flickered, and I noticed the change in scenery.

Gone were the decorative hotel walls and pristine floors. Concrete walls with bright fluorescent lights and long hallways came into view, and it was my turn to suck in a breath. These hallways I remembered from my brief time in captivity with Mark. Henri's progress across the screens stopped on a room that looked much like the room I had been held in.

Pushed up against the far wall was a bed covered in what looked like metal boxes. Tall metal tanks ran the length of another wall. In the middle of the room was a long table covered in microscopes, jars, tubes, and an assortment of other items I couldn't make out on the small black and white screen. Two visibly human men in long lab coats worked side by side at the table. Henri paused on the screen, studying it intently.

"Is that what you were looking for?" I asked softly.

"Yes," Henri said sharply.

I looked up at his face, taking note of his clenched jaw and pursed lips. Henri looked angry, and that was making me nervous. I sat back, alternately studying Henri and the monitor. His anger radiated into my mind, putting me even further on edge. "What is it?" I asked softly.

"That," he began, his words clipped, "is research you don't want in Petrivian's hands."

"What kind of research?" Jared asked.

Henri ignored him and began flipping through the screens faster. Anger radiated from him and I found myself scooting further across the couch. I pulled my knees to my chest and watched from a distance until Henri finally stopped his manic computer search.

"Here, wolf, go ahead and look for the bitch," Henri snapped as he pushed the laptop away and stood up. He stalked toward me and I found my heart pounding loudly in fear. "Come with me."

I stood, as though pulled up on puppet strings, and followed Henri into the bedroom, casting a backward glance at a worried Jared. He took a step toward me, but I shook my head and pointed back at the computer. I could see the indecision on Jared's face, but he stopped walking and watched me with yellow eyes. I turned back toward Henri and bumped right into him. Large hands grasped me around my arms as he hauled me into the bedroom and slammed the door.

"Henri?"

"I need to calm down," he said through gritted teeth.

"Okay," I said tentatively, not sure what to do. The only thought that seemed to make it through my fog-filled brain was, "Please don't kill me."

"I don't plan on killing you, my sweet," Henri responded to my unspoken words. He stalked toward the bed and gripped the frame, squeezing until it snapped and splintered. With a loud roar, he flung the broken pieces across the room.

The bedroom door opened and Jared stood in the doorway, his eyes wide. "What the fuck?" he asked, staring at the bedframe.

"Go away, wolf, before I kill you out of sheer annoyance."

"You could try," Jared responded, stepping into the bedroom.

I raced across the room, pushing Jared back. "Jared, no!"

"Out of my way, Izzy."

I pulled the gun from my side and leveled it at Jared's chest. He stared at me with bright wolf eyes. "You can't come in here," I said.

"Fucking blood-sucking vampires!" Jared spat as he backed up out of the room.

Immediately the need to hold my gun was gone, and I holstered it. I was breathing hard, with Henri's fury echoing in my brain. One more second and I was sure Jared would have been dead. The only thing I was unsure about was who would have killed him. The thought echoed in my mind that it could have been me.

"I suggest you leave us, wolf," Henri said as he walked toward me, removing his shirt as he did. "Unless you want to watch me fuck her? Is that what you like, wolf? Do you like to watch?"

"Keep your hands off her!" Jared growled.

"Isabella, take your clothes off," Henri's words echoed softly in my mind even as he spoke to Jared. "Isabella enjoys the feel of my hands on her body."

Both gun holsters dropped to the ground loudly and I began removing my shirt even as I slipped my shoes off. My bra was on the floor before I knew it and my hands were reaching for the button on my jeans. I wanted to take my clothes off and have Henri run his hands across my body.

"Izzy, you don't have to do this," Jared pleaded with me. "This isn't what you want. Please."

I looked up at Jared, frowning. What was he talking about?

"What don't I have to do?" I asked.

"You don't have to have sex with him. He's a monster!"

"So are you, wolf," Henri retorted as he moved across the room and grabbed my breasts with both of his large hands. "Take off your clothes," he whispered.

I unzipped my jeans and began lowering them down my hips. Henri moved back as I stripped my remaining clothes off, eyeing me appreciatively. All thoughts drifted away as Henri's presence pushed into my mind. He needed me, and I needed him in return. My thoughts and desires echoed his, until they encompassed all thought. Sex, desire, blood, pain, death, and destruction were foremost in my mind as Henri grabbed me and tossed me onto the broken bed. I heard a door slam, but I paid it no mind. The only thoughts on my mind were of Henri, and his strong, muscular body. His thoughts pulsed into my mind again. Sex, blood, pain, destruction. Henri moved his body over mine, pushing himself into me with enough force I cried out in a mix of pain and desire. Sex, blood, pain. His mouth found my neck and he bit down, drawing a scream from my mouth. Sex, blood. He thrust into me again, and all thought of pain drifted away on a sea of mindless pleasure. Blood. It always came down to blood.

Chapter 19

I don't know how long I slept, but when I woke, I felt famished. The vast bed was empty and I was wrapped in blood-soaked sheets. I felt at my neck, knowing I should feel concern at the amount of blood on the sheets, but I couldn't seem to muster the feeling. Licking my lips, I felt the salty taste of blood. I couldn't remember it, but I knew I had shared blood with him once more.

"You're awake," Jared said from across the room. I sat up and looked to where Jared stood in the doorway of the bedroom, his feet carefully just outside the room. "You must be hungry. I made canned green beans and spam for dinner, even though it's almost morning."

Nodding, I climbed out of bed and walked naked across the room. I could feel Jared's eyes on me, but for some reason I didn't care. "I am hungry," I said as I walked by Jared toward the living room.

"Aren't you going to get dressed?" he asked in a strained voice as I walked through the living room and toward the dining room, where the smells of food were coming from.

I paused and looked down at my naked body. Dots of dried blood littered my pale skin, but I shrugged and continued to the dining room. The need for food was overwhelming. Henri sat at the head of the table and I smiled when I saw him. His hair was wet from a shower and he was dressed in head to toe black, making his pale skin seem to whiter than usual. He grinned at me as I sat down in front of a plate of food.

Jared followed me in and sat as far from Henri as possible at the rectangular table. The smell of food made my stomach rumble, and I eagerly dug in. Usually, I hated canned meat, but I was too hungry to think about it as I forked it into my mouth. My plate was empty in minutes and Jared quickly took it from me. I licked my lips, wishing I had more food.

"Go shower and get dressed," Henri told me, and I immediately stood to obey.

Before I knew it, I was back in Henri's bedroom pulling my clothes on. I brushed wet strands of hair from my face as I put my gun holsters back in place. I eyed myself in my all black outfit. Henri and I would match. Something was missing though, I thought, as I finished pulling my boots on. Henri had told me to get dressed, but I felt incomplete.

I wandered around the room, unable to determine the source of my agitation. Henri opened the door and looked at me as I paced the room. "What are you doing?" he asked. "The sun is up and we must hurry."

"I'm missing something," I responded as I looked under the bed for whatever item I was forgetting.

"What are you missing?"

"I don't know."

"You aren't missing anything, Isabella. Let us go," Henri ordered as he turned on his heel and left the room.

I sighed, feeling my agitation diminish slightly as I followed Henri to the front door. I paused, looking back toward the bedroom once more as Henri opened the door. "Izzy, what is it?" Jared asked as he moved up beside me. He held the laptop and a couple cords in his hands, and his backpack slung over one shoulder.

"I'm missing something," I responded absently as I turned

and followed Henri into the elevator. My leg throbbed suddenly, and I ran my hand across my thigh. There should have been something there, on my thigh, but I couldn't figure out what it was. I shook my head, trying to shake off the uneasy sensation.

Henri stared at me as the elevator doors swished closed behind us. He put a hand on my arm and I felt his presence in my mind, pushing my thoughts away and replacing them with his own. Blood and revenge were on his mind, and my thoughts echoed his. We would make them pay. We would get it back from them and we would kill them. No, we would torture them first.

"Here," Jared said as he passed the backpack to me. "You should keep this. It has all the ammo in it. You'll need it more than me."

"I thought *you* were here to keep her safe, wolf."

Jared growled behind me. "I am, but that doesn't mean she shouldn't be prepared. I doubt you'll be there to protect her. You only care about yourself."

"You know nothing, wolf."

"Whatever," Jared muttered under his breath as he wrapped an arm around my waist protectively.

I pulled the backpack onto one shoulder and leaned back against him as Henri turned to the control panel and entered a series of numbers. The elevator began moving, and I watched the numbers decrease. We passed the ground floor and the elevator numbers stopped moving, while the elevator continued. I felt the anxious desire for blood well up inside me, and I instinctually knew it was coming from Henri. My mouth watered at the thought of piercing into raw flesh.

The elevator stopped moving and Jared pulled away from me even as I pulled out the Glock. The door swished open and Henri rushed out in a blur of speed. I stepped out, but Jared pushed his way past me. Two men stood before the elevator doors with guns drawn. I had no chance to react as Henri ripped the head off the first man with ruthless efficiency. Jared grabbed the second man and sent him flying into a crumpled heap far down the hallway.

I blinked and followed Henri past the first dead man. His head rolled across the floor and I kicked it casually back to his body. The gun was still in the man's hand, unfired. Both men were dressed in dark suits and shiny black shoes. Jared hurried back to my side as Henri took the lead down the hallway. I knew exactly where he was going. His belongings were in one of these rooms, and he was going to get them back.

These halls looked familiar to me. My short time in captivity under this hotel was in hallways the same as these. Everything was concrete and white, with no discerning features. Henri stalked down the hallway intently, but I held back. The doors all looked the same, and I had to resist the urge to open them and try to find my old room. Were there more people in these rooms being held against their will?

We reached an intersection and I looked right even as Henri marched forward. I knew this place, and I turned down the hallway. Jared stayed beside me, his presence a comfort, as I walked directly to the room Mark had been held in. I opened the door and peered inside, anxious about what I might see. The room was empty, but Jared pushed in beside me, sniffing loudly.

"Mark was here," he said knowingly.

I nodded absently as I turned around and went back into the hallway. The next room was where I had heard the doctor arguing before. I opened the door, but Jared rushed past me before I had stepped inside. The room was obviously an office, and a large table littered with papers took up most of the room. Across those papers was a thick layer of dried blood, but thankfully no body.

I put my gun away as I walked around the desk and began sorting through the papers. A desk plaque indicated this office belonged to a Dr. Maxwell Douglas, and the paperwork scattered on the desk seemed to back that up. I didn't see anything of note in the desk papers, so I started pulling open drawers. Jared stood near the door, watching the hallway while I looked through the office.

The top desk drawers held the usual office supplies, but the large, bottom drawer held a small amount of files. I flipped through the files briefly before grabbing them and joining Jared at the door. He frowned down at the files in my hands as I stuffed them into the backpack.

"What's that?" he whispered.

"I remember this doctor when I was here with Mark. I thought there might be some info from our capture in these files," I responded.

"That doctor's probably dead, if the blood in there is his."

I nodded, sad at the thought, even though I'd never seen or spoken to the man. Had he been killed when Petrivian's men had taken over? "I hope there's something useful in here," I added.

"Don't tell the bloodsucker," Jared muttered as we moved back into the hallway. We turned down the hallway Henri had gone down, and found him in the fourth room on the left.

"There you two are," Henri murmured when we walked into the room.

The room we entered was the one we had observed on the computer. Henri stood at the lab table, carefully placing items into a large, black case. Two men in white lab coats were dead on the ground with their heads turned at unnatural angles. A third man sat on the floor, staring at us with wide eyes.

"What is all this stuff?" I asked, walking around the table. I had been around my brother's science experiments enough to recognize the usual items, but it was the unusual that I was referring to. Silver liquid swirled around in a large, enclosed container. Wires ran from the container to a large battery pack. Henri picked up the container gingerly and placed it into the case along with the battery.

"These are the belongings I was looking for," Henri replied. "Most of them anyway," he added with a sharp look at the man cowering on the floor.

A small beaker of the same gray liquid bubbled over a Bunsen burner on the table. Jared leaned toward it, holding his hand close. A frown marred his forehead as he examined the liquid. "I can feel it," he said softly.

"Feel what?" I asked.

"There's silver in this liquid. It's not all silver, I don't think, but enough," he responded, looking at the remaining scientist.

"Yes, it is primarily a silver alloy mixed with some other ingredients we hadn't quite deciphered," the man muttered.

Henri smiled and nodded his head. "Be glad you didn't," he said as he turned off the burner. "Can't have Petrivian figuring this out."

"What is it?" I asked.

"All in due time," Henri answered as he grabbed the beaker of liquid and stoppered it before shoving it into the case with the rest of the items. "Good thing Petrivian acts first, thinks later."

"What do you mean by that?"

I frowned at Henri and placed my hands on my hips. I was tired of his cryptic responses. Henri glanced at me, grinned, and closed the case before turning toward the scientist. The man scurried away from him, backing himself further into the corner. With one hand, Henri reached out and hoisted the man up onto his feet. The man stumbled back, but Henri struck out with lightning speed. His teeth sunk into the man's throat, but Henri didn't just drink his blood. With a jerk, Henri tore the man's throat open and dropped him to the floor.

I swallowed the bile that rose in my throat, when suddenly Henri was before me, blocking my view. He placed a hand on my arm and I looked up into his brilliant eyes. Blood turned his lips bright red, but I had no time to notice more when his mouth was suddenly on mine. I tried to pull back, but he was in my head, feeding his cravings for blood to me. I swallowed the dead man's salty blood down like it was a fine wine. Jared made a gagging noise behind me, but I ignored him.

Henri pulled back and I licked the remaining blood off my lips. He smiled at me before grabbing the case off the table and heading toward the door. "He didn't answer your questions again, Izzy," Jared said suddenly, startling me out of my stupor.

"What questions?" I asked, looking from Jared to Henri, who had stopped in the doorway.

"About the stuff in that case he carries," Jared prompted.

I stared at Jared, trying to make my muddled brain catch up. I could feel the thoughts there as I looked at Jared. Why couldn't I concentrate properly? Blood, mmm, yes, that was so tasty. What? I shook my head, trying to throw Henri's thoughts out, but they overwhelmed me.

"I will tell Isabella all she needs to know, wolf. Now is not the time or the place," Henri snapped over his shoulder. "There are other vampires still awake, and likely alerted to our presence. We should hurry."

Jared growled, but I put a hand on his shoulder and he quickly quieted down. "Henri, please, tell me," I pleaded. I couldn't remember what I was asking him to tell me about, but it seemed important.

"When Petrivian took over this place, he killed everyone!" Henri roared, and I stumbled back, startled at his sudden outburst. Outwardly, he had appeared so calm, but now I could see it as well as feel it in his presence in my mind. "He killed my researchers, my pets, and my experiments! That was a big mistake for him, and he will pay for it in the end. My research will ensure it! That is all you need to know!"

I stared at him, wide-eyed, fearful of the anger radiating from Henri. Jared touched my hand with his and took a small step forward, partially blocking me from Henri. "When you say pets, I'm assuming you don't mean cats and dogs," Jared said softly.

"Do not confuse me with Sarah," Henri replied acidly. "Yes, I mean my human pets, but I assure you they were well taken care of.

They lived long, happy lives here, serving me. They wanted for nothing."

"And your experiments?" Jared urged.

Henri smiled smugly, but I could still sense the anger radiating from him. "I'll have to start all over with new experiments."

"You mean people. You're a monster."

Henri laughed, but there was no humor in it. "I believe we've had this talk before, wolf. You are just as much a monster as I am."

"No, I'm not."

"Not yet."

"We've stayed with you far too long. Izzy, let's go," Jared said. He grabbed my arm and tugged past Henri into the hallway.

"Isabella, you will stay with me," Henri ordered.

I stopped in my tracks, with Jared tugging on my arm. He stopped and looked back at me, and I read the worry and fear there. "Izzy, please, just come with me."

"I'm staying with Henri," I replied, slipping my hand out of Jared's grip. Jared growled and his eyes turned yellow, indicating his rising wolf. He dropped the laptop he'd still been carrying as his hands elongated and morphed. Fur began to quickly cover his skin, changing him from human to wolf.

"Isabella, take out your gun," Henri ordered. The gun slipped into my hand easily, and I stood waiting for his next order. "Put the barrel in your mouth. If Jared attacks me, you will pull the trigger."

The gun tasted of metal as I held it in my mouth. I could feel Henri's orders pressing at me as I watched Jared. I struggled to pull the gun from my mouth, but it was as though I had no control over my own body. Even my thoughts were a jumble. Part of me wanted to obey Henri, while the other part of me wanted to pull the gun free and shoot Henri with it. My leg pulsed again, and that invisible pressure urged me to pull the gun away.

"Stop," Jared panted, and I focused on him. His eyes were still yellow, but the fur had already disappeared. "Damn it, stop!"

Henri smiled wickedly and shrugged, as though nothing was of consequence. "Isabella, remove the gun from your mouth. Jared won't hurt me, will you Jared?" Jared shook his head as I pulled the gun from my mouth. "Let's make things interesting, wolf. Isabella, point your gun at Jared. How do you think Isabella will feel if your death is on her hands? Would she mourn you? Would she feel so guilty she took her own life?"

I turned the gun toward Jared, my hands shaking. No, I didn't want to do this. "Please," I squeaked out, but no one was listening to me. Both men stared at each other, sizing the other up.

"I have left you alone, wolf, but you push things too far."

"No, you do!" Jared shouted back.

Henri laughed again, and I could feel his confidence. He knew exactly what he was doing. "When I leave this place, Isabella will come with me. You have three choices. Either you come with us, you stay and be Sarah's plaything, or you die. What'll it be?"

"You know I won't leave Isabella."

"I'm counting on it," Henri replied smugly. "You wanted to know what was in this case, so I will show you. You will be my next experiment, and Isabella will be a treasured goddess at my side. Life can be good, wolf. I treat my things well."

Jared stood still, turning only his eyes toward me. "I will stay with Isabella," he replied softly, his shoulders dropping in defeat.

"I thought you might decide that. Isabella, you can put your gun away. You shouldn't need it now."

I holstered my gun and Jared picked the small laptop up off the ground. Henri turned and walked through the doorway, with us on his heels. A part of me felt thankful that I hadn't been forced to shoot Jared, but the other part of me yearned for blood. Deep inside, I knew that other part was Henri. We had shared too much blood, and I was his now. I had been warned, but I hadn't listened. The thought drifted away as Henri took my hand. I smiled up at him, admiring his strong jawline and piercing blue eyes.

"Where are we going now?" I asked as I adjusted the backpack on my shoulder.

"We have some revenge to take care of," Henri responded with a laugh. "Let's go find Sarah's location."

"Finally something we agree on," Jared murmured from beside me. I looked into Jared's yellow wolf eyes and smiled. Yes, revenge was something we all wanted.

Chapter 20

We wound our way through the hallways, following Henri's lead. He led us to another office, where we were able to hook the laptop up as we had in Henri's apartment. Henri clicked through the surveillance video until he found Sarah's location. She was in the dungeons where we had found Henri, and she was still awake, along with several other vampires and humans with guns. A new victim was hooked to the device Henri had been in, and he didn't appear to be enjoying himself.

"The sun grows higher. She won't be there for much longer," Henri mused as he clicked past several screens. The hallways leading to Sarah were filled with hired guns, mostly human. "We can sneak past her and make our way back to the house."

"No," Jared said immediately, shaking his head. "This may be my only chance to take the bitch out. I'm not going to miss it."

"Aren't you concerned about Isabella's safety?" Henri asked, turning toward Jared.

Jared clenched his jaw in anger, and I set a comforting hand on his arm. "Sarah needs to pay," I stated, looking back at Henri. "I'll stay back, but we're taking care of her now. We already agreed on this."

A grin spread across Henri's face as he looked at me. "Good. I have some payback of my own for her."

"She's mine," Jared growled.

"Now, now, wolf, you must learn to share," Henri replied with a chuckle. He turned toward the computer screen once more, clicking his way down corridors. More men were hurrying toward the dungeons, and taking up critical positions along the way. "She's expecting us to come for her. She never kept more than a few bodyguards before."

"We should hurry, before more arrive," I mused, anxious to fight Sarah. I could feel Henri's excitement echoing in my mind.

"We don't want to be flanked," Jared commented, pointing out adjoining corridors. "Check there."

"They won't come from that direction, wolf," Henri argued as he started closing the laptop.

Jared grabbed the computer, stopping Henri. "Check the corridor."

Henri sighed loudly, but opened the computer and clicked through the corridors. "See, wolf, they won't come from that direction."

"Where does that go?" I asked, leaning around the two men to peer at the screen. The corridors appeared to go deeper underground, past the reach of surveillance.

"Another safe house."

"There are more? Yet you never mentioned it. Why am I not surprised?" Jared added.

"You didn't really think that was my only escape route, did you? We will be leaving by a different path. I wouldn't want to run into your Pack in broad daylight, after all."

"My Pack?"

Henri turned toward Jared and shook his head. "Now, now, wolf, do not lie to me. You have been conversing with your Alpha. I'm sure your plot to meet up would have been a grand one, but I have always had a different plan in mind. Your cell phone won't work below the hotel levels, so don't bother trying to update him. Unless you plan to run upstairs, but that would mean leaving Isabella behind."

"Damn," Jared murmured, his eyes flashing toward me in worry.

"Not to worry, wolf. We'll meet with your Alpha in due time. For now, I have a better suggestion."

"And what's that?" Jared sneered.

"Kill Sarah, of course," Henri replied with a shrug as he picked up his black case and strode out of the room. Jared exchanged a quick glance with me before we both followed Henri into the hallway.

Jared stayed close to my side as we followed Henri's lead. His eyes remained yellow, but I wasn't too worried about Jared losing control. "Why didn't you tell me?" I asked while we were still on the upper levels. I knew there wouldn't be time to speak soon, and Henri was too preoccupied to fill my mind with his own thoughts.

"You mean that I was talking to Jed?" Jared asked, and I nodded. "Because you're under the vampire's control, that's why."

"No, I'm not, Jared."

"You almost killed yourself because he told you to stick a gun in your mouth. He's controlling you!"

"What are you talking about?" I asked, confused.

"You don't remember?"

I shook my head. "I think I'd remember something like that," I replied.

"Damn, it's worse than I thought."

"What's worse?"

"Nothing," Jared murmured, shaking his head. He stopped in his tracks and grabbed me by both arms, turning me towards him. "Don't forget me," he said softly, and I felt a lump in my throat at his words. Without warning, he pulled me toward him and kissed me.

"Wolf!" Henri barked.

Jared pulled away and looked down at me. His yellow eyes

were moist and he smiled weakly down at me. "Izzy?"

"This isn't a fairy tale. A kiss doesn't break the spell, wolf," Henri murmured as he grabbed my arm and pulled me away from Jared. "Nice try, though."

I stumbled behind Henri, and he released my arm. "What was that all about?" I asked Jared as he came up beside me.

"The wolf thinks you're under my spell," Henri answered for Jared.

"Jared, it's not like that," I said softly. "I mean, I guess it's sort of like a spell."

"Hah!" Jared shouted in triumph, but I laid a soft hand on his arm. He didn't understand what I was trying to tell him.

"Jared, being in love is like a spell."

"Love?"

I smiled at Jared, feeling sad that he didn't understand what I was feeling. "Jared, I'm in love with Henri. I'd do anything for him."

Jared's face fell, and I felt sorry for him. Had he developed feelings for me stronger than friendship? "Izzy, you don't love him. He's manipulating you. Can't you see it? He's controlling you with that damn vampire blood."

"Oh, Jared."

"Enough," Henri cut in. "We are almost to the dungeons. No talking from now on."

I clamped my mouth shut and nodded in response. Henri and Jared both had their game faces on, and seemed ready. I pulled the Glock out and adjusted the pack on my back. We reached the end of the hall we were in and Henri opened the door, revealing a set of steep stairs going down. I followed Henri, with Jared close by my side, as we descended toward the dungeons.

At the bottom of the stairs, Henri stopped to listen, cocking his head to one side. After a moment, he took the left corridor, motioning us to follow him. The lights in the halls dimmed as we descended further, making it difficult to follow Henri in his black clothes. His pale skin and blond hair were the only things visible to my human eyes.

We moved quickly, and I found myself struggling to keep up with the vampire and werewolf. The floor and walls shifted from tile to stone, and I knew we were getting close to the dungeons. Henri had no trouble finding his way down the twisting corridors, and he led us swiftly deeper underground until he finally stopped and waited for me to catch up.

Henri pulled me in close, placing his mouth to my ear as he spoke. I could feel Jared leaning in close as well to hear. "This corridor reaches a juncture up ahead, and there are seven human men waiting for us."

Jared sniffed the air and leaned his mouth next to my other ear. "I smell vampires too, but I can't tell how many."

"Yes, there are vampires as well. The wolf and I will rush ahead and defuse the situation. I want you to stay here and shoot anything that comes down that hallway," Henri added. I opened my mouth to respond, but found I was unable to speak. "Go ahead and speak, quietly."

"I don't want to accidentally shoot you," I said softly.

"You won't," Henri replied. "I'll call for you when it is safe to follow. Bring the case."

Henri set the case down on the ground beside me and rushed off in a blur. Jared hesitated before pulling me into his arms and pressing his mouth to my ear once again. "Your knife is in the bag," he whispered into my ear, and I felt a throbbing in my thigh in response. I reached my free hand back, touching the bag. "Put it on, Izzy. Do it for me."

Jared didn't give me a chance to respond as he raced after Henri down the corridor. I hesitated, unsure what to do. My leg thrummed and tingled where the knife usually rested. Why did Jared have the knife? I had purposely left it behind because it had been causing me to do strange things. But, maybe it hadn't.

I backed myself up to the wall and pulled the bag off my shoulder. The hall was too dimly lit for me to see more than five feet in front of me and I worried I wouldn't be able to react in time. Jared didn't ask me for much though. I pulled the bag open and reached my hand in, thinking I'd have to dig around to find the knife, but it came to my hand easily.

I awkwardly pulled the knife out with my left hand and held it up. The knife felt warm in my hand, and strangely comforting. I had a moment of indecision, holding the knife in one hand and the gun in the other. There was no sound coming from the direction the men had gone, and I took that as a good sign. I put the Glock back in the holster so I could use both hands to strap the knife to my side.

As soon as the knife was in place, I felt warmth radiate across my body. The knife throbbed suddenly, jolting me with an electric shock. I pulled the Glock out of its holster and leveled it down the darkened hallway as instinct took over. Several seconds passed as I strained to see or hear down the corridor. A faint breeze tickled my cheek and I pulled the trigger repeatedly on impulse. By the time I emptied my clip, the vampire was dead at my feet. I quickly reached into the pack and replaced clips in the Glock before leveling it down the corridor once more.

"Isabella, it is safe now. Bring the case," Henri ordered.

I holstered the gun, slung the pack across one shoulder, and picked up the case before walking toward the sound of Henri's voice. The urge to obey him was overwhelming and my feet moved of their own accord toward the vampire. Henri waited for me further down the passage, where the halls intersected. Human body parts littered the ground down each corridor. I counted three piles of ash as well, indicating dead vampires.

"Where's Jared?" I asked worriedly, looking down each hallway in turn for the werewolf.

"He's having wolf difficulties," Henri responded.

"What does that mean? If he's having trouble controlling his wolf, I can help him."

"Do not worry about it," Henri stated irritably as he pulled the case from my hand. I let go and frowned up at him, ready to argue further, but the words died on my tongue. Jared needed me, and Henri was telling me not to worry about it! I was worrying about it. "He'll catch up. Let's go."

I clamped my mouth shut and followed Henri down the left corridor. More body parts littered the ground and I worried Henri had injured Jared while I'd been out of sight. Henri stopped suddenly and I held my breath, listening for danger.

"I have not harmed the wolf. Stop worrying about him," Henri said harshly, and I realized he'd been invading my thoughts.

Henri moved in close and stared down at me with his piercing blue eyes. Blood coated his lips red, and I realized he'd likely fed off the humans. Of course he had fed off them. He's a vampire, after all. Isn't that was vampires did? They fed, they consumed, and they took control. My mind spun as I felt Henri press his thoughts into me, and pull the stray thoughts from my brain. I needed to be more careful.

"What do you need to be careful of?" he asked sharply.

"Vampires," I responded automatically. "I can't see or hear as far as you can and one could easily sneak up on me."

Henri smiled and ran a hand through my short hair. "I will protect you. We must hurry though," he added, his eyes sighting down the corridor behind me. "The wolf comes."

My lips twitched into a smile, but I quickly turned my face so Henri wouldn't see my reaction. Jared raced into view, his yellow eyes glowing brightly. He was still in human form, but thick hair covered his arms and I doubted he'd stay human for much longer. Henri yanked on my arm, pulling me after him down the corridor. As soon as I turned to follow him, Henri released my arm and hurried ahead.

I had only gone a few steps when Jared rushed by me, growling. The hair stood up on my arms at the sound and I stopped in my tracks, straining all my senses. Sweat coated my palms as I gripped the gun, waiting for someone or something to jump out at me. After several minutes, Jared called to me and I hurried down the hall toward the sound of his voice.

I followed the trail of dead bodies until I reached Jared. Sweat covered his forehead and drenched his shirt, and I knew his hold on humanity was waning. He said nothing as he turned and led me down the hallway. I kept my gun in hand, but my eyes darted worriedly to Jared. Long claws tipped his fingers and he ran hunched over, as though he was ready to run on all fours at any moment.

Jared sprinted ahead without a word, and I ran after him. The sound of fighting stopped me in my tracks, and I realized it was probably a bad idea to be chasing after the werewolf. The sound of gunfire dropped me to my knees, and I backed up quickly. The corridor ahead of me was empty, but I could hear the fighting nearby. I inched forward, crawling toward the sounds of battle with the Glock held in front of me.

As I crawled closer, I realized the fighting was from a side passage to the right. I clung to the wall as I inched forward. A gunshot ran out again, and I stopped my progress. What was I doing? Fear held me against the wall. The gun grew slick in my hand from sweat, and I quickly wiped my hand on my pants.

Tears welled in my eyes as another shot rang out. What could I do? I was just a stupid, measly human. The knife pulsed against my thigh, sending jolts of electricity up my body and startling me out of the fear that had been closing in around me. Hadn't I already killed a vampire? I had stood toe to toe with a blood-sucking creature of the night, and come out the other side. Slowly I stood, gathering my courage. I may be human, but I wasn't going to be a victim any longer. I would fight, or die trying.

I moved forward and peeked quickly around the corner, surveying the situation. My mind couldn't make sense of the chaos in the corridor, and I wasn't going to stand around trying. I stepped forward, aiming my gun at the first man I saw. The vampire jerked as the holy bullets hit him in the back, knocking him to the floor in a pile of dust. I sighted on the next man and pulled the trigger, wincing as blood spurted from his leg when my bullet hit him. The man turned toward me with a gun in hand. My hesitance at shooting a human evaporated quickly at the sight of the gun, and I pulled the trigger again, making sure I aimed for his chest.

The bullet took him in the shoulder and he dropped the gun, clutching at his wound in surprise. He dropped to the ground, and I hurried past him toward the sounds of distant fighting. My eyes skimmed over the blood that coated the floor and walls as I raced down the hall with the pack bouncing on my back. I stopped at an intersection, looking both ways. Dead bodies littered the floor, but I didn't care about the dead. The living was all that interested me.

The sound of howling urged me toward the right pathway and I ran ahead. By the time I reached the next intersection there were only dead bodies to greet me. I paused once more, listening for sounds of fighting as I caught my breath. Gunshots rang out, and I followed the sound once more.

I wandered down the paths, chasing sounds and arriving too late every time. My legs ached and my side burned, but I pushed myself on. I didn't see any piles of ash, but the floor was covered in slick, red blood. I jumped over dead men and slid on blood and entrails until I skidded around a corner and came face to face with a very large werewolf. The wolf turned his massive head toward me and dropped the arm he had in his mouth.

The wolf's fur was brown and white, and blood dripped from its muzzle. He moved toward me, and I froze in fear. I knew the wolf was Jared, but I wasn't sure if the wolf knew that. The wolf stepped toward me, then stopped, turning to look behind him. He turned and ran, his claws clicking on the stone floor as he raced toward the vampire down the hallway.

I paused for only a second before chasing after the werewolf. The vampire's eyes widened in recognition, before he turned on his heels and raced away. My lungs burned with exertion, but I pursued him with all my waning strength. That vampire would lead us back to Sarah. The vampire and werewolf were both soon out of sight, but I hurried after them. I reached an intersection and stopped, wondering which way to go. The knife pulsed on my thigh, and I suddenly knew. I turned left and stopped thinking about where I was going and what I was doing, letting the knife guide me toward the vampire. Jin would die first, followed by Sarah.

Chapter 21

The corridors twisted and turned and I wondered if I was going the right way due to the lack of dead bodies. That thought died quickly when I raced around a corner right into two men in suits, who seemed just as startled to see me as I was to see them. They raised their guns, but I moved faster, sending a flurry of bullets into their bodies. They dropped to the ground without firing a shot, and I quickly switched guns to the Browning.

I had barely pulled the gun out, when a vampire was on top of me. I fired off a round, but the vampire grabbed my arm, pulling it out of the shoulder socket with a loud pop. I screamed and dropped the gun, but the vampire held tight to my arm. He tossed me through the air and I curled my body, ready for impact. My back hit something soft and I rolled to the side as Jared in wolf form moved in front of me, ready to meet the threat.

The vampire was dressed in a black suit, much like the humans, but his pale skin was a dead giveaway that he was not human. His superhuman strength and fangs were also a pretty good indicator. Jared and the vampire rushed toward each other, but I couldn't follow their actions with my eyes. I scooted away before standing and looking around. Jin was nowhere to be seen, but there was a distinct pile of dust in the middle of the room. No way to know which vampire it belonged to though.

Jared snarled loudly and I whipped my head back toward the fight. The wolf had the vampire on the ground; his powerful jaws crushing his throat. With a sickening snap, the vampire's head detached from his body. The werewolf tossed the head to the side, and I watched as the vampire's body slowly began to disintegrate.

I walked past Jared and retrieved my gun, using my left hand to pick it up. The wolf waited for me, his golden eyes watching me intently. "Where's Jin?" I asked, not sure if Jared would understand me or not.

The big wolf turned and loped down the hallway before pausing to look back at me. I smiled and walked past the dead vampire, who was quickly turning to ash. The wolf continued down the corridor, leading me to another juncture. He stopped there and looked up at me. The knife pulsed against my thigh, and I knew there were vampires to my left. I started to turn, but Jared moved in front of me, stopping me with his massive body.

"Jared, what is it?"

The wolf moved around me and snagged the pack with his teeth, pulling it from my back. I winced as the bag jarred my shoulder, but I let it drop to the ground. He nudged the pack with his nose and looked up at me expectantly.

I knelt down and opened it up, wondering what a werewolf would need from a backpack full of ammo. "I have the knife on, Jared," I said softly, wondering if that's what he was looking for.

The wolf regarded me, and I imagined he could understand my words. He nudged the pack with his nose and looked up at me again. I sighed and holstered my gun before digging through the bag. I wasn't sure what Jared wanted me to find, as I pulled out the extra ammo he had packed. My hand grasped something that wasn't ammo and I hauled it out.

The small, gray cell phone was simple, but I recognized it

from the cottage. So, this was how Jared had been communicating with Jed. There was no signal on the phone since we were underground, but I'd hang onto it for later. I shoved the phone in the pocket of my pants and grabbed a replacement clip for the Glock before pushing the ammo back into the pack on top of the papers I had taken from Dr. Douglas's office. I swapped clips and replaced the Glock on my side before carefully pulling the pack over my shoulders again. With my left hand, I grabbed the Browning and stood up.

"No cell signal underground, Jared." The wolf growled and turned down the opposite corridor. "That's not where the vampires are," I stated. Jared shook his head and spun in a circle before turning toward the same corridor again.

"Isabella," Henri said, startling me. I turned toward the corridor I had sensed vampires down to see Henri walking toward me. I took in his appearance, noting the absence of the black case he had been carrying. Other than a light dusting of ash on his shoes, Henri looked immaculate.

"Henri, there you are," I said as though I'd been looking for him.

"I have cleared the way to Sarah. She and several other vampires are in the dungeons she kept me in. Let us finish this," Henri stated.

"What's that direction?" I asked, pointing toward the path Jared had been indicating.

Henri glanced at the werewolf and back at me, a scowl marring his handsome face. "That leads to the safe house, and the werewolf Pack. We are not going that way. Come, Isabella," Henri ordered. I felt his words press against my skin, urging me to obey.

I walked toward him, even though I didn't want to. The Pack was nearby? Jared had been trying to tell me, but it was too late to figure it out now. I stopped beside Henri, wincing as he grabbed my injured arm. He frowned down at me, his eyes roaming across my body.

"My shoulder," I muttered, nodding toward my injured arm.

Henri ran his hands across my shoulder and I bit down to keep from crying out in pain. He grasped my arm and jerked, popping it back into place. I cried out in pain, feeling tears well in my eyes. "Best to have you in working condition," he said as he bit his wrist and held it in front of me. I hesitated, finding the thought of drinking his blood repulsive. Henri glowered, but I grabbed his arm, smiled and pressed his wrist to my mouth, feigning eagerness.

The blood welled in my mouth, and I swallowed it down, feeling the healing benefits react quickly. With the blood, I felt Henri's presence strengthen in my mind, while the knife on my side pulsed angrily. I pulled away and licked my lips before transferring the gun to my right hand. "Let's go kill a vampire," I said with a grin.

"Yes, let's," Henri replied as he turned and led us down the passageway.

I hurried after Henri and placed myself by his side. He looked down at me and smiled, and I felt a returning smile plaster across my face. The knife burned against my thigh, reminding me there were vampires nearby. Of course, there was a vampire right beside me. Three months ago, that would have scared me. It should still scare me.

I felt stronger and more certain of myself than ever before. Henri's blood coursed through my body, invigorating and strengthening me, but I wasn't sure if that was the source of my confidence. The knife pulsed on my side, as though reminding me of its presence. Was the knife making me confident? Jared loped along on the other side of me, and I grinned widely. I had a vampire on one side, a werewolf on the other, and a mystical vampire-killing knife strapped to my thigh. No wonder I felt confident. The smile slipped from my face as we turned down the narrow corridor toward Henri's old cell.

Three vampires waited for us, with Jin in the forefront. He smiled maniacally at us before charging toward us at top speed. I was faster than a normal human was, but I had barely raised my gun when

Henri and Jared both moved. Henri raced forward, knocking Jin backward before barreling toward the next vampire. Jared growled and pounced on Jin, tearing at his throat in a matter of seconds. I squeezed the trigger on the Browning, sending a stream of bullets down the corridor.

The third vampire ignored me and focused on Jared. He lifted the massive werewolf off Jin and tossed him into the wall. I emptied my clip at the vampire, but he seemed unfazed as he turned and stalked toward Jared. The Browning was empty, so I holstered it and pulled out the more powerful Glock. I aimed at the vampire's chest and only managed to fire off one round before I was knocked off my feet.

I landed with a thud against the ground and stared up at the ceiling, trying to regain the ability to breath. Hands grabbed my ankles and pulled me up into the air. I twisted and turned, struggling to detach myself as the blood rushed to my head. A loud growl raised the hair on the back of my neck, and I braced myself for impact as the large wolf leapt at the vampire holding me.

The wolf knocked the vampire backward, taking me with him. I dropped to the ground again, but I was prepared this time and rolled out of the fall. Somehow, I had managed to hang on to the Glock, and I aimed it at the vampire. There was no need though, as Jared ripped into the vampire's throat. The wolf shook his massive head, tossing the vampire back and forth. He finally dropped the remnants of the vampire and looked up at me.

I slowly walked forward, examining the holes in the vamp's chest before he disintegrated. "Why didn't he die when I shot him? I emptied the entire clip into him," I added, pointing at the many holes in the vampire's chest. My aim had definitely improved.

"My guess is those bullets weren't blessed. Let me see your extra ammunition in the pack," Henri ordered.

Jared growled, obviously not wanting me to hand the bag over the vampire, but I didn't have a choice. My hands moved as though pulled on puppet strings as I handed the pack to Henri. He smiled at me and took the proffered bag, opening it gingerly as though he expected a snake to jump out. The bag didn't contain anything but ammo and the paperwork I had taken from Doctor Douglas, so I wasn't too concerned. Henri ignored the papers and pulled the box of Browning ammo out, lightly touching it with his fingers. Nothing happened, and he dropped it back into the bag before pulling out one of the pre-loaded clips. This time when he touched the first bullet, he immediately jerked back as though stung.

"Not all of these are blessed," Henri mused as he handed me the clip in his hand. "This one is. Use it well."

I took the clip and reloaded the Browning while Henri continued to rifle through the bag. After several minutes, he came up with another clip for each gun and handed them to me. I shoved the clips into my pockets and Henri tossed my pack onto the ground. Jared growled, but I understood. Down the hall was a room full of vampires. I wouldn't have time to search through my bag for an extra clip.

"Sarah is waiting for us," Henri stated, and I looked up into his blue eyes. I felt Henri's anger well up inside me, and my own anger echoed his. "Stay back and wait for my move. I'll go in on the right and the wolf can take the left. Don't trust your eyes. Trust me, and your instincts."

Henri turned and walked down the hall toward the dungeon room. I followed him, walking past the remnants of three vampires. Jared had killed two vampires, Henri had killed one, and I'd managed not to die. My confidence wasn't high as Henri reached the metal door and pulled it open.

"Ah, there you are," Sarah drawled as soon as the door was open. I shivered at the sound of her voice. It was like fingernails on a chalkboard.

Henri moved past me, followed closely by Jared. As soon as they entered, I followed behind them, quickly taking in the cell. The smell of lavender was thick in the room, coming from several tall candles Sarah had placed along the walls. A dozen vampires stood around the room, all dressed in black suits, with their pale faces turned toward us. In the middle of the room was my brother's ex-girlfriend.

Sarah was completely naked except for a pair of knee-high pink boots and a bright pink headband in her thick blonde hair. The man she was currently torturing was held off the ground by chains, much as Henri had been. Sarah held a small whip in her hand as she straddled the man. Blood poured from small cuts across his body, but he was very much alive and awake. His wide eyes stared at us in fear.

"Haven't you come up with any new games, Sarah?" Henri asked as he walked further into the room.

Sarah's eyes flashed in anger, but she quickly changed it to a smile as she thrust her body into the man. He cried out, and I realized exactly where she was straddling him. My face flushed even as I tried to concentrate on the danger and not on the fact that Sarah was having sex with her captive.

"As I recall, you liked my games, Henri," Sarah replied as she began riding the man with renewed intensity. She stopped talking as she thrust against the man with vampire speed, until he screamed loudly. Sarah stopped and moved off the man, staring down at him in disgust. "Damn humans. They just can't wait!"

"Really, Sarah, he is just a human," Henri stated as he crossed his arms over his chest.

Sarah sauntered toward Henri, but her eyes flicked toward me. The room changed suddenly, and we were all on a sandy beach with a bright sun shining down and a vast ocean beyond. The door leading back out was still visible, looking odd in the middle of sand. Several of the vampires panicked and ran out of the room in a flurry of screams. Henri laughed loudly as Sarah stomped her foot in anger.

The scene melted away, turning the room into a nightclub, complete with booming music and strobe lights. "Stop it!" Sarah screeched, stomping her foot again like a petulant child. "I said, stop!"

"We're going to play my games this time," Henri responded as he stalked toward Sarah.

Several of the vampires moved in closer, but Sarah held up a hand stopping them. Her demeanor changed as Henri drew closer. She arched her back, pushing her breasts out. Henri reached out and grabbed her around the waist, drawing her close to his body.

"Do it," Sarah said breathlessly, her hands snaking up his chest. "Fuck me hard. Just like last time. Hard. Fuck me hard!"

Jared growled beside me, but I couldn't take my eyes off Henri and Sarah. Her words echoed in my mind. *Fuck me hard.* I had never uttered such words in my life, until the incident with Lucas. I had said those exact words. Damn!

"Fucking vampires," I muttered, pointing my gun at the two in the center of the room. Which one did I shoot first?

Henri cast a frown at me over his shoulder, and I felt his thoughts in my mind. "Isabella, wait for my move. Lower the gun."

His order pressed in on me, and I lowered my arms. Fucking vampires! Henri turned back toward Sarah, pulled her against his body, and kissed her. Eww! I cringed, watching as he groped her breasts with one hand. After several disgusting seconds, he pulled away from the kiss and looked down at her. "YOU ARE WORTHLESS," he stated, biting off each word as he shoved her backward.

She stumbled and glared up at Henri angrily. "Fuck you!" she screeched.

"We already did that, you sadistic bitch. You are nothing but Petrivian's whore."

Sarah screeched again and ran at Henri, but he moved with lightning speed toward the right, grabbing one of the other vampires and tossing him at Sarah. Henri raced toward the next vampire while Sarah was distracted. Jared bolted to the left, leaping on the first vampire who came toward him. I took that as my cue and raised my gun, firing in Sarah's direction.

The scene shifted again, and bright sunlight glared down on us. Several of the vampires screamed in surprise, covering their faces. I took advantage of their distraction and opened fire, emptying my first clip in the Glock and quickly replacing it. In the blink of an eye, the bright sunlight disappeared and we were left in utter darkness.

I stopped firing and backed up until I felt the dungeon door behind me. Growls rose from my left and the sounds of more fighting came from the right. Jared was left, so I figured I could safely shoot toward the right. I opened fire, taking intense satisfaction at the sound of screaming vampires. My second clip empty, I switched to the Browning and waited.

The room changed once more, and we were back on the sunlit beach. To my left, Jared was corned between two vampires. I didn't hesitate before firing on the closest one, freeing Jared up to take care of the other one as I examined the room. Three vampires had Henri surrounded, but it was the two vampires stalking toward me that I was worried about. They moved as a team, both rushing at me. I fired the gun repeatedly; hoping some of my bullets hit their target.

The beach vanished and suddenly we were in space, with nothing beneath our feet and only a vague sense of light illuminating the area. One of the vampires dropped, his body turning to ash. The other grasped the single bullet wound in his chest, desperately trying to claw the holy bullet out before he turned to ash as well. I fired again, this time taking the vampire in the head. His eyes opened wide in surprise as the hole in his head burned him from the inside out.

The room changed again until we were back in the dungeon. Henri stalked toward me, ash coating the front of his black shirt. "Sarah ran out," he stated bluntly. Jared loped beside me and we followed Henri into the next room, where Sarah stood waiting for us.

"Damn you, Henri," Sarah said as she stalked back and forth. "Those were some of my best men."

"That was your best? Pretty pathetic," I commented. Jared snorted beside me in what I could only guess was a werewolf's version of a laugh. I reached out and rested my hand on his head, running my fingers through the thick fur.

"Who's your pet, Izzy?" Sarah asked, looking down at Jared.

Jared growled in response, sending shivers down my spine. "You remember Jared, don't you Sarah?"

Sarah glanced at me sharply and I smiled at the sudden worry etched on her face. "I'm going to drain your blood until..." she began.

Jared pounced, knocking Sarah off her feet and cutting off her words. His massive jaws clamped around her throat even as she thrashed around, attempting to dislodge him. Jared's claws pressed into her flesh as he held her down with his massive body. Henri moved in close to me, putting a hand on my cheek. I cut a glance to him, wondering why he wasn't attacking Sarah.

"Put in this clip, Izzy," Henri ordered as he held a clip for the Browning out to me. His fingers brushed along the bullets, but they didn't seem to bother him. I pulled the clip out, which still had several bullets in it, and took the clip from Henri's hands. "Hurry now," Henri ordered, and I pushed the new clip into place even as the knife grew warm on my side.

I looked back at Jared, who still maintained his grip around Sarah's throat. She had her hands in his fir, sending streams of blood down his body. They were too close together. If I shot at Sarah, I might hit Jared. "Help him," I said to Henri. "I thought you wanted to kill Sarah too."

"He's doing a good job," Henri mused as he touched my cheek again. "You want to help though, so go ahead. Shoot, Isabella."

"But I might hit Jared."

"The wolf is more trouble than he's worth. Shoot him," Henri ordered. I stared up at Henri, watching in horror as his eyes turned from blue to black in the blink of an eye. His hand ran across my cheek and gripped the back of my neck. His fingers pressed into my skin as he turned my face toward his. "Take your gun, aim it at the wolf, and pull the trigger."

Henri's orders sank in and my arms moved of their own accord. No, I wouldn't shoot Jared. My hands shook as I held the gun in hand. "No, please. I can't shoot him."

"Do not disobey me, Isabella. You will shoot him."

The knife pulsed on my side and unshed tears blurred my vision. "I can't."

"Oh, you can and you will. Fire the gun, now!"

My finger pulled the trigger, and I jerked. The shot went wide, hitting the far end of the room. Jared snarled and pushed Sarah across the room, digging his claws into her stomach. "Fire!" Henri ordered, and I pulled the trigger again.

This time, the shot hit closer to Jared, but still missed him. "Please, Henri, don't make me do this."

Henri squeezed the back of my neck and pushed me in front of him. His mouth found my ear, and he spoke in a harsh whisper. "I will fix this disobedience once and for all. You will aim the gun at the wolf and pull the trigger. Those are silver bullets, Isabella. He will die. Then you will come with me and be my queen. We will crush Petrivian. We will conquer the werewolves. I will rule over all, and you will sit on top of the world at my side." Tears washed down my cheeks at his words. I could feel him imposing his will on me, and I was slowly losing the battle. "Shoot the wolf!"

I stared down at Jared as he struggled against Sarah. Blood was pouring from his body, but he still hung on. He bit down again, and I heard a loud crunch as he broke the bones in her neck with his bite. Sarah screamed one last time as the werewolf's jaws clamped down further. With a loud growl, he ripped her head from her body. Henri's order pressed in on me, and my finger pulled the trigger, sending the first bullet into Jared's leg.

Jared whimpered and looked back at me, his yellow wolf eyes staring at me in surprise. "Jared, I'm so sorry," I said as I pulled the trigger again.

Jared's body bucked as the bullet struck him, and he collapsed on top of the remnants of Sarah's body. Tears filled my eyes as I stared at my friend. "Very good, Isabella," Henri said as he removed his hands from my neck. "Follow me."

I holstered the gun and followed him out of the room, stepping past Jared's bleeding werewolf form. Henri walked several paces ahead of me, knowing I would follow him. I paused in the hallway to glance back at Jared, praying my aim had been good. He opened his eyes and looked at me, then quickly blinked his left eye. I felt a small flutter of relief, but I quickly squashed it back down before Henri sensed anything.

I hurried after Henri until I was beside him. He glanced down at me, but didn't say a word as we made our way to the next corridor. I retrieved my backpack and slung it over my shoulders before continuing. The next hallway had several cells, and Henri stopped in the first one to retrieve the case he had left there. We continued rapidly down new corridors, leading away from the stone-covered halls.

Within minutes, I was completely lost. The paths twisted and turned, descending rapidly deeper underground. The halls changed to dirt, and I had to grip the back of Henri's shirt to continue as we left the lit pathways. Onward we traveled, down corridors that pressed around us and forced us to walk in a crouch until Henri finally stopped.

I still couldn't see anything, so I had to wait and listen. Henri banged against something in front of him, and dirt rained down on my head, choking me. I coughed, covering my face as more dirt fell on top of me. Fear of being trapped had my heart racing. I released the back of Henri's shirt, and began inching my way backward.

Henri continued his pounding, and more dirt fell down. I backed up faster, afraid the tunnel would cave in. When the tunnel widened, I turned and began hurrying down it, keeping my hands stretched out in front of me. A hand grabbed my arm, stopping me in my tracks.

"Isabella, what are you doing?" Henri asked, his voice sounding irritated.

"Running for my life! Are you done trying to cave in the tunnel?" I retorted, turning toward the sound of his voice.

Henri sighed loudly and tugged on my arm, pulling him back behind me. "I wasn't caving in the tunnel."

I didn't respond as Henri tugged me behind him back down the narrow tunnel. He stopped and released my hand before disappearing. I waited, reaching out my hands to feel only empty air. Hands gripped my outstretched arms, and I was suddenly pulled upwards. I squeaked in surprise, until my feet were back on solid ground.

Henri gripped my hand again, and led me behind him. The air smelled different, almost stale, but not like the dirt tunnels we had just been in. Henri pulled me behind him swiftly, but I reached my free hand out to the side to feel for the wall. The walls were hard, like wood, and the corridors were tall enough to walk upright in.

We travelled on, winding our way in the darkness upward. My legs ached as we continued, but I said nothing of my discomfort. After what felt like an hour, we came to a steep set of stairs. At the top of the steps, Henri knocked on something. A responding knock came from the wall, which suddenly opened to reveal a door.

Henri pulled me through behind him, and I looked around at our new surroundings. We were in a large room that I guessed was a basement by the concrete floor and the rickety stairs leading upward. We weren't alone in the room, and the man who greeted us was not someone I was expecting to see.

"Is the car ready?" Henri asked.

"Yes, sir. It's in the garage. I have a path ready for you," Leon replied, bobbing his head at Henri. His dark brown hair just brushed his shoulders and looked as scraggly as ever. "Everything went according to plan."

"Good. Thank you, Leon," Henri responded.

I stared at the werewolf, who was a newer edition to the Pack, in complete confusion. "What the hell?" I asked to no one in particular.

Henri chuckled and grabbed my hand as Leon led us up the stairs into the main house. "Leon here is one of mine," Henri responded.

"One of yours? What does that mean?"

Henri lifted the case in his other hand and smiled at me. "He is mine, just as you are mine. In time, you will see."

I blinked in confusion, my mind racing as I replayed the last few months in my mind. "What exactly is in the case?"

Henri stopped at the top of the stairs and looked at me with a confident smile plastered on his face. "This contains the secrets to my werewolf serum." I stared at him blankly and he continued. "It helps me influence the wolves, so they are more willing to help me."

"You mean control them."

Henri shrugged his broad shoulders and turned away, but I could feel the smugness emanating from him. So, this was Henri's plan all along. The pieces began clicking into place in my mind, but I still had many unanswered questions.

"Come along, Isabella," Henri ordered.

My feet moved of their own accord, pulled by Henri's command. How was I going to get out of this? I couldn't disobey any of Henri's direct orders. My hand strayed to the cell phone in my pocket. If I could get away for a little while, I could contact the Pack. No, I mustn't think about that. I wasn't sure how much of my thoughts Henri could read.

I followed Henri and Leon through the house, not paying attention to my surroundings. The werewolf led us to the garage and flicked on the lights. Inside was a black limousine, with blackened windows. Leon opened a door and Henri led me inside. The interior was completely dark inside, until Henri flicked on the overhead light. The interior was spacious, with enough room for several people to lie down and sleep.

Leon climbed into the driver's seat and started the car. "Are you ready, sir?" Leon asked.

"Yes, Leon, take us home," Henri responded.

Leon nodded and pressed a button on the console. A blacked out barrier rose, blocking our view of the front of the car. I sat in the far corner, attempting to look out the window, but even as I felt the car move, I still saw only darkness.

"It is getting late in the day, and I must retire," Henri said, and I turned to look at him. He stretched out on his back across the seats, with his hands folded behind his head. The black case rested on the floor beside him. "You should get some sleep as well. We have a long drive ahead of us."

I nodded my head and pulled the backpack off, setting it on the floor beside me before settling back in my seat. I felt suddenly tired and yawned, knowing Henri must be pressing his will on me again. The knife throbbed against my side, but I ignored it. Maybe I should just open the door and let the light in real quick. Would that solve all my problems?

"The doors are locked and cannot be opened," Henri said suddenly. I swallowed hard, knowing he must have read my mind, and turned to look at him. His eyes were two black coals as he stared at me. "You will sleep until I wake you. Now, lie down and sleep."

My eyes grew tired and I hastened to obey him. Try as I might, I couldn't stay awake. The knife throbbed and burned my thigh, urging me to keep my eyes open, but I couldn't. I should have known better than to trust another vampire. Hadn't I learned my lesson last time, with Patricia? I was stuck now. I couldn't defy Henri's direct orders. I felt depression welling inside me, threatening to overtake me. How did I fight?

The knife burned again, and I slowly smiled. I still had options. He could control my body, but not my mind, not anymore. Justin was working on a cure, the werewolves would find Jared, and I would fight with my last breath to regain control. My breathing slowed, and I knew I'd soon be asleep. The knife pulsed, sending comforting waves of warmth across my body. Before I drifted off to sleep, one phrase kept replaying in my mind, like my own personal mantra.

"Fucking vampires!"

About the Author

Laura Hysell is the author of the Isabella Howerton series, which includes *Bloody Beginnings* and *Bloody Consequences*. She lives in the countryside of the Willamette Valley in Oregon with her husband and two daughters. She has been writing since childhood and has received Honorable Mention in two short story contests. Her hobbies include archery, photography and playing piano.

Follow Laura on the following:

www.laurahysell.com

facebook.com/laurahysellauthor

twitter.com/laurahysell

Printed in Great Britain
by Amazon

30253061R00153